Winter Games

RACHEL JOHNSON

PENGUIN BOOKS

PENGUIN BOOKS

Published by the Penguin Group
Penguin Books Ltd, 80 Strand, London WC2R ORL, England
Penguin Group (USA) Inc., 375 Hudson Street, New York, New York 10014, USA
Penguin Group (Canada), 90 Eglinton Avenue East, Suite 700, Toronto, Ontario, Canada M4P 2Y3
(a division of Pearson Penguin Canada Inc.)
Penguin Ireland, 25 St Stephen's Green, Dublin 2, Ireland (a division of Penguin Books Ltd)
Penguin Group (Australia), 707 Collins Street, Melbourne, Victoria 3008, Australia
(a division of Pearson Australia Group Pty Ltd)
Penguin Books India Pvt Ltd, 11 Community Centre, Panchsheel Park, New Delhi – 110 017, India
Penguin Group (NZ), 67 Apollo Drive, Rosedale, Auckland 0632, New Zealand
(a division of Pearson New Zealand Ltd)
Penguin Books (South Africa) (Pty) Ltd, Block D, Rosebank Office Park,
181 Jan Smuts Avenue, Parktown North, Gauteng 2193, South Africa

Penguin Books Ltd, Registered Offices: 80 Strand, London WC2R ORL, England

www.penguin.com

First published by Fig Tree 2012
Published in Penguin Books 2013
001

Copyright © Rachel Johnson, 2012
All rights reserved

The moral right of the author has been asserted

Typeset by Jouve (UK), Milton Keynes
Printed in Great Britain by Clays Ltd, St Ives plc

ISBN: 978–0–141–03889–6

www.greenpenguin.co.uk

Penguin Books is committed to a sustainable
future for our business, our readers and our planet.
This book is made from Forest Stewardship
Council™ certified paper.

ALWAYS LEARNING   **PEARSON**

To my grandmother, Lady Fawcett (née Beatrice Lowe, 1913–2000) and my mother-in-law, the Lady Margaret Stirling-Aird (née Boyle, 1920–), whose time in Bavaria in the 1930s was the inspiration for this novel.

I

Park Town, North Oxford
November 1935

Jacob Linden came into the dining room where the girls were having breakfast, both wearing hand-knitted Shetland jerseys with wavy piecrust collars, Demeter's a pale pink, Daphne's racing green. It was a clammy, cold day and the branches of the monkey-puzzle tree brushed against the tall sash ground-floor window in the breeze, making a ghostly scratching sound the girls no longer noticed.

'Good morning, nymphs,' he said in a cheerful tone. The girls looked up suspiciously. Fa didn't usually talk in the mornings. Let alone to them. Jacob Linden laid a printed brochure by Daphne's plate.

'*Schloß und Burg Marquartstein*,' it said in bristling Gothic script. Daphne moved her plate next to her cup and saucer, then brushed her toast crumbs off the white linen tablecloth into a cupped hand. When her hand was out of her father's sight she splayed her fingers so the crumbs dribbled on to the large Persian rug under the dining-room table, and only then gave her full attention to the document.

On the frontispiece, there was a picture taken in summertime of a white-painted castle, slightly obscured by spreading deciduous trees. It had an east wing and a west wing, gabled roofs and three floors of painted shutters. It was topped with a turret that ended in a pointy cupola, like the bishop in chess. A gravelled drive swept clear of leaves led to wide front steps.

'*Das neue Schloß*,' it said. Below was another picture of another house, set halfway up a forested mountain. '*Die Burg*,' it said. The next word made her spirits lift.

'*Koedukation*'. Daphne didn't need her German to know what that meant.

Boys.

She'd hardly ever met a boy, apart from the grocers' lads in the covered market, who had chapped hands and cheerful voices despite early starts followed by long days in the cold selling root vegetables to dons' wives. But they didn't count. Nor did the endlessly recurring under-graduates who came to Park Town to sit at Fa's feet in the study to read out their pointless essays. Daphne thought it was so embarrassing when people read out loud, because then they used their reading-aloud voices.

Then she spotted that the pamphlet was in English underneath the German.

'Old and New Castles Marquartstein, Oberbayern. A Country Boarding School for Boys and Girls. Recognized by the Government. High School preparing for the University/ Formation of Character and Mind in Communal Life/ Bodily Training/ Sport/ Handicrafts.'

She turned the page. There were more sepia landscapes, showing different views of the castle in all seasons. Photographs showed a class composed of pupils of both sexes in shorts and bare feet sitting on a wall in bleaching sunlight; a view from the castle into the Achen valley, it said. The village, with traditional gabled wooden chalets with busy window boxes, exuded warmth and charm.

There were also photographs devoted to displaying the wholesome curriculum of the school, which showed lusty boys and girls with pale musculature and fair locks lying on makeshift camp-beds in Alpine meadows ('Rest after Dinner' was the caption), canoeing, sitting at lessons at tables in the shade, climbing up stiff slopes with stout boots on, carrying rucksacks, always framed smiling against a backdrop of snow-capped peaks.

'Can I see?' said Demeter, grabbing it.

One daughter was named after a nymph and another a goddess but both had thick, curly brown hair with golden glints in it, and lively eyes.

When women asked why Demeter, aged eleven, was so much younger than Daphne, their mother, Winifred, would sigh even more than usual. Only if pressed would she explain it was because she had 'trouble starting babies', at which point people would give knowing looks. The sisters were too young to know that some grown-ups liked bed very much, and some not at all, and, in their parents, they had one of each kind. No one would dream of going on to say that Linden was the sort of fellow who liked bed so much that he would sleep with other dons' wives, and even his own students. It was not the sort of subject that ever came up, not at one of the Lindens' famous dinner parties, at any rate.

Germany? Daphne thought again, her mind racing. It must be something to do with the trip to Oberammergau, last year, when they'd gone to see the Passion play.

And that trip had been conceived at a dinner party, here in this very room; there had been ten or so grown-ups present. Laurence Lowther, warden of Merton, had been talking about how the Nordic races in Europe were superior. 'All other nations are lesser breeds,' he had explained in his silky way. Priscilla Lowther had gazed round the table, to check that her husband, who was the ranking academic present, held everyone's attention.

Priscilla had shoulder-length blond hair, a gleaming forehead, a short straight nose, and was entirely beautiful, apart from when she laughed and opened her mouth wide to show a band of pink gum above her teeth. Then, to the girls' delight, she looked like a neighing palomino.

'Look at Hitler. He may not be entirely sound' – Lowther emitted a cough, to show that he was well aware the leader was not entirely without stain politically – 'but no one can deny he's pulled Germany's chestnuts out of the fire.'

It was all quite strange, Daphne had thought, to talk of 'lesser breeds', as if people were like dogs, some smaller and hairier than others. It was especially odd, talk like this, here at the Lindens' house, in Park Town. Her mother was English back to the Normans but, on her father's side, the Lindens had only been in England since just before the war. Her father's father, Tomas, and his wife, Lore, had arrived from Litau in Latvia, and they had all became citizens in 1911. Daphne supposed that Lowther was, in his way, paying her family a sort of *compliment*, but as with all compliments, Daphne had quickly realized – like 'This essay's better, much better' or 'Your hair's looking nice and tidy today, Daphne' – it contained an implied criticism.

Winifred Linden liked to serve the final course as if they were in formal Hall. Nesta, the cook, and Mosey, the maid-of-all-work, would array the fruit, cheese and nuts on a vast bobbled glass platter, a Lithuanian heirloom. One girl would take in the platter, and the other would bring the decanter, coddled with a white napkin round its neck like a tubercular child.

On that occasion, it had been the turn of Daphne to hand it round, so she took it, as instructed, first to the woman on her father's right.

'Listening to Laurence, ha ha, I'm glad I don't know any Germans, thank God, but the problem with Englishmen as opposed to Frenchmen,' Priscilla was saying to Linden, then lowered her head and her voice, so she was looking at him from under her lashes, 'is that they never make approaches.' She pouted a little, as if put out. 'Is it because they're frightened of rejection?'

Linden gave Priscilla a contemplative look, as if deciding something. 'Far more likely, if they're Englishmen,' Linden said, and leant in very close so that only Priscilla and the hovering Daphne could hear, 'is that they're frightened of acceptance.'

Priscilla pealed with laughter, and passed the port to the man on her left. The merriment emanating from the couple cast a slight pall over the rest, who were quieter, as they sipped from little port glasses, and picked at nuts and grapes. Daphne had successfully circumnavigated the table without dropping the historic plate, past Mr and Mrs Cayley, the Berridges and the Ropners, and was just waiting to serve her mother, hoping against hope not to drop the platter, when Priscilla spoke again.

She started explaining in a bright, determined voice that it was the tercentenary of something in August of that year. 'And I've decided that you, darling Winnie, should join us, in Oberammergau – for the Passion play. We've been invited. We really should go, you know. The first performance was in 1634 so it's the three hundredth anniversary this year, 1934.' She beamed across the oval table, covered for the occasion with another Lithuanian heirloom, a white damask cloth. Winifred hated being called Winnie. But this wasn't the reason why in the next second she managed somehow to knock over the crystal decanter of Saint-Estèphe that Laurence had presented on arrival for the Lindens from the legendary College cellars.

But Laurence, a former diplomat, met the disaster with the words, 'Don't worry, Winifred dear. 1930 was a very poor year for Bordeaux,' and covered the unsightly plate, his Stilton stained with claret, with a deft conjuror's whisk of his napkin.

In her confusion, Winifred had agreed to Priscilla's suggestion, and regretted it instantly. Priscilla had placed a proprietorial arm in triumph on Jacob Linden's back, out of sight of everyone but Daphne. Then she had applied a significant pressure, as if promising something.

'And bring the girls, too,' Priscilla had said, leaving her hand where it was, in prospect of ownership.

This scene flitted across Daphne's mind now, as she applied herself to her egg while Demeter hogged the *Koedukation* brochure, and her father, Jacob Linden, disappeared into the grey tent of *The Times*, and it was followed by a further series of scenes: Oberammergau. With the Lowthers. The Lindens. And 'the girls'. That was when it had all started.

Or it was when the girls, at any rate, had realized it was going on.

It was on the first night, in that hot dark *Gasthof*, with mahogany covering the floor and ceiling, the house crowded with heavy carved furniture. Every surface had some sort of white cloth on it, embroidered with flowers, or a doily, on top of which sat some ceramic animal, cow-creamer, candelabra, dried-flower arrangement, or a clock. At least the *Gasthof* was spotlessly clean, as promised in Lowther's copy of *The Link*.

As the girls had established with a cursory glance when bored on the little train from Murnau to Oberammergau, *The Link* was even more boring, if that were possible, than *The Times*. There seemed no point to it at all. At least *The Times* had Court and Social pages, and small ads and, best, the Invalids column. They would read aloud to each other choice entries in the soothing tones of a ward sister bringing hope to an anxious relative. 'The Brazilian ambassador was stated last night to be a little better'; 'Mr R. S. Hudson is on the high road to recovery after his recent operation for appendicitis.'

The Link, however, didn't even have Deaths on the front page. Deaths were thrilling, a reminder of all the people who'd just done the one thing that no single person reading the announcement had yet done, but all of whom would. *The Link* just had endless articles about understanding. When Daphne steeled herself to ask Laurence what understanding was – she was encouraged to initiate adult conversation whenever possible – Fa jumped in.

'It means not minding whatever Germany does,' he'd said on the train, with his eyes closed.

When they'd arrived at the *Gasthof*, it smelt all lemony, as if recently cleaned in their honour, and the astringent aroma was overlaid with a meaty waft from the kitchen.

Frau Mayr showed them up to their rooms. The Lowthers were at one end of the corridor, in a large double room with a lumpy bed covered with an embroidered counterpane, a large wardrobe and a view of the church. The Lindens were in two smaller rooms down the corridor.

There had been nothing to do until supper.

Daphne and Demeter threw their cases on their single beds and opened them, Frau Mayr having bustled off to show the Lindens the bathroom they should use, and which one was for the Lowthers.

'We will serve the evening meal at seven o clock,' she said, popping her nose into the girls' bedroom. She darted them a bright look. 'We are eating *Klopse*,' she said, as if they would be pleased.

'What's *Klopse*?' asked Demeter after she'd left, launching herself on the bed and opening Daphne's copy of *Modern Girl*. 'I do hope it's not *hooves*, 'cos that's what it bloody sounds like.'

'Don't worry,' said Daphne, unpacking. She moved a china shepherdess from her dressing table to make room for her Pond's cold cream and hairbrush. 'And don't swear! Look on the bright side. It can't be as horrid as farmhouse mould.'

Dem looked anxious, and so she might. Nesta, their cook, had made the mistake of asking Demeter to read out the ingredients of farmhouse mould so she could make a shopping list, and the first item in the recipe was 'one cow's heel', and Demeter had almost fainted. She put down her copy of *Modern Girl*, and her eyes started filling at the prospect of *Klopse*.

'Come on, Demeter,' said Daphne, 'it's almost suppertime. Go and have your bath, stop worrying, and leave the water in.' Demeter was half out of the door. 'Oh, and could you run and get the Izal, will you, from Mother's grip? She's down the corridor, past the Madonna and Child, last door on your right, I think.' Dem clattered off. 'On your *right*,' shouted Daphne after her.

The meal had started with a golden, parsley-flecked noodle soup, which was so delicious, even Dem could eat it.

Everyone had talked about this play they'd all come to see, which was going to go on for seven hours, and talked again about how there'd been a plague in Swabia and Bavaria, the place where they were now, and how the villagers had sworn to perform the Passion tragedy faithfully once every ten years if the plague stopped, which it did.

The Lindens believed in exposing their daughters to adult conversation, but this didn't stop Demeter from sometimes saying the first thing that came into her mouth.

'I'm Demeter and I'm ten,' she said, to the Mayrs' son, Kaspar. Then a strange expression chased across her face, her eyes widened and darted, as if she'd just remembered something important.

'Fa?' She leant forward and called down the table. The Lowthers ignored her and carried on talking. 'Fa?' Demeter called again, louder.

The party was sitting at a large round table, its dark wood cloaked in a white cloth. It was decorated sweetly, with little posies of fresh white daisies and carved candlesticks and napkins in gaily painted wooden rings. The children sat at one end, Kaspar in his uniform, as he'd been to an *Appel*.

The grown-ups sat at the other end. In the middle, their hosts, the Fräulein and Herr Mayr, sat opposite each other, presiding over the steaming tureen. Candlelight shone on ruddy cheeks, and the glasses and silver sparkled on the table. Winifred was crumbling dark bread with her left hand on to her side plate, and gazing ahead.

Jacob looked questioningly at his younger daughter. He avoided looking at his wife, who never put a brave face on things. 'Fa!' Demeter called again.

This time, everyone fell silent, and spoons floated mid-air.

Though this was a guesthouse, there were no other guests present. Frau Mayr broke the silence. '*Edeltraut! Herein!*' she barked.

A girl in plaits emerged, and Frau Mayr rattled out instructions regarding the main course.

'What is it, my child?' Linden asked. He was in an expansive mood, on his third glass of Bocksbeutel, with a fruity Silvaner on its way, Priscilla at his elbow and his whole family at his command.

'No . . . it doesn't matter,' said Demeter, head bowed.

'Yes, it does matter,' said Linden. 'If you want to stay up to supper, you must sing for it, same as at home. So pipe up, Demeter.'

'Yes, do kick on, young lady,' said Lowther.

'Well, when I was looking for the Iz . . . something –' Demeter hesitated. She knew there was something unmentionable about Izal, the toilet paper, as there was with almost everything to do with the body. 'And I got lost.' She paused. 'I couldn't find the right door, and I by mistake opened the door when you were with Mrs Lowther,' she blurted. 'I saw you.'

Jacob stared at Demeter. Winifred Linden's mouth set in a line and she gazed across the lit candles into the middle distance, but a telling red flush stained her neck and upper chest. She had been mistaken, she realized, to assume that not even Jacob would be so cruel as to make love to Priscilla on a family holiday, during the Long Vac.

'Oh, how sweet, did you, darling?' laughed Priscilla Lowther. She shook her head and gazed round the table with an indulgent expression, as if little children must be humoured.

Priscilla Lowther sipped her wine. She was looking more refulgent than ever in the candlelight. She had twisted her liquid blond locks into a French knot, and she was wearing a cream silk blouse, so everything about her was creamy, sheeny: her skin, her hair, even her neck gleamed golden. Winifred's coarser brown hair was pinned back above her ears and she was wearing the same clothes she'd been travelling in. After they'd arrived, she'd lain down in her clothes on the bed, Jacob had slipped out of the room and she'd fallen asleep, so she hadn't changed for dinner.

'I had a headache earlier, and your papa helped me. I'm feeling much better now, thank you, now I've had a little rest.'

She nodded and smiled at Jacob Linden from beneath perfectly arched brows, as if such a bold display of eye contact between the two of them would be quite enough to dispel any suspicion of impropriety. 'Well,' she sighed, 'isn't it lovely, to be here?'

She tilted her glass towards the Mayrs in a toast so the yellow syrupy wine sparkled in the crystal glass in the candlelight. The grown-ups followed suit, and Kaspar raised a pewter tankard. Priscilla had glossed over things so brilliantly it was as if Demeter's contribution had never taken place.

Daphne pinched her little sister's arm tight.

'What did you see?' she whispered, smiling as Kaspar passed his bowl up for seconds, even though the other bowls had been removed by Edeltraut, the maid in a pinafore with her plaits wound tight above her head. She moved her leg without thinking as she passed her bowl on and realized that it was now touching Kaspar's leg, and moved it away, but not before Kaspar had responded eagerly to the pressure. She shifted her thigh. She had felt an astonishing tingle of electricity between them – and she wondered if he had felt it too. She was wearing a knee-length frock that had ridden up, so her leg was slightly sticking to the wooden chair. It was August, and very hot. The windows in the dining room were small, and no breeze could in any case steal past the shutters and curtains.

'You must tell me.'

Demeter shook her head.

'It's fine,' said Daphne. 'You see . . . I saw them, too' she lied.

She hadn't; she'd been in their own room, but she didn't really need Demeter to explain. At the words 'I saw you,' it all fell into place. It had been going on for months. Since the dinner party at least, if not before. That's why Winifred had stopped talking and started crying in her bedroom.

'Were they . . .?' she asked.

Demeter gulped. Then she stared into her plate and nodded, before looking up, eyes brimming.

'Don't worry, D.,' she whispered, tucking her napkin back so she didn't spill *Klopse* – whatever *Klopse* were – down the clean front of her dress. 'They're all . . .' she struggled to find the words that would explain the behaviour of Jacob Linden and Priscilla Lowther to Demeter, and failed.

'Give that back to me now,' she snapped at Dem, and held out her hand for the brochure.

Only the day before, Daphne had been offered a place at St Anne's College, Oxford, to read Modern Languages. She knew that she'd been expected to win an award to Somerville, but still. Not everyone who was expected to win a scholarship to Oxford always did.

'It's been decided. No daughter of mine will go to Oxford as a commoner,' confirmed Jacob Linden, from behind his paper.

'But Father,' Daphne protested. Linden laid his paper down and looked at his daughter.

'It's for the best, believe me,' said Linden in a pleasant voice which meant he wasn't going to change his mind. 'You're only seventeen,' he went on. Daphne knew what he was going to say next, about how her mind was a sponge.

'At this age, your mind is a sponge. Now is the time to learn the language properly. Your French is already very good. You could bring your German up in few months, and then you'll get an award.'

Daphne thought of her best friend, Betsy. Betsy Barton-Hill lived in Suffolk, and her father was a landowner. He never told Betsy that her mind was a sponge, because Betsy's mind was empty and even her father called her an abject fool. And Betsy was going to the Lucie Clayton Academy of Charm, while she was going to have to go to Germany and learn German.

It was so unfair.

'Just for one term,' Jacob Linden said, helping himself to more coffee from the silver pot. It kept the coffee wonderfully hot, and the stream of dark liquid steamed in the morning light. 'Or term and a bit. I need to look at the dates. It'll be like a holiday, a long *Sommerferien* for you,' he went on, taking a slice of toast from the silver toast rack and scraping butter along it with the butter knife. Demeter carried on eating her porridge with milk and white sugar, quite tepid, which was how she liked it. Winifred, as ever, was having her breakfast upstairs on a tray in bed. 'Here, I've finished with this. You can read the leaders.'

Fa made Daphne read the *Times* leaders every day, as preparation for the Oxbridge entrance exam, and had forgotten his daughter had already sat them. He passed Daphne the paper, folded to expose an advertisement at the bottom of the page.

Come to Happy, Friendly GERMANY
where your £ buys more of everything . . .
from Sea-bathing to Winter Sports!

It was an advertisement from the German Railways Information Bureau. It continued:

Everybody is busy building Germany's prosperity –
yet everyone has time to be genuinely courteous,
friendly and helpful to visitors.

Daphne let out a big breath that sounded like a sigh.

'It's not as if there's going to be a war,' her father said. She glanced at him sharply, because it wasn't that she was worried about, even though he'd taken them to see a terrifying film called *The Shape of Things to Come*. This showed what happened after war was over. Everyone was crouching in caves. Daph and Dem had had nightmares for weeks.

'One war is enough,' Jacob Linden continued, with confidence. 'Our chap, wet though he is, will never allow it to happen again. Not even the Hun want to live through two wars.'

Daphne's eye lingered over the sterling sign in the *Times* advertisement; it had sown suspicion in her mind. She wondered whether she was being posted to Germany, to this Marquartstein place, because the pound went further there. But she wondered whether she was also going because – she could hardly bear to think this –

'Oh no, the last thing you need worry about is that there will be a war. There won't. Anyway, you'll be fine over there. You're *English*.' Linden spoke with tremendous assurance, and his hooked nose disappeared into his coffee cup, as if it was all settled. He placed great faith in the nationality of his daughters and wife, who had an immunity he could not claim. To Linden, a Jew whose father had been born in Moscow and whose mother was Lithuanian, being English was a bulwark against all threats.

Daphne listened to this, her stomach tight. She felt frozen. She was being sent to Germany because her mother couldn't bear the sight of her after what had happened with John.

'Germany is just the place for you,' her father continued. 'Remember how much you loved Oberammergau? How moved you were, by the villagers, the hundreds of them, joining together in Christ, to bring the Passion play alive again?'

Her parents were getting rid of her on the cheap, Daphne thought. There had to be some human sacrifice after baby John had died, exactly a year after their return from Oberammergau. She should have known it would be her.

Daphne flicked back to the week she'd spent in Oberammergau with the Lowthers: the forced visits to freezing-cold *Rokokokirchen* to peer at ill-lit frescos, or to wood-carving workshops to watch bearded men grunting as they fashioned ox and asses, or to the damp grottoes in the florid excrescence of that so-called palace called the Linderhof – experiences that she had found difficult, tiring, boring, even uncomfortable, at the time, but which seemed golden, almost magical, in restrospect. Indeed, the trip to Oberammergau had been recorded in the Linden family annals as a comparative triumph.

'My dear girl, there is nowhere better for languages, for music – and the opera in Munich is world renowned.

You will be safe there. The Germans are practically cousins. I envy you. How I wish I was your age again, with everything before me!'

Daphne managed to raise an eyebrow.

'It's only for a term, my darling, then you can spend the rest of the time – there's a very good place I know – with a *Gräfin*.' He looked a little misty for a moment. Daphne knew what that meant.

'Maybe one of your schoolfriends –' Jacob Linden paused. He wasn't very good at names. He knew the name of one of Daphne's friends, the sexy one, who lived in Suffolk. As a specialist in Roman philosophy and law, he could quote large chunks of *corpus juris* verbatim, but it took a second to pluck a name, especially a girl's name, from his overstocked cerebellum. 'Maybe Betsy, er, Barton-Hill' – his voice sounded uncertain, but he'd got the name right, so Daphne allowed him to continue – 'could travel out and join you. Term starts in a couple of weeks, and then you could stay with friends over Christmas, and be in Munich early in the New Year, in January sometime anyway. Terribly exciting to be there in the Olympic year, old girl, eh? I could call her people today.'

Daphne let out a breath, and felt cheerful. Betsy. Now there was a thought. If Betsy came to Munich, that would change everything.

Her world up to this point had been Oxford, where children learnt Greek paradigms before breakfast. The scraping sound of scales on quarter-size violins drifted out of windows even on sunny days, when children should be in the parks, or smelling the cherry blossom in Norham Gardens and Fyfield Road, or watching the undergraduates glide down the Cherwell in punts drinking cheap wine and puffing stagily on cheroots. Daphne's world was contained by the high, long-walled lanes and bosky streets, her life conducted to the sound of organ voluntaries drifting from chapel to quad and the rhythm of the Michaelmas, Hilary and Trinity terms and orchestrated by a bereft mother who found daily life unbearable.

Her life had been none of the things an English girlhood should be: jolly, outdoorsy, loud, playful, with japes, like apple-pie beds, and pillow-fights, and constant teases. It had not been bouncy at all.

She would miss Nesta and Mosey. And Dem. She watched Dem eating her egg, with love. At least baby John had died, so she wouldn't have to miss him too, she thought, wondering if that was an awful thing to think.

'And then, after Munich, you can hold the St Anne's place as a fall-back, but you can sit Oxford entrance again,' Jacob Linden continued. 'You've plenty of time.' He picked up their cat, Antigone, from the top of the radiator, which was emitting only the faintest of heat, and stroked her vigorously, pressing a forefinger down from her head to the base of her spine and tail in one firm movement while making a special crooning noise intended to heighten the cat's pleasure.

Daphne picked up the brochure and looked at it more closely, as if gazing into a crystal ball. Her father stepped into the passage, his napkin still tucked into his shirt.

'*Ma!*' he roared.

Betsy was so lucky to have brothers and Sir Bache as a father, thought Daphne. Fa didn't care about her marriage prospects in the slightest. She flipped through the pages again. Fa wanted to send her away to a school where you had to wear a sort of swimming costume made of clinging cotton – in other words, leaving very little about the place called 'between the legs' to the imagination – and prance about in high meadows, whatever they were, and do housework, i.e. *Hauswirtschaft*, and learn how to mend and darn and iron.

But then again . . .

Boys. And Betsy.

Father's roar had, as intended, winkled Winifred from her bedroom. Demeter was sent upstairs to the nursery to read.

'It's all been agreed, dear,' said Linden, after his wife had made a silent entrance and sat down.

'Daphne will not be taking up the offer of the place at St Anne's, as she wants a proper chance to go to Germany to improve her German. She wants to reapply next year for Somerville, of course. After all, she's only seventeen.' Daphne looked at her mother, hoping she would scotch this crazy scheme.

But Winifred had stood up, and was looking out of the window.

'Mother?' Daphne said in a meaning way. There was the sound of a front door slamming on the other side of Park Town.

They were, for once, supposed to be discussing her

future. But her mother was gazing out of the window, her much-admired violet eyes – especially striking when brimming with tears – trained on the garden path of the house opposite.

This was the Garfield house. Like the Lindens', it was of rather noble, Georgian appearance, its grey ashlar-stone façade lichened green by exposure to the damp air of the river. The Lindens and the Garfields lived opposite each other on the approach road to the Park Town crescents, which faced each other across an ovular communal garden, which meant that, if you looked at the layout on a map of Oxford, their road resembled a picture in a basic biology textbook of a vagina opening up into a womb.

The Linden house, number twelve, faced an identical row of large, detached and semi-detached houses. These houses were considered among the best in Oxford. Just the words 'Park Town' immediately called forth six-bedroom family residences with gardens front and back, nurseries upstairs and nannies who took only an afternoon off a fortnight.

Priscilla Lowther was walking out from the Garfield house in a belted Burberry and a headscarf. Her slim ankles exuded the burnished gleam of the finest Wolford stockings. Being very pretty and married to the head of a college, and not being dumpy and dowdy and a mere don's wife, with sad hair in a grey bun, gave Mrs Lowther a certain confidence in her standing in Oxford society, and she revelled in it.

But now, not long past nine o'clock in the morning,

Priscilla Lowther was leaving Josiah Garfield's house, which was strange.

Josiah Garfield was the world's leading authority on early Christianity, and provided endless fodder for the feverish fantasies of the Linden girls. He was a fellow of All Souls, and had the bushy eyebrows and burning gaze that suggested a mind on higher things – as if daily life, with its meals and family and servants, was merely an irritating distraction. This lofty mien seemed almost to be compulsory, Daphne had noticed, among the dons, as if any concession to creature comforts implied possession of a 'second-class brain'. Having a second-class brain was about the worst thing anyone at the University could say of anyone.

The Linden girls thought Priscilla Lowther was unimaginably glamorous, but dangerous. There was the business in Germany, for a start, with their father. They didn't know that Priscilla was also very unusual: she got what she wanted and, unlike so many women, once she'd got it, she then proceeded to enjoy it.

As Daphne watched Priscilla stalk down the path, she felt pleased for her mother and sorry for her father. Perhaps Priscilla had tired of her father and had taken up with Garfield, whose name often appeared in *The Times*. Could it be, Daphne wondered, because they – the Lowthers – didn't have children?

Daphne had no idea why some women could have children and some women couldn't. It was a total mystery, even after her Little Talk with Mother.

Daphne remembered the Little Talk quite clearly.

It was the last time she remembered her mother being happy.

Her mother had been heavily pregnant, her skin plumped and pink. She had started the baby quite soon after they returned from their holiday in Germany, to the girls' surprise.

Mother had been resting, lying lustrous on her bed, and Daphne sat on the chaise longue upholstered in blue-and-cream toile de Jouy at the end. 'Mother?' Daphne had asked. Distracted and embarrassed, she shifted from the chaise longue to the stool at her mother's glass-topped dressing table. She lifted the glass stoppers on her scent bottles, sniffed and replaced them, played with the powder-puff and looked at her mother's reflection in the three-way mirror. 'You know you're having a baby . . .' She paused.

Winifred struggled to sit upright, and looked over at her elder daughter. She was wearing a violet empire-line woollen dress that matched her eyes, and lisle stockings, and her slim feet rested under a pale pink cashmere rug.

'Ah,' she said. 'Well.' She seemed to be lost in thought. What Winifred was thinking was that this was probably a good moment. Jacob had asked her when she was going to tell the girls and, specifically, Daphne, the facts of life. Winifred had replied, 'When they ask, dear.'

'Have you talked to them about solitary gratification, Winifred?'

'No I haven't, Jacob. Do you really think it necessary?'

'Maybe not,' sighed her husband. 'Let's leave it till

they ask, as you say, if you think that's right. You are their mother, after all.'

And so far, they hadn't, until now.

Winifred spent a few moments rearranging the special pillow behind her back, an oyster satin one, edged in antique lace the colour of old people's teeth. 'You've been . . . in bloom for how long now, dear?'

Daphne counted backwards. 'Three years. Maybe two. Two and a half.'

'Of course, of course,' said Winifred. She stared out of the window for a moment. The curtains were open, and all she could see was grey Oxford sky, the spiked bosom of the Radcliffe Camera and the spires of the colleges in the distance. Oxford was always colder than London. She wished they lived in St John's Wood.

'The important thing to remember, dear,' Mother had said, 'in your twenties, maybe sooner, you will meet someone, and you may want to marry him. And if you and your husband love each other very much, then, well, you can have a baby.'

Winifred Linden felt this conversation was going well. Contraception was available only to married women. Therefore, the only sensible thing to do was to tell the girls that intercourse was impossible until they had rings on their fingers.

'So, darling . . .' she said, unsure how to continue. Winifred's own sex education had comprised one single event, which was when her own mother had given birth to her little sister, Margaret. Winifred, who had been amusing herself on her own in the nursery, had rushed

24

down when called. In her mother's dressing room, she had been shown not the newborn babe but the placenta, redly filling a white kidney dish to the brim prior to being weighed by the midwife. Winifred had shuddered. She could not eat liver under any circumstances.

'Does that answer your concerns? I hope I've never shirked my duty in preparing you girls for . . . motherhood, have I?' she appealed to her older daughter. 'I'm glad you raised this, very glad, actually.' She wondered if this was the moment to mention . . . solitary gratification.

Daphne sat very still. She couldn't believe that was it. Even the nuns had told her more than that about 'relations', after Sylvie Fulcher had been expelled for being found in a bush with a boy and her underwear – a pair of pilling navy gym pants – had been found in a puddle. They'd done human reproduction in the next biology lesson. They'd also dissected a frog in science, which left indeterminate body parts smeared on a glass tile from which the girls were instructed to draw their own conclusions.

To crown this, in the final term of school the girls were treated to a talk about birth control in which they were told that it was permissible to take your temperature with a thermometer to determine whether your ovaries had released an egg. It was possible to tell this because, according to the nuns, body temperature went up very slightly when the ovary was releasing, or had recently relinquished, an egg. Daphne had listened carefully.

'Of course, at your age, you will meet men, young

men – and all I want to say to you is this. There is a terrible danger of going too far.' Winifred held her daughter's gaze for this bit, so violet eyes locked with hazel.

'If you go too far, then a girl can get herself into the most terrible trouble. Remember that girl at school? Sylvia someone? It really can ruin your life, that sort of thing. It is paramount, at all times, whatever the circumstances, to remain a lady.'

Daphne went over and adjusted her mother's pillows, as the satin one had slipped down. It was hopeless trying to talk to her.

Winifred patted her arm, confident that her daughter knew everything that she needed to know. She knew that the best protection she could offer her daughters was to persuade them that intercourse could happen only between man and wife. She sank back on to her pillows, relieved that the girls were too young to be told. It did not seem to be necessary at this point to tell her daughters anything about childbirth, let alone marriage or getting old.

It was one of the things that mothers could never tell their daughters. There was no question of Winifred telling them that their husbands would find passion elsewhere, as Jacob had with Priscilla Lowther, *inter many alia*. There was no point.

The girls would find out how awful it all was for themselves, eventually.

And now, they all gazed out of the window, talk of Daphne's future forgotten. They watched Priscilla's hourglass shape in the mac turning left at the pillar box towards the Banbury road. It struck Daphne that Priscilla Lowther didn't seem to care two hoots whether she had children or not. She seemed perfectly happy enslaving distinguished diplomats and professors, one after the other.

It began to rain, hard.

Daphne glanced at her father. She felt of no more consequence to her parents than a child's glove impaled on a railing.

Her parents left her in the dining room to get on with their lives. She didn't see them again till breakfast time the following day, though she'd heard her mother crying. Daphne didn't imagine for a second that her mother was weeping over her, and her imminent departure.

She was weeping over the baby that had died, upstairs in the night nursery, at the age of three months. Mosey had said that John had gone to sleep in Jesus, but that didn't make it any better: her mother was still weeping over him.

They knew that, after that, they couldn't expect anything to be the same again. And it wasn't. The Park Town house felt like a mausoleum, entombing them all in their mother's grief, a place where the baby had died and was now waiting to receive the rest of them.

It was a wet and windy morning in the middle of the Michaelmas term at Oxford. The pavements were wet, the high street a sea of scarves and umbrellas, the coffee shops full of steaming undergraduates hunched over toasted buttered teacakes. The trees in the University parks had already shed their burden of leaves, to brace their branches against the raw Oxfordshire skies.

But Daphne was already in the mountains, wearing a belted jacket, heavy trews and long woollen socks turned down neatly below the knee, and perhaps the red knitted tam she'd spotted in Boswell's on top of her curls, speeding down a slope in the glittery sunshine and high, tonic air, in search of hot chocolate while young men called Franz and Werner and Hans – she very much hoped anyway – panted in her wake.

She knew she would have to escape, and go to Germany. Her mother blamed her, and her father didn't even know her age.

Daphne was eighteen.

2

Berchtesgaden/ Obersalzberg, Bavaria
February 2006

Francie handed her company credit card to the man at the check-in desk of the Mountain Resort and Spa, Berchtesgaden, Bavaria, Germany.

She waited for the check-in guy to check her out, but only because men almost always checked her out.

She was pretty, quite tall but nicely rounded, straight nose, mouth that reminded men over a certain age of Carly Simon, bosoms, proper bottom, and she also had – everyone agreed – great hair: a sort of stripy, tawny brown, thanks in part to the 2006 Aveda Colour Collection. As Francie, who worked on a glossy magazine, knew only too well, it was no longer enough for cosmetics merely to be organic. No. To absolutely everything in mags and fashion and beauty there has to be a season – every January, the New Year New You special; every June, the Beach Body special – and so now, even shampoos and dyes had their own 'spring' and 'winter' shades.

She gave the log fires, the open brickwork, the soaring ceilings, the businessmen talking into mobiles, the couples sitting on sofas not talking a practised once-over: it was obvious that architects, interior designers and brand consultants had been hard at work here for years. Millions had been sunk into putting this place back on the map. The reception area dropped down to a seating area and bar chill-out zone. A wood fire blazed in a monumental iron brazier on a trendy raised plinth in the middle of the floor. Around the fire sat low-slung modular sofas, and extravagantly tufted fur rugs cosied up the stone floor.

The action, such as it was, was taking place in the bar to the left, towards the bank of lifts. Francie wondered how many tens of thousands of Euros had been lavished on 'hotel conceptualizers' for them to come up with the name 'Rocks' for the hotel bar, a name that was spelt out in pink neon. 'Fifties-diner style,' Francie murmured, and made a note in her Moleskine notebook. Below the neon sign, a ponytailed waiter was polishing a glass with a cloth. At the bar, two businessmen sat on stools, hurling peanuts down their throats and slurping beer from huge jugs.

One side of the great room presented a bland sweep of drawn curtains in the shade of curtains and carpets all over the world, a sort of porridgy greige.

Presumably, by day, the vast picture windows framed marvellous panoramic views of rich Alpine meadows dusted and sprinkled with flowers like stars pinpointing in a green Milky Way, milkmaids, long-lashed cows tinkling with bells as they safely grazed the upland slopes, not to mention Lindt-chocolate-wrapper vistas of white mountains, yellow sun and cornflower-blue sky.

While she was scribbling her notes (description in

travel pieces was impossible unless you wrote things down straightaway), a large woman with big Elnetted hair made a very deliberate entrance. She minced past the reception desk in a tight wrap dress and a glittery necklace made of a golden shower of coins. With a secret smile, she took up a position at a mic-stand near Rocks American Bar that Francie hadn't noticed before but now clocked with a sinking feeling.

In order not to make eye contact with the lonesome songbird, she dug into her bag to see if she'd had a text from Nathan since she last looked, which was at least ten minutes ago.

Nathan was her boss. He'd warned her not to mention skiing or the Nazis in her copy about a mountain resort built in the exact spot where the top Nazis played musical chalets while the rest of the world lay broken, otherwise he would 'personally spike it and put a house ad in its place'. She knew why. If she did, this hotel group would stop advertising, probably with the entire IMAG group.

Nope. Nothing. She resisted reading his previous texts and replaced her mobile.

Oddly, there wasn't even one from Gus.

Whenever Francie whinged to girlfriends about Gus spending long evenings curating his iTunes or on his unlikely new obsession with yoga, her interlocutors would sternly remind her that Gus was 'adorable' (i.e. a male heterosexual, with his own hair and teeth, who was not obviously sociopathic) and that he, Gus, would be snapped up 'before he even went on the market', while she, Francie, would be stranded for ever on the dusty top shelf of life marked 'divorcée' were she so self-deluded as to cut him loose for a second.

If there was so much as a whiff of splitsville in White Cube – their friends' name for the couple's minimal maisonette in Little Venice – flocks of predatory harpies would gather, Francie was told.

It was as if her friends loved him more than she did.

Francie knew of course that Gus was – or would be – a catch. But that wasn't the point. Of course Gus was kind, nice-looking, solvent, energetic (he'd co-founded his own ad agency, Village, which had the obligatory Wurlitzer, ping-pong table, beanbags, Coke fridge, etc., in its Soho offices). He was an early-adopter (Facebook, Apple, Young British Artists, minimalism). Gus was skinny, fit, with a full head of very short hair (he looked a bit like a Danish marine).

She knew that the only snag with Gus was this: she had married the first man who she felt loved her. It was not his fault. It was hers.

And what she could not admit to her friends – not even to lovely Miranda, her best friend at work, the deputy editor of *Event*, forty, tall, dark, calm and beautiful – was her shameful, totally pathetic feelings for Nathan. Who was married-but-sort-of-separated-at-the-moment anyway.

She thought about Nathan now almost continuously, while also being grimly aware that he had done nothing, so far, to merit her attention.

There was hardly a girl in the office he hadn't, at some

point, seduced, or been seduced by. There was Cat, who Miranda had found sobbing in the Ladies and, when she'd tried to comfort her, Cat wouldn't say why she was crying, but it was pretty clear that she'd had the Nathan treatment.

And then there was the features-desk secretary who was like a ripe peach when she arrived but a few months later had withered on the vine and moved, a shadow of her former lush self, to *InStyle* magazine via, it was rumoured, a stopover in the Priory, a series of events in which Nathan was, needless to say, implicated.

But she and Miranda had discussed them, analysed each story, and neither actually believed the gossip. Not all of it. Apart from when it came to Samantha. Sam was a well-upholstered, jolly 27-year-old who dive-bombed Nathan during an office party when he was sitting on a sofa so that his dark, Piero della Francesca head – the man was so beautiful he should be frescoed on to the wall of an Umbrian church – was completely obscured by her boobs. The next day she'd confessed to Miranda. Miranda was the sort of person everyone confided in. She was a fantastic listener.

Sam had first sworn Miranda to total secrecy by the Dyson Airblade, and then blurted to Miranda that after said party she'd been to bed with Nathan or, in her words, they'd 'bonked each other's brains out'. Obviously this was too good not to pass on.

Miranda duly passed on the scoop that Sam was Nathan's 'new office bike' to Francie in Costa Coffee within seventeen minutes of swearing blind to Sam that it was 'total secret squirrel' and she'd 'never, ever tell a soul'.

As Francie stood there, mourning the amount of time she'd wasted on Nathan, without anything having even happened yet, she realized something with awful clarity: that the reason there were so many fewer great female writers, composers and whatnot than men was not because women were domestic slaves, trapped in childbirth, uneducated, unempowered, disenfranchised – except of course, nowadays, magazines banged on about self-actualizing, which meant that a woman had to be bullied to become a 'person in her own right' or 'her own person', which was all crap, basically, like when a fashion spread told readers to 'build their best beach butt ever' or 'get the pre-collection Navajo look for Fall' – no.

That wasn't the reason at all.

The reason women fell behind after storming their GCSEs, A Levels, and so on, was love.

A woman in love spends literally 90 per cent of her time trapped in an underground mental prison, a virtual solitary confinement, thinking about the man she's in love with.

She obsesses about the 'status' of their 'relationship', two words men will never willingly use in one sentence, except if they're on Facebook. The woman worries about what he thinks about her; what she's going to wear, say or do at their next meeting, and so on.

Which was why it was a jolly good thing that women were so good at multi-tasking because, for the last few weeks, Francie had been on autopilot at home and at work while wondering what Nathan was doing at that moment, who he was flirting with now, who he was in bed with, and what he was like in bed.

Like last night, for example. 'When you're in love, or when you were in love with girls Before Me' – she corrected her own question to Gus, as he was cooking supper. Gus with his new, even shorter, stubblier haircut, in a butcher's apron. Whatever he did, he did with authenticity. One of the things he was most proud of was that he was a media creative and he hadn't ever had to wear a suit to work, and for him, wearing designer trousers by Comme, or Yohji, or Paul Smith, was a part of his job – 'how much did you think about them? What per cent of the time?'

'What do you mean?' said Gus. He was concentrating, grating the rind of an unwaxed lime into some marinated chicken. It was as if he didn't want to hear the question. She asked it again. Then he ran a hand over his hair – he did that a lot now it was so short – and said, 'About two per cent of the time, maybe five? It's different for girls, isn't it?' he said, grinding a melange of pink and black peppercorns over the mix. ''Tis woman's whole existence.' It was weird. Gus only ever read the sports section but seemed to know everything: history, politics, poetry – you name it.

She sighed as the check-in man tapped away. The Nathan thing was a disaster. A total disaster. And it hadn't even happened yet She knew it would, even though she was married, and he was anybody's, and therefore it was all like the tagline to a lame, straight-to-video Hollywood romcom.

Marriage. No one prepares you for these things, Francie thought. As their couples counsellor called it (Mrs Gluckstein's preferred title was 'marriage enhancer', but neither of them could bring themselves to use it), Gus and Francie, after five years of marriage, were having what she designated as 'issues around intimacy'.

Which wasn't, Mrs Gluckstein had told them, surprising, after she'd found out about Francie.

Francie's father had died in a plane crash when she was little, and her mother, Vanessa, had bolted to South Africa when she was eight and married a permatanned man called Geoff who wore pilot-style, short-sleeved shirts with epaulettes when not in full safari rig.

As a result, Francie's expectations of marriage to Gus (painfully normal childhood, C of E primary in East Sheen, St Paul's, Central St Martin's) had started from a low base, even though – after her mother had bolted, that is – Francie had had a blissful time with her grandparents, Daphne and Jeremy Fitzsimon, on their dreamy estate in Hampshire on a chalk stream, with ponies and a kitchen with a four-oven Aga and a succession of chocolate Labradors, all called Cadbury.

Mrs Gluckstein had told them to compile a list of what mattered to each other to see how well they 'understood each other's needs'.

For Gus, her list went: work, photography, Sky Sports, Apple products, sex, coffee, and herself last. She put sex after Apple as a joke, and herself last as a test.

For Francie, Gus had listed: Gus, shopping, sleep, luxury travel (except glamping and designer yurts),

36

flowers, and Ladurée macaroons. He had even meticulously noted the two flavours she liked: the surprisingly green pistachio ones, and the two-tone addictive toffee-salted caramels.

Then they swapped. It was a huge relief to Francie that Gus thought he came so high up in her life, but it was a bit of a blow that Gus had failed to mention her work.

Mrs Gluckstein, meanwhile, never even asked to see the list at the following session, so it was, they both agreed, a bit random. Like so much of adult life, it felt like homework completed, handed in but never marked by a teacher one wanted to please, and therefore unfinished business.

But the Gluckstein exercise still bugged Francie. I mean, she'd always *worked*.

She'd had a secure, loving childhood in Hendridge despite the total absence of her parents, and despite this lingering sense there were things she didn't know about her past. Every time her mother came back from South Africa, to see her in the holidays, there was a tension that couldn't be explained, a sort of gap in her life that she knew only to plug one way . . . with *plastic*.

Francie went to a nice girls' school (Heathfield). Then she went to St Andrew's and, post-Finals, to Phuket, where she had sex on the beach, an experience she vowed never to repeat. On her return in September she applied to magazine group Emap, where she was appointed to work on the 'fulfilment' side, having made much first on paper, and then in interviews, of her place

37

on the St Andrew's Summer Ball committee and rather less of her 2.1, as literally everyone got a 2.1.

Emap had led to work on monthlies, then to Gus, then to weeklies, then to dailies, and now she was the travel editor of Emap rival IMAG's newest and shiniest title, *Event*. All the while, wunderkind Gus was 'growing' Village, his ad agency in Soho. The magazine was divided into sections: Event Fashion, Event Beauty, Event Books, Event Cuisine.

Right at the back was her section, Event Travel. The coverlines of *Event* invariably included the words 'Now!' and 'New!' and were spattered with exclamation marks and, occasionally, cover-mounts in the shape of a give-away gift, but there was only a certain number of Cath Kidston plastic make-up pouches or free waterproof mascaras that readers could take. But it was all good, basically: Francie, a girl who had started off as an orphan, (Grandpa Jeremy and Grannie Daphne had been very much *in loco parentis*), was in possession of a job, a child-and clutter-free flat in Clifton Villas, open shelves lined with glass jars, top-of-the-range everything from sheets to Smeg fridge, and a husband – and, well, as her friends assured her: he was top of the range too.

Indeed, Francie had reached her thirty-fifth birthday and could honestly say that one of the worst things she could remember happening (she was too little to remember her father's death) was about two weeks ago.

She realized she was falling in love/lust with Nathan the day Gus'd asked her to help him move the wormery on the verandah and it gushed inky fluid on to her new

Jimmy Choo baby-girl-pink suede ballet flats that she'd bought online from the Cruise Collection on Net-à-Porter, waited in for the bike to deliver, and had unwrapped that very day. 'Worm-bin juice!' she'd screamed as she ripped them from her feet. It wasn't Gus's fault, what happened, but she knew the ruined shoes allowed her to be angry with him; it wasn't a good reason, but it was something she'd been waiting for.

'They're brand new, not even worn, now they're ruined,' she'd said, almost in tears.

'As rarely a day goes by, even a Sunday, when this flat doesn't rustle to the sound of tissue paper in the hall, or the arrival of the bike from Pret-à-Porter, I don't see why you're so upset,' he'd said, as he dabbed at the dark patch, which only made it worse.

'It's Net-à-Porter, Gus,' was all she said.

But even Francie had to admit – Gus had a point.

What she was really good at was shopping. Grannie had said as much, the second time in a row she'd seen her granddaughter with a large yellow Selfridges carrier, and Francie had tried to take it as a compliment, until Grannie had next wondered out loud whether 'people bought things nowadays because they had nothing better to do'.

As for *work* – the awful thing was, now it was mainly travel-and-beauty puff pieces. Nathan was tormenting her and demanding she churn out bridal-beauty copy 'to bring in the advertising'. Plus, he kept sending her on trips, but it wasn't as if she was exactly *Martha Gellhorn*.

She'd literally just come back from Los Cabos, Mexico.

She had completed and filed a write-up of a resort's new 'offering': the Bride's New Beginning Ritual, designed by the Director of Romance to create positive energy and intimate exchange beginning with a Holistic Twilight Ceremony where crystal bowls resonated with beautiful harmonic tones and concluding with a Mayan ritual perfumed by sage smoke conducted by a shaman. When she read this guff on the email from the PR even Francie felt depressed. She couldn't believe her career had come to rewriting copy about holistic pre-bridal therapies.

When she'd got back from the panic-inducing pampering freebie in New Mexico, she was so freaked about being lumbered with Event Bridal for good that she almost 'fessed to Miranda that it was Nathan she was mooning over. But something told her that even though Miranda was amazing and such a good friend and a properly beautiful person, it was better not to.

For Miranda was Nathan's deputy, and the two were thick as thieves. Plus, she and Miranda had spent too many lunchtimes discussing what a dick Nathan was. Nathan had left his wife Meredith and two little girls, Hope and Charity. Nathan had had a succession of girlfriends. God knows what his current 'relationship status' was. But most of all she held back from sharing her feelings with Miranda because she was married, and it was all so bloody ridiculous.

She shook her head and tried hard to refocus her thoughts on the hotel, just as tomorrow she'd have to start properly noticing this part of Germany. Nathan might be a dick, but he was also a multi-award-winning editor. And her boss.

Just then, there was a tap on the mic.

'Good evening, Mountain Resort,' the singer said in a husky voice. No one looked up.

She started on an Ella Fitzgerald number, flashing her for-hire eyes and tossing her hennaed mane at the boozing businessmen.

Time to go, thought Francie, feeling suddenly lonely, and hungry, and slightly wretched. She returned to the desk and leant over it winningly to catch the concierge's attention.

'Excuse me, is the *Stube* still open?' Francie asked.

Thanks to due diligence on the dining options at the hotel on the Lufthansa flight from City airport, Francie knew that the *Stube* was a gingham-curtained faux-rustic zone on the lower-ground floor that served Bavarian specialities. She could quite imagine spending an hour in the *Stube*, reading *Eat, Pray, Love* at her table for one, before flopping.

Francie had gone off piste with *Eat, Pray, Love*, as her book-group book was too heavy to bring in her hand luggage: as usual, it was a punishing 600-page military history, as all the women in the group worried that they 1. would have nothing to say to men at dinner parties or 2. that childbirth had wiped everything they'd ever learnt from their brains at school or University, like an iPod being restored to factory settings. So this month it was *King Leopold's Ghost* about the Belgians and the Congo, which was amazing actually, but maybe not the best thing to read over *Bratwurst*.

As she spoke, she felt her mobile vibrate in her bag.

Her heart lurched, even though the text, she knew, would be from Gus. Francie glanced up and saw that the time, according to the clock on the wall above the gleaming head of the concierge, was 10 p.m., so only nine in England. There was a part of Francie that considered her own internal clock should override other time zones, and she was almost surprised to find that other countries stuck to their guns even after she, on GMT, had manifested there in person. She decided she wouldn't look at the text, though.

If she didn't look, she wouldn't discover it wasn't from Nathan *so soon*.

'Your room number is 212, on the second floor, and your spa treatment, yes?, is tomorrow at 4 p.m.,' the receptionist told her, circling her room number and the appointment in the spa in blue biro as he spoke. He handed her back her credit card and passport, and a folder in which the room's passkey had been tucked.

'Thank you, that's great,' Francie said, as if a free, two hundred Euro spa treatment was no more than her due. 'And a couple of things: can I go up to the Eagle's Nest tomorrow?' As the words left her lips, it hit Francie again.

She was standing on the very site of the mountain retreat where the *Führer* had planned the invasion of Russia and conducted the war. A few hundred yards away from where she was, right now. If that. Even Francie found it a bit weird. Maybe it was a good thing Nathan had forbidden her from writing any of this in. 'No way can we have some horrific mash-up of the Final Solution and hot-stone massage in the same piece,' he'd said.

'And can I get something to eat in the *Stube*,' she repeated. 'Or is it too late?'

'*Ja*, it is too late, we are no longer serving at twenty-two hundred hours,' the receptionist replied in a voice that said: I am merely delivering information. No acknowledgement that this was not the answer Francie was looking for.

Francie began to wonder how much she was going like the Germans.

He pushed a leaflet towards Francie and did the annoying thing again – enclosing the relevant information in a blue speech bubble of biro.

'During the winter months or during inclement weather when access to Eagle's Nest is restricted, you will instead visit the world-famous Salt Mines. Wearing traditional mining gear you will descend into the depths of the mine, where you can see glowing salt grottoes and a subterranean salt lake.'

As Francie read the pamphlet, she pondered whether the entire difference between the English and the German attitude to life was expressed by the choice of the verb in that sentence. In Germany, it was you *will*. In England, it was *if you can be arsed*.

'But tomorrow you have your itinerary,' the concierge continued. 'Your car will be outside at 0930 a.m.' He reached down and produced a folder that some PR had clearly prepared earlier: several sheets of printed material, a brochure, and the inevitable DVD – and a car key. Francie slipped both folder and pamphlet into her satchel and gave the lobby one last *tour d'horizon* before heading to her room. Her mobile buzzed again. Another text. And then another.

The first was from a German network congratulating her on having joined it. The second was from Nathan.

'Are you still sulking? Xxx' She stared at it, confused. With Nathan, one x was a formality (everyone, from his PA to his children's teachers, got one x). Two xx meant he was in a good mood. Three xxx meant he was in a grrrreat mood. And four xxxx meant the flirtiest male editor in women's glossies was feeling frisky.

The third was from Gus. 'Call me urg. It's your grand-mother.'

Francie's heart pounded. She only had one grand-mother.

Grannie Daphne was in her very civilized care home in Oxfordshire, the sort of place that had fresh flowers not plastic ones, and still believed in the Digestive biscuit. Something must be wrong with Grannie.

'Shit,' she said out loud, thinking, but Grannie's only eighty-seven – or is it eighty-eight now – that's young these days, isn't it?

'*Bitte?*' asked the receptionist.

'Nothing,' said Francie, hurrying to the lifts, wheeling her red Tumi behind her, anxious to be alone upstairs so she could speak to Gus.

She stood in the lift, noting that –1 was the Wellness Centre and Mountain Spa for future reference, then pressed the button that said 2. She gazed at her reflection in the mirror, smart-casual in her camel double-breasted coat, a garment she'd bought because it went with her hair. She automatically came in close to examine her skin. She looked pasty, and the thought popped into her head, even though she was worrying about Grannie, she just couldn't help it: why was Nathan asking her if she was still sulking? Had she been sulking previously?

It was only after she'd spoken to Gus and she was lying under the billowing white duvet, so puffy it was like being inside cumulus cloud, feeling hungry and anxious, that she allowed herself to cry a little bit, about Grannie, who might have had some sort of stroke, and was apparently asking for her, and in the middle of this, she also cried a tiny bit harder because it had occurred to her that Nathan's text was probably a misfire, and hadn't been meant for her . . . and if hadn't been for her, then who the hell was it for?

3

Das Neue Schloss Marquartstein, Oberbayern

Alpen

Bavaria

3 November 1935

Dear Pa and Ma,

Thank you for your letter, Pa. So glad Dem's been made lax captain and has decided to do French & Italian rather than German. German's so difficult to speak and even harder to listen to, they all talk as if every sentence ends in an exclamation mark! And every word is uttered as if in italics!

Ma, I do so hope you are feeling better and ~~that you are feeling the benefit of only having Demeter in the house~~ *you're managing to rest more. How is Antigone? You never said.*

You asked about the uniform, it's ghastly of course, but I knew that from the brochure: baggy nutbrown tunic over cream cotton shirt, tied with girdle. All shapeless. School tie. Underneath — BLOOMERS *(brown of course, same as everyone's uniforms on the street) with elastic around the waist and legs* ~~which are so difficult to wash that all the girls are all issued with 'linings'.~~

I've had my dirndl made. Can't imagine I'll ever wear it much after Munich, unless of course I marry a German which I might as the boys are terribly jolly here ~~or end up as~~

serving-wench in a beer cellar. I'm still quite enjoying Marq.
even though some things are drear and dread. Like the early-
morning run. A handbell is rung at six-thirty, & we all have
to get up, the whole school, & girls put on their bathing suits for
Morgenappel, the morning assembly. At which we all stand with
our BARE FEET in the SNOW in front of the Schloß, shiver-
ing. We wait until Herr Ellermann comes out & of course HE
is wearing woollen socks, stout boots, gloves etc!

Then we have Morgenlauf ie morning run, & have to
do hare and hounds after Heinz, the school's champion
cross-country runner, while Herr Ell or Fräulein Erika
follows waving a big stick shouting SCHNELLER,
SCHNELLER! There's so much to say – my German is coming
on, I'll try to write the next in German, Ma, I'm doing
Hauswirtschaft. The food is fine. Brekker = cereal & boiled
eggs and coffee & black bread. As we leave the dining room a
maid holds a tray, full of baked potatoes, you keep them in your
pocket to warm your hands and eat them at 'second breakfast',
after they've cooled.

Right, have to go and change for Appel – the parade of
Bund Deutscher Mädel. It's such fun – we just march about,
singing.

Pa – skip this bit! Ma, pls pls can you go to Boswell's, &
possibly buy me a Kestos brassiere and send it to me?

Don't skip this bit. This is a long letter as I won't be able to
write one probably next week as I'm in a play (Hamlet).

Best Love,
Daphne

Dear Betsy,

Thank you for your long letter – will try to send this to you in the afternoon post, have to go to village anyway.

I am making a huge effort in letters home (well, my first letter) to convince them what a wonderful time I am having in the wholesome Alps. I'm used to it here and I don't miss Park Town AT ALL.

We ski to lessons in the science block, the little ones sled everywhere, with red cheeks, in mittens, so sweet. I am eating like a horse, you have to, to keep the cold at bay – but I haven't been banting even though I'm eating like a horse, we have TWO *brekkers, a normal one followed by baked potatoes or, even nicer, white buns filled with dark chocolate. I do Hauswirtschaft with the other girls, I've learnt how to use a sewing machine, how to darn. I even know how to wash & dry a pair of lederhosen. All of this will no doubt be of great use to me in later life.*

Everyone talks about a place called the Hoch Alm, where you sleep in mountain huts and eat fried patties of flour and fat called Schmarm and ski down, but that doesn't happen this term.

I miss Dem a lot but I've made friends with a girl called Sophie. Her father is prof at the University in Munich called Ludwig Maximilian something so we have lots in common. The headmaster, Herr Hoffmann, says she may have to go to take her Abitur (it's an exam) in Stockholm, so she may have to

leave. Everyone here sits it in Munich but she can't, they'd
FAIL *her, simply because she's Jewish. Sophie's being very good*
about it, so is Prof Hoff, who is wonderful.

*He makes these stirring speeches about placing ourselves
in service of the community. I haven't got a clue what he means
but it's marvellous. Everything sounds so important in
German.*

*We have assembly in a hall called the Aula. Marble pillars
and heads of elk high on the walls, hideous bust of Hitler we
have to salute constantly. When I'm not running around the
castle naked holding baked potatoes, I am made to march about
in a Girl Guide uniform, singing. It's v well organized. Your
father would approve.*

*Am hiding fact from Ma and Pa that the place is literally
crawling with boys – young men really. When you asked me
how German boys compare to English boys then I thought –
but I don't know any English boys. Apart from your brothers
of course but they don't count.*

*Only a few more weeks before Munich! Hurrah! It feels odd
to say finishing school. How can you be finished before you've
barely begun? Pa has found a house with a countess and
everything near the English Garden, and presumably not too
far from the Opera. But I'm not sure I want to go. I want to
stay here. Can't wait for you to join me there. We'll have the
time of our lives, I promise. I'm so pleased you're coming.*

*Tinkety tonk
Daph
PS No wild oats yet*

Dear Betsy,

Such awful news. You won't meet Sophie in Munich after all. She's disappeared. Frankly, if it goes on being this thrilling, I may have to start keeping a diary, like Ma keeps saying one should, though I bet people who keep them are even drearier than people who tell you their dreams. What happened was, we went to bed, after rehearsal for Hamlet, Prinze von Dannemark, & when I woke up her bed was all made but her hanging cupboard was empty, no case under her bed, she'd gone.

I expected Prof Hoff to explain at Appel what had happened but he didn't say anything at all. Not one word. Someone said it's because he could be reported and that Sophie's probably escaped into Austria across the border, which is only a mile or so away. We hear guns, sometimes, in the night. I heard firing & asked one of the maids what it was & she didn't really look me in the eye & said, hunting chamois, but even I know you don't hunt in the dead of night. In today's rehearsal when we got to the bit about the bourn/ traveller I started sniffing audibly. I think it was about Sophie but I know it was also about John. I suddenly missed Ma terribly and understood a little more, I think. How ghastly it has been for them both.

Oh yes, oh JOY! Yesterday we went skiing! A place called the Geigelstein. We had hot chocolate in the tea house halfway up, and on the way down one of the boys, Klaus (!), taught me how to do a stem Christie on a mountaintop while looking certain death straight in the face down a precipice. They all ski like angels here and I'm learning.

I wonder what will happen to them, you know. I feel sorry for you in a way because of your brothers. I've prayed they wouldn't get killed, if there's a war, just in case you were still officially not praying after that time the baker's boy would look up at the window, and see you, and wave, and he didn't.

I BEG YOU TO WRITE
TTFN,
Daffers

PS Pa did write to me saying that there won't be a war. I have to assume he's not just saying that. I know it would be an awful bore for him and Ma if I came home again just when they'd finally got rid of me, and I'm so looking forward to the next bit, and I'm so glad AGAIN you're coming.

4

Francie sat on her bed in the fluffy white robe and nibbled nuts, seeds and fruits from her palm, like a grazing koala. She'd opened the mini-bar when she woke and found a note welcoming her to the 'Health Bar' and a line-up of vitamin waters, crunch bars and sachets of grains.

She felt pensive.

The fact was, for a professional travel writer, Francie was no more than average at being on her own. Gus didn't want to come as a plus-one to Berchtesgaden, but, for want of anything better to do, she often accompanied Gus on his trips. Gus liked to combine long haul with self-improvement, so he spent hours online planning excursions to Indonesian rainforests so they could both listen to pygmy song or spot whales in Baja California. 'Let's do it while we still can,' he would say. Francie knew what that meant.

The fact that they hadn't had children yet; another crunchy issue for Mrs Gluckstein.

She'd fallen in love with a man who promised to while away the expected longueurs of their marriage in the darkroom with a £25,000 Leica. 'You can't beat 35mm,' he would say. 'All the greats still use film.' But a year after they'd bought the flat he'd had his darkroom repainted a suspiciously sunny yellow, and gone digital. In other words, Gus was ready to take things to the next level.

Francie sifted through the seeds and picked out the toasted sunflower ones that tasted Marmitey, and considered the situation.

Francie knew that if they had babies they would end up moving out of the white-on-white, airy flat in Little Venice to a dark terraced house near a park with a café in it. In the park, women younger than her, pregnant with number four, would be doing 'pushy mums' sessions with baby in a jogging stroller with tractor tyres. She and Gus would have a hallway full of baby-transportation equipment and a sitting room full of plastic. Even the trendy couples they knew who started off only buying wooden toys and making sweet-potato purée and laundering their own nappies cracked at the arrival of what they called 'number two', at which point life as they knew it ended.

Women who BC (Before Children) only ever read the *Guardian* and visited farmers' markets and watched art-house movies would, AC (After Children), perfectly happily eat McDonald's in Legoland and watch daytime TV at the arrival of their second baby. Everyone – however cool and North London prior to that point – cracked at number two, and turned into less smiley, and more broke, clones of Jools Oliver who actually paid good money to spend their Saturday mornings in soft-play areas, trying to read the *Guardian* Family section while their children peed on slides.

Francie had been to too many dinner parties with London parents, especially toned, university-educated career women who, when pregnant, said: 'I don't care if it's a boy or a girl so long as it's healthy,' and who then – when they had duly birthed their perfect offspring without analgesia – went into a frenzy of competitiveness and bought Baby Mozart CDs and sent them to pre-pre-school in Japanese. Francie hadn't yet recovered from meeting an old schoolfriend at a party, asking her how she was, only for her to go swivelly-eyed. 'We've got exams,' she gasped, as if having an asthma attack. 'We're sitting Common Entrance in three weeks,' thereby proving to her old friend that her failure to 'separate' was pretty much total, and that she and her husband were only too happy to serve as indentured slaves to their own children till the end of days.

Francie also couldn't stand the naked ambition of parents full stop, the way they claimed, 'I don't care what Josh and Polly do so long as they're happy,' but then proceeded to monitor the comparative progress of friends' children and their own progeny's achievements with naked panic. Francie knew that, in 2006, 'healthy' or 'happy' only scratched the surface of what parents demanded their children to be, at any age, which was a glorious reflection of their parents' own fabulousness.

And most of all, Francie worried that as soon as she had a child, she would behave exactly like all the pushy mothers. So Francie was not, for the moment, taking folic acid tablets or watching what she ate. She did not consider her reproductive organs as a gardener might approach an allotment, as soil to keep fertile and loamy prior to seeding.

All this went through her mind as she sat on the bed. She wasn't ruling out babies. She just wasn't, she decided, in a hurry, whatever the *Mail* said about her fertility falling off a cliff and how she was biologically extinct at thirty-five.

Somehow, being away from Gus – and from Nathan – put things in perspective, allowed her to think and breathe.

Francie scuffled off the bed, wrapping her white robe tight around her. She unlocked the French windows and stepped out into the cold air on her own balcony, which faced out towards the Watzmann mountain (according to her book, the third highest in Germany), its three peaks looking like a particularly pointy profile. She sucked in the fizzing air, threw her head back and, for some reason, said out loud, 'Just do it!' to herself. That made her feel better.

She went back in, pulled on jeans, a longjohn grey top made of very fine, almost translucent cotton, a heavy navy cashmere sweater and her brown leather rigger boots, and headed down, tummy rumbling.

She took a lift to the lower-ground floor. Then all she had to do was turn right and follow the noise of chink-ing cutlery and the scent of bacon until she came to the huge open-plan dining room, picture windows framing Alpine scenes, just as she'd envisaged the night before.

She went up to the help-yourself area, the spread

confirming her theory that breakfast-buffet options offered in different parts of the world were just as telling as language, religion or history. Here, in Bavaria, the buffet told guests, you never have to ask where's the beef (or pork, or any form of protein). Here there were platters of ham, salami, onion, gherkins, cheese and covered chafing dishes where bacon, egg, sausages, and other items steamed away, giving off a slight whiff of tinfoil-dished airline meal. Slightly nauseated despite her hunger, Francie sat down with a small glass bowl of muesli, a large bowl of fruit salad and the *FT*. A glance at the front page told her that Bush was a lame-duck president; the hundredth British soldier had died in Iraq. The main story was about the FTSE 100 being 6000, and the basement slot was about City bonuses pumping up the property market in London. There was a short piece about radical Islamists protesting against the cartoon of the Prophet that had been published in a Danish newspaper. Francie only read one piece in its entirety: a 200-word extended picture caption, really. The photograph showed David Cameron cycling to work to save the environment and establishing his green credentials, a few paces ahead of a 3-litre Jag, which conveyed his suit, red boxes and whatnot.

Half an hour later, she was cruising down the road in a VW Polo, its sat nav programmed with her itinerary. The road was empty as she beetled past sites of special historical interest to Third Reich anoraks, such as Hitler's chalet, and past Göring's summer residence, and quickly found herself in the sweet cobbledy town centre of Berchtesgaden.

It was always nice to be somewhere else, she thought as she parked by a closed bank with a green façade and lit ATM, even if she was worried about Grannie, and probably shouldn't have had that second cup of coffee.

It was really quite nice here. The houses were all frescoed, and you could see mountains, and the sun was about to come out and make it look picture-book pretty, she could tell. She'd buy Grannie something here, she decided.

She sat in the car and checked her guidebook, which said that, according to the explorer Alexander Humboldt, she was sitting in one of the most ravishing towns in the world. Then she read that Humboldt was German, and that Salzburg was also up there in his top ten, which explained things. It was like a first-time mother believing that her howling nine-pounder really was the most beautiful baby that had ever been born. Francie had witnessed the onslaught on objectivity wrought by patriotism and motherhood many times.

Anyhow, now she knew: these painted houses everywhere were called *Luftmalerei* houses. She locked the car, and wandered off towards one, which was painted with monkeys wearing clothes. She looked at her guidebook again and found a picture of the house in the Berchtesgaden section. It was, she read, the Gasthof zum Hirschen. It was obviously a destination house, as it was covered with frescos showing monkeys/ apes as bankers, bakers, kings, doctors, wearing hats, holding sticks, with little dogs at their feet.

The setting, with mountains jutting away whitely in the background, and the blue-and-white-shuttered foreground and medieval half-timbered houses covered with pretty pictures was all . . . She struggled for an adjective better than 'Alpine' or 'German' or 'Heidi-ish' as she passed a shop selling penknives with carved handles – and only penknives with carved handles – for whittling. Within, a tiny Rumpelstiltskin of a grey-haired man in an apron sat at a workbench, bent over a small piece of wood. They nodded at each other.

She came to a square with cafés where people were, incredibly, already embarked on elevenses. They were sitting at little round tables, outside, guzzling pale sausages and salt-studded pretzels of the same fat girth, and washing down the snack with bladder-bursting *Steins* of white beer.

Francie winced, and turned into a cobbled shopping street, in hope, only to pass shop after shop selling identical bosom-cupping frilly wench shirts, the dainty, gingham, pinny-fronted dresses as worn by all the waitresses in all the cafés, and hunter's hats perky with pheasant feathers in deep forest green.

'Who would buy this shit?' Francie scribbled in her Moleskine.

She mentally made a note also to be very clear about shopping opportunities in her copy for Nathan. *Event* was always very hot on the consumer angle on everything, and she could see the box on shopping already:

Berchtesgaden. Great for 1. carved wooden crib sets 2. gear for rock-climbing 3. cuckoo clocks 4. gingham dirndls with silver-buttoned bodices and 5. shepherd's crooks. Not great for: everything else.

On the positive side, however, as she passed butcher's shops and sausage eaters, she could at least say without reservation that Bavaria was pretty unbeatable in the category of pink, meat-based comestibles of almost every description.

She would have preferred to spend the next hour or so lounging in the après-ski area by the blazing fire, sipping herbal tea and reading *Eat, Pray, Love*, but she felt an obligation to complete her itinerary. She had a vision of some girl, in some marketing department of some regional tourist board, taking the trouble to print it out and slip it into a folder all for her, along with the dreaded DVD.

Plus, they'd already programmed the sat nav.

She walked back to the bank, and got into the little car, feeling more purposeful. Next stop, the lake, apparently one of the most numinously beautiful sites in the country.

It was only ten kilometres to the Königsee, so after twenty minutes or so of listening to German pop music on the radio (the alternative was German speech radio, or Wagner) she parked next to a snack-stand selling Coke and Frankfurters, and set off up a well-worn path alongside the lake.

After a kilometre's gentle climb, glimpsing blue flashes of water that sliced through the greeny-black shade, she arrived at a clearing. There was a sign, telling her this was the Mahlerwinkel, the painter's spot.

She stood at the Mahlerwinkel and imagined standing here in front of an easel, creating an eyesore that would try and fail to convey the undoubted majesty of the scene: the greeny-blue water of the sleepy lake, darkened at the edges in the overhang and shadow of towering peaks wreathed in cloud. The Watzmann, its sheer craggy flanks limed with snow, rising almost perpendicularly from the lake. The steamer chugging through the middle, leaving a straight line of white wake, as if deliberately placed there as an aid to composition by an unseen hand, towards the white church with orange bulbous domes on the opposite side of the lake.

Yes, Francie could see why artists were compelled to give such scenes a bash.

But it was almost lunchtime. According to her itinerary, she was meeting Margit – her official guide – in half an hour, back at the car park. So she turned back, only pausing at the tatty parade of tourist shops and kiosks selling T-shirts and suncream and bottles of water, just to confirm there was nothing she wanted, there was nothing, at that moment in her life, she needed to buy or eat. She still hadn't got anything for Grannie, though, and at the last concession but one, there were some white plastic tubs, in different sizes, arrayed on a trestle. She stopped. She picked up a tub and read the label.'*Murmeltier Fett*,' it said. A woman had emerged from the recesses of her emporium in the hope of a sale. 'Excuse me, sorry, *Bitte*, I mean, but what is this?' Francie enquired of her. 'Is it honey?' Grannie loved honey, and Francie loved to give her honey, Manuka honey, lavender honey from Provence, heather honey from Scotland, even honeycomb suspended in golden goo . . .

'*Nein, nein!*' the woman said, almost crossly, as if she couldn't believe Francie didn't know what it was. 'It is *Murmeltier Fett,*' and she picked up a tub, pointing to the side where it was written. 'It is fat. From the marmot.' She gestured towards a poster that she'd tacked to the wall. It showed a plump toothy rodent, emerging from a hole in the ground as if to undergo expensive orthodontic treatment. Then she mimed slathering the fat on her forearms. '*Effectiv,*' she said.

The plastic tubs were dusty, as if no one had touched them for a while. There were sample pots of the fat, and jumbo tubs. After deliberation, she selected a large and handed over ten Euros to the marmot-fat seller with a familiar sense of satisfaction. She was glad that Gus wasn't there, because he simply didn't understand that after a day or two away from the shops, women have this itch to scratch, and will, after a certain point, buy anything.

When she returned to the car, plastic tub clunking against her leg, Margit was waiting, in a cagoule and sensible shoes. Margit turned out to be a blond dynamo, who within minutes confessed to Francie that before she'd had her only daughter, who was now at the *Gymnasium,* she, Margit, had been a junior ski champion, much as those who had been to Oxford and Cambridge insert this key fact into the conversation within twenty minutes of meeting anyone. Now, she confided, her daughter was already acing skiing competitions all over Bavaria.

'We will have lunch now, *ja*?' Margit went on, after Francie had run out of polite questions about her daughter. The Germans all seemed to have a very clear idea of what Francie should do with her day. 'Lunch, yes,' said Francie, with a grateful smile. She hopped back into the VW.

'Lunch, yes, and after lunch, the Documentation Centre,' said Margit, getting into her VW. 'Follow me, please.'

They drove in convoy along wet roads (it was by now raining) to the bottom of the Kehlstein mountain, and then parked outside a restaurant and just by a *Langlauf* trail. Francie craned her head to see if she could spot the Eagle's Nest, Hitler's tea house, but she couldn't: the mountain was bearded with dark-green firs, and the summit was wreathed in cloud. There were few cars outside, and a wind was getting up. Margit led the way into the restaurant, which had wooden tables and benches outside, against the walls.

They sat at a table that had clearly been kept aside for them, not that the place was full. The waitress whirled over, whipped off the 'reserved' sign, and handed out plastic folders containing the menu, pages of dishes that Francie would pay a lot of money not to eat. Then, silently, she handed to Francie a separate folder containing photocopied pages of correspondence dated 1940. At Francie's request, Margit gave the gist.

'Martin Bormann sent this letter to the owner of this restaurant, the Scharitzkehlalm,' she said, as Francie agonized over whether to have the pork chop or the *Schnitzel*, both of which were accompanied by *Bratkartoffeln und bunt gemischten Salatteller der Saison*.

'He said unless they handed over the place, they would be sent to Dachau.'

Francie remembered that, in Germany, '*salat*' meant meat. Meat slathered in mayonnaise. And the pig was basically a *vegetable*.

'So what happened?' asked Francie as she sipped a fruit punch, feeling the heat pumping into the room from a tall woodburning oven tiled in challenging shades of mustard and green. Here I am, she thought to herself, I am sitting in a restaurant that was requisitioned by the Nazis. What should I be feeling? And why has the tourist board taken me here? In order to show how totally fine they are with it when foreign hacks write stuff about their challenging past?

Margit was now instructing her about the chalet at the top of the mountain under which they sat. 'It is a mountain road that takes you up to the tea house,' she said. 'To the top to the Kehlsteinhaus, the road takes you 1,600 metres, and with only one hair-pin curve.'

Francie wasn't sure whether she should be impressed by this feat of National Socialist engineering or not. She frankly had no idea about the etiquette around Nazi tourism at all. The waitress was now talking to Margit in German.

'Gretl is saying that Adolf Hitler would come here, he would eat *Windbeutel* with a glass of milk,' Margit said. Francie automatically started scanning the menu for

Windbeutel, went through the dailies and the specials and the menu.

Windbeutel was still there! As her eyes locked on to the word, she saw it had become the hostelry's *signature dish*.

'This place started off as a hut selling *Alpenmilch* on site in 1805. At 1,024 metres.' Francie noted that, in the Alps, everyone seemed very keen to remind you of the altitude the whole time, as a point of pride.

'It was owned by a man called Simon Hölzl. He was the man Bormann asked to sell up. You saw the letter. He declined. His father and grandfather had lived and worked there. He was kicked out in 1940 and had to buy it back in 1949.' The waitress shrugged. She moved to an ancient couple sitting by the woodburner in silence. The man was wearing a hat with a pheasant feather sticking out from the brim.

Francie looked out of the window, veiled in a light veneer of emulsified animal fat, and up to the looming peak of the Kehlstein, where the Eagle's Nest squatted out of reach. Martin Bormann was a piece of work. He not only stole this restaurant from its owners, he built Hitler a tea house on a crag. She tried to imagine the dialogue.

MARTIN BORMANN: Leader, I've got you a present. It's just a little tea house I've had built, right up at the top of the mountain at 1,834 metres.

THE LEADER: Ah so! How very kind.

BORMANN: And I've put in a bronze inlaid lift that can take you from the foot of the mountain to the top in thirty seconds.

THE LEADER: But I don't like heights.

BORMANN: That's OK. It only cost 30 million Reichsmarks. It's your fiftieth, after all! I wanted to do something special. The fireplace is a special present from Mussolini, by the way. You don't have to go there or anything. I just wanted you to know how I feel about you, that's all.

As she looked up at the monumental *Berg*, the last sixty-five years of peace in Europe seemed to fall away like strands of gossamer. She looked about the restaurant, its cosy pine tables and chairs, its wooden floor, its belching ovens tiled in poison-ivy green, the kitchens that had tirelessly fed and fuelled and welcomed and warmed all-comers, friend or foe, for the past eighty years.

Then she took out her phone, and checked it for messages from London. She hadn't come to Germany, she told herself, to get hung up on this. It was OK for other travel journalists to come to Berchtesgaden, and to drone on righteously about how a whole world of evil masqueraded as an Alpine holiday. Before she'd left Little Venice she had taken the trouble to do some research – i.e. Google the hotel – and found out what other travel writers had said. 'Nowhere better epitomized the arrogance of the Third Reich, its lofty disdain for the rest of humankind, than the summer retreat for Hitler and his cronies, high in the Bavarian Alps,' wrote someone in the *Guardian*. But she was writing this for *Event*.

Francie looked around again. She couldn't help it. The past seemed very close. She was sitting in a restaurant that Hitler used to come to, at the bottom of his Eagle's Nest, but the truth was, no one at *Event* gave a shit and *Event*'s readers would only learn, from Francie, about the important stuff, like the thread-count of the sheets, and the spa.

Francie remembered when, the other day in the office, a harrowing first-person account of a child who'd survived the death camps had crossed the desk of Clemmie, the features ed. 'Oh no,' was Clemmie's reaction. 'Not another Auschwitz memoir!' So yes, everyone was fed up with it, it was a publishing cliché. She looked at another photo of Margit's daughter slaloming down a ski-slope on Margit's mobile phone. Nathan's last instructions to her before she left echoed in her ears:

'No Nazis. No skiing. Or I spike it.'

Francie sort of got that. It was so much easier that way. In her copy, she would foreground the painted houses in Berchtesgaden, the limited shopping opportunities and major on the spa. Obviously, it was not possible to turn the clock back.

It was time to move on.

She ordered the steak, and a 'salad' (i.e. potato slathered in mayo) as a side. Gretl came back and whisked away their plates. 'Do you have children?' Margit asked, clearly expecting the answer yes and already smiling, braced to hear all about them.

Suddenly, it occurred to Francie that it would be easier to lie. To say she had.

The waitress returned and placed a round Marmite-jar-shaped dish on the table. 'No, I don't, not yet,' Francie

66

said. Had Margit ordered this enormous pudding course as some sort of punishment?

The dish was piled high with what looked like dumplings or profiteroles, oozing cream, and laced with a bright-red sauce.

'*Windbeutel*,' the waitress announced with pride. '*Immer mit Schlag, selbstverständlich!*'

Francie wished Gus was there so he could make a joke about how he was 'always with a slag' too (everything on the pudding menu was served with cream), rather than with the earnest Margit. But it was weird. Not only were *Windbeutel* still on the menu, but she was about to be spoon-fed Hitler's favourite pudding.

They drove slowly back in convoy to Berchtesgaden and Obersalzberg, passing the little road that took you to the Interconti.

Francie wasn't sure she wanted to spend the next hour in the Documentation Centre, with its thousands of photographs, documents, maps, and so on, about the Nazis and a tunnel that linked to a warren of underground bunkers.

In fact, Francie was surprised that this was on the schedule *at all*, when she could, as her welcome letter from the PR & Marketing Manager pointed out, be 'experiencing the gastronomical delights of the resort and relaxing in our awarding [sic] Mountain Spa'.

Margit signalled to the left, and they parked. It seemed they were the only visitors.

Inside the centre, Margit had whisked her past the desk, and they went into the first room in an endless suite of rooms. Francie's eye immediately rested on a large, grainy black and white image. It was a photo of the parallel train tracks leading directly into Auschwitz, a pile of shoes heaped on the snowy tracks. 'Obersalzberg and Auschwitz belong together,' she read, in a breast-beating caption that told her that the region she was in, a small chunk of Germany hugged on three sides by Austria, was intended by Hitler to remain a 'place of pilgrimage for the German people'.

She moved through the rooms, past photographs of Hitler lifting babies to kiss, past images of cowled Jewish women with yellow stars safety-pinned to their blanketed breasts, Hitler in lederhosen and woolly socks, and smiling German girls in pinafores with brown skin and blond pigtails, photographs of his house, the Berghof, the ruins of which were only a few hundred yards away.

There was a photograph of the Duke and Duchess of Windsor on the steps of Hitler's house. This wall was devoted to the leader with dignitaries from overseas: Lloyd George. The Aga Khan. Halifax.

Francie was about to move on, but her eye latched on to another picture. In this photograph, Adolf Hitler stood between two girls, both wearing demure button-down dresses, with slides in their hair, smiling. One was blond and buxom, the other had shingled chestnut hair. It looked as if Hitler had an arm round both. There was something about the girl on the left's naughty expression, the way she was wrinkling her eyes and smiling. Something familiar. Francie stepped forward to read the caption.

'The *Führer* with two English admirers, Nuremberg, 1936,' it said.

'Jesus, Mary and Joseph!' Francie exclaimed.

'What is the matter?' asked Margit. She had clearly been to the Documentation Centre many times before and had been using the downtime to send a series of texts to her athletically gifted daughter. Francie could hear the tri-tone bleeps as the replies whizzed back.

Margit came over and stood next to Francie. 'What is the problem?' she asked.

'Nothing,' said Francie. She took out a notebook from her bag, and a pen. She wrote down the caption. Then she remembered she had a little digital camera. She found it, switched it on and framed the photograph of the English girls with the *Führer* in the viewfinder. Her fingers, she found, were trembling.

She was about to press the button when she discovered that in her shock at seeing these girls posing up with Hitler she hadn't switched it on after all, so she did so – this would need a flash – when there was a tap on her shoulder.

'No photography please,' said a woman in uniform, wagging her finger in Francie's face.

'Please, can I just take this one picture?' Francie pleaded. She had to have proof. She pressed the button, and there was a flash. She didn't bother to check the image, in case the attendant confiscated her camera, or became even more officious. Her heart was thudding.

'It's not history, it's her story I'm going to get,' she said, pointing out the photograph to a puzzled Margit,

69

who had finally dropped her Nokia in its case into a leather bag covered with bronze studs, a bag that Francie already felt she knew very well.

'Look at that picture,' she said. 'The girl on the right.'

'*Ja?*' said Margit.

'That's my grandmother,' said Francie.

5

They threaded their way to an empty round table where large armchairs awaited their bottoms, already a tight foursome.

A bustling *Kaffee und Kuchen* service was well underway in the lobby, with teams of waiters pushing gleaming silver trolleys with domed crystal lids across marble floors.

'So,' said Siegmund, the blond one, gesturing to two armchairs for the girls to sink into, before settling into his. 'Here we are.' He looked around with pride. 'This is supposed to be' – he paused as if overcome – 'the drawing room of Munich.' The girls gasped in appreciation, and widened their eyes for Siegmund's benefit.

The truth is, they were quite struck by it all. The drawing room of Munich! Daphne felt grown-up, and somehow more *rounded*. She still missed Dem, and felt awful she hadn't replied to Dem's last letter, but the thing was, she felt happy, especially now Betsy had arrived and, in her honour, yesterday, the *Gräfin* had produced these cousins, as if her work was done.

'Otto and Siegmund will take very good care of you,'

she had said, as they stood around her drawing room yesterday.

Betsy had just arrived from the station, popping like a Champagne cork from a bottle after three 'utterly desperate' months at the Lucie Clayton Charm Academy learning deportment, flower arranging, how to make a white sauce and enrobe a Christmas cake in royal icing, and other essential accomplishments for the aspirant bride.

Betsy was thrilled as the maid took her bags upstairs to the room with a little balcony she was to share with Daphne. After she got back to England in the summer, she was, like her sisters, going to come out.

Esmé, Betsy's mother, Lady Barton-Hill, wife of Sir Bache Barton-Hill, had explained that the point of the coming-out exercise was not to find a husband as such, but to acquire a nice group of young friends from whom a suitable husband might, God willing, *emerge*.

Esmé also explained that what was even more important, if that was possible, than the emergent husband were the *house parties*. For it was at house parties that one made one's *friends for life*.

As Betsy had brothers as well as sisters and played strenuous mixed doubles on a hard tennis court next to the walled garden at Tiddington, Daphne couldn't see that finding a suitable chap for her was going to present much difficulty to Lady Barton-Hill, even if she did have Sir Bache to contend with.

Sir Bache was known as the Basher or, to give him his full title, the Basher of Vladivostok. He'd rescued

British subjects from the Bolsheviks in 1917, and been an enthusiastic supporter of the Anglo-German Naval Treaty of June 1935. He had firm views about what constituted a suitable husband for his daughters. Anyone darkly complexioned, who lived in Hampstead – and everyone knew what that meant – was officially a contemptible malformation of humanity. Such types were not allowed within forty miles of Tiddington Hall, and as for all the rest, they fell into three categories: menials, defectives, and degenerates.

By the time the Barton-Hills' last child, Betsy, was coming of age, though, Esmé and Bache had eased off. They didn't mind if Betsy was wild, so long as she wasn't considered *fast*. When Linden had called about Munich, therefore, the Barton-Hills had agreed that Bavaria was just the ticket. After all, despite the war, the Germans were basically cousins, the chaps were a decent bunch, and the country was on the up, Sir Bache assured his wife.

Betsy, already thrilled to leave Lucie Clayton, had perked up even more when she met the two young men the very day of her arrival.

'It is just as well you meet some nice suitable German boys, apart from Eric, of course.' The *Gräfin*'s eyes lit up when she mentioned her son. Even though she was fond of the cousins, who were her son's age and had been introduced to her as plausible German 'debs' delights' by him, she only smiled when Eric's name came up.

Eric was her tall, anxious only son. He didn't want to have anything to do with the succession of Pamelas and

Peggies who arrived with their cases and capes at his mother's house and whirled their way through Munich for several months, and needed taking to the Opera, waltzing at a ball, walking round the English Garden or driving to one of Mad King Ludwig's castles. Eric had his foot on the first rung of the *cursus honorum* that was the National Socialist movement. He wore uniform, with shapeless jodhpur trousers so baggy they seemed to be winged on either side.

That morning, Eric had left the establishment on Königin-Luise Strasse earlier, before the girls had got up, breakfasted and had their first lesson, which was fine by them. Eric seemed a cold fish. He only seemed to have two expressions. Uniform off (drippy, anxious) and uniform on (drippy, anxious and stern). But still, three boys were better than none, which was what Daphne was used to, up to now.

So, sitting in this exotic, foreign hotel lobby, it all seemed so far away – Park Town, her mother, the awfulness, the kitchen with Nesta and Mosey, the gas-lit nursery, her bedroom – her past melted away as she looked forward to trying the airy, flaky *mille-feuille*. So this was life, this was living, she thought as she gazed around the self-important, marble-encrusted, lamp-lit lobby.

'Just tell the girls the truth. That we're in the Nazi hotel,' said Otto, the dark one who looked like a Spanish painting, as he shifted on the green velvet chair, as if reluctant to sit there for very long, which was a shame, as the afternoon cake session was shortly to segue into the cocktail hour. A pianist in black tie tinkled away at a glossy Bechstein, waiters in natty, nipped-in uniforms slung with snowy-white tea-towels dipped and darted like swallows among the tables, or leant over sofas, adjusting ancient Chinese lamps that gave off a yellow glow. A fat pastry cook stood glowering behind a glass counter, as if daring anyone to approach his confections of whipped cream and puff pastry, marzipan, spun sugar and jam. Behind a mahogany bar, where battalions of bottles shone, soldierly waiters in crisp whites stood waiting for the sun to go over the yardarm.

Siegmund had marshalled them to a low table bang in the middle of the room, underneath a vast glass ceiling light that radiated outwards from a yellow centre, like a sun. In each quadrant there were the plants and flowers of spring, summer, autumn and winter. Daphne studied the light and admired the soft glow of reds and browns and yellows it emitted, and then it clicked – this was the celebrated circular glass ceiling-light fitting that displayed the fruit and foliage of each of the Four Seasons – which was the translation of the name of the hotel: Vier Jahreszeiten. Betsy put on her 'Isn't this lovely?' face, which wasn't hard.

Both boys were handsome, clever. Not only did they speak English, they didn't seem to mind talking English, and talking English to girls, which was an extraordinary stroke of luck, the girls felt.

'Is that the famous light?' Daphne said, pointing up, thinking this was the right sort of interested-sounding remark to make. But before Siegmund could confirm it, a large group of five uniformed officers had jostled rudely past their table, and Otto's comment suddenly made sense.

'Oh, so is this why you call it the Nazi hotel?' Daphne asked. 'Is this where they all come?' She wasn't so sure this was a good question, and she soon regretted asking it.

'They are acting as if Germany is already theirs,' Otto said with force. He was staring at Siegmund accusingly. He struck his cushion with one delicate hand, startling a waiter who was passing. He waited to take their order.

'Munich is the home of the National Socialist Party, Berlin is its business address, Berchtesgaden, its Winter Palace,' Otto told the girls. Betsy and Daphne didn't dare reveal that they weren't sure where the other two places were. Otto sounded so impassioned whenever he said anything. 'Here, Herr Hitler is leader of a gang. In Berlin, he is Chancellor of the Reich. And in Berchtesgaden, where he has a chalet, he is a tourist.'

Daphne had never met boys – men – who talked like this, let alone to each other.

'Oh, I'd simply love to see his chalet,' said Betsy, which made Siegmund glance at her with approval, before he told the waiter what they would have.

'Of course, Munich's the capital of the movement,' Siegmund snapped. At the words 'capital of the movement', the girls' eyes flicked briefly but failed to meet. Betsy and Daphne's efforts not to titter when foreigners said things that sounded funny in English were proving increasingly successful. 'You are so stupid, Otto. Stop speaking like this. You know you have to join. I have.

You have to, as well. Otherwise, you know . . . you can forget your hopes of becoming a surgeon. Forget them completely.'

'*Nein*, Siegmund,' said Otto, flashing him a dark look. 'Plenty have, but not me. A few slogans. A pretty uniform – there's nothing so stupid it would not find thousands of willing believers in Munich, but I'll never be one of them.'

Luckily, at this point a waiter brought their cakes, on a pagoda-like stand. The girls leant back in their chairs, not wanting to help themselves and appear greedy. Siegmund lit a cigarette and, as he blew out smoke, he asked, 'Now, do you both ski, and what do you think of Eric?' And the atmosphere eased.

The girls leant forward. At last! This was better. They were going to stop talking about drear subjects and places and start talking about people.

'Eric's a *Hundertfünfundsiebzig*, you know,' Siegmund said.

Otto glowered at his cousin again. 'Really, Siegmund, half the Party's the same, but did you really have to mention that?' he said, pouring them all coffee from the tall silver pot that steamed, centre table. 'After all, he can't help it.'

Still, Daphne and Betsy demanded to know what the *Hundert*-whatsit meant, and Siegmund seemed to take an almost refined pleasure in telling them that this was the way people referred to paragraph 175 of the criminal code, the paragraph that defined the crime of homosexuality, which was punishable in various ways. The cakes froze on the way to the girls' open mouths, as they tried to decide how shocked they were, or should be, by the turn the conversation had taken.

There hadn't been a moment for Betsy and Daphne to compare first impressions of the cousins. So it had not yet been decided how they were going to pair off. They were all enjoying the open sense of possibility this gave rise to.

Otto, the medical student, was pale, and serious; he spoke less, but when he did speak you listened, because for someone so slight he had a deep voice, much deeper than Siegmund's, which seemed to emanate from within a locked vault. He had a high forehead, and dark hair that sprang away from his temples but curled into question marks at the nape of his neck. Siegmund was muscular and blond with smooth buttery cheeks tinted with pink. But there was something cruel about him.

Siegmund is a creature of the sun, and Otto the shade, thought Daphne. Siegmund was so blond, so meaty, there was something feral around his mouth, animal . . . whereas Otto had dark curly hair and was pale, poetic.

Daphne had read Goethe for the Oxford entrance exam and she decided he had more than a touch of the Sorrows of Young Werther about him. Yes, the cousin she found she wanted to look at was Otto.

Ignoring his cousin, Otto now turned towards the English tourists and said, 'I can't remember now who said it, but it might have been Harold Nicolson.'

The girls tried to look intelligent, as if familiar with the sayings of Harold Nicolson.

'He said: the Germans appeal to the adolescent, the French to the adult.' He declined the offer of cream for his coffee, as if to display his own Gallic asceticism, as if he would be much happier drinking an espresso on a Left Bank boulevard. 'Cousin Siegmund is the living proof of that theorem.'

Siegmund sat straight-backed. He was wearing a green Loden jacket with floral embroidery around its small, almost symbolic collar, frogging, a silver pin and a formal white shirt. He stubbed out his cigarette, reached for a cake, and his blue eyes flashed. He was staring at Otto – in a dark, narrow suit and a white shirt, no tie – in the predatory way he looked at everyone: boys, girls, waiters, women.

'Well, we English prefer being foreign here to being foreign in Paris,' Daphne said. It was lucky, because Paris was the only other place she'd been, apart from Germany in 1935, and Deauville, where the Lindens went every other summer. She had only been two years old, so she hoped no one asked her about it, and that Betsy wouldn't pick her up on it. Betsy could be quite cutting and competitive sometimes in company. 'Everyone's so friendly here, aren't they, Bets?'

She eyed the tower of pastries on a silver cake stand on the low table, but held back. Ever since she'd left Marquartstein, she'd spent the entire time eating. She sipped her coffee, and decided that, if she had one wish, it would be to eat whatever she wanted, and never put on an ounce. She wondered who would be coming that night.

The *Gräfin* was hosting a little cocktail party for what she called '*Mein* English *Kinder.*' The fact that the crumbling countess knew Jacob Linden and clearly still felt a *tendresse* for him helped – it was clear, already, that she preferred Daphne to Betsy, just as she preferred Siegmund to Otto, and Eric to everyone.

The cousins were not, of course, staying with the *Gräfin*. They both had family residences in Munich, a set of circumstances that allowed Eric to evade squiring duties while he concentrated on his career. The aristocracy had been brought to its knees in turn by war, revolution, inflation and economic depression. English girls who came, like Daphne Linden, and Betsy Barton-Hill, had English pounds they converted into Reichsmarks at the tourist rate. The tourist rate was double the rate paid out for sterling to German citizens. So the Betsies, Margarets, Daphnes, Deborahs and Nancys were all that kept the Montdragons and their ilk from starving, and for that, of course, the English girls could never be forgiven.

Betsy wasn't listening. She was gazing happily at Siegmund and thinking about her new clothes.

She'd arrived from London in the finest of fettles, not only because she'd escaped from deportment lessons but because she had with her a whole new wardrobe from Marshall & Snelgrove: a skating dress in smooth scarlet facecloth, with Swiss peasant embroideries at the centre of a zip-fastened bodice; a white windproofed skiing jacket, a warm jersey ski-hood, hand-knitted ski-mitts, and Tyrolean accessories, all of which she'd shown to Daphne.

Daphne had been very brave about it. Apart from her dirndl, and her Marquartstein uniform, Daphne had only a few plain dresses, navy gaberdine trousers for skiing, jerseys and a hopsack skating skirt.

'Everyone's frightfully friendly,' Betsy agreed happily. 'This is all such fun. And speaking of skiing, Siegmund, guess what? I can't believe I haven't said! You'll never believe this. But my cousin, Celia Collins, is competing in the Olympics. She'll be here any day now, I expect,' Betsy concluded with deliberate vagueness.

Daphne turned to Betsy. She'd never heard of this cousin.

'My second cousin,' Betsy said.

'Well, in that case, it's settled!' Siegmund had said, reaching for the cake stand.

'You must both come to Garmisch, and stay with us during the *Winterspiele*. We have a chalet there.'

Betsy squealed out loud.

Siegmund pushed cake into his mouth in triumph and turned to Otto. Daphne's heart sank slightly. She'd seen Bets's wardrobe, and it was no wonder Betsy was hipped on this plan to go to the Winter Games. She had all the right clothes, and Daphne didn't.

'Why don't you come too, Otto,' he suggested, chewing, as Daphne wondered whether her school jersey and gaberdine trousers would be warm enough or whether she could borrow something of Betsy's. 'Put some colour in those white cheeks.' And then he'd pinched Otto fondly. 'I know my parents have several spare tickets for the opening ceremony.'

Daphne was just reaching out for the other rectangle of dark *Sachertorte*, glistening with apricot filling, when, out of the corner of her eye, she noticed that Siegmund swivelled in his chair and suddenly grasped Otto's leg. Daphne noted that his hand gripped Otto's thigh at a point quite high up the leg. But after a term at Marquartstein, she was unshocked. The Germans were always taking their clothes off to commune with Mother Nature. They all seemed very open about this sort of thing.

'Cousin,' Siegmund said, still gripping Otto's thigh, 'you must come to the *Winterspiele*. Our new English friend Betsy's cousin will be skating for Great Britain. Whatever you think about politics, you must admit – this is history.'

'I don't want to get into a row, not here,' Otto said, and he attempted to remove Siegmund's heavy hand.

'Nonsense!' Siegmund barked. 'Nonsense!' He knew what Otto was objecting to. 'There are Jews competing on our teams, our national teams, representing Germany. It's the Olympic Games. It's sport, not politics!' He held his arms out as if holding a pair of poles and wiggled in his seat, as if weaving between poles in the slalom.

Betsy's fingers had been straying for some time in the direction of a sponge oblong coated in smooth pink fondant and laced with chocolate in the shape of a leaf. As Siegmund spoke her fingers clasped the cake, as if his remark would provide cover for her greed. So far, she'd had three, all with different-coloured icing, and Daphne for some reason hadn't even finished her *Sachertorte*. Otto hadn't wanted to take tea at the Four Seasons. It was Siegmund who had insisted. After only a couple of hours, it was clear to Betsy. It was Siegmund who had leadership qualities.

'Shall we go to powder our noses?' she asked Daphne, so she could find out which cousin she liked. She hoped it wasn't her one.

'Well?' said Betsy.

'Well, what do you think?' Daphne asked. She knew what she thought. She'd known the first second she'd clapped eyes on him.

They had both emerged from their respective cubicles and were standing in the Ladies of the Four Seasons. It was lovely in there, practically the nicest place she'd ever been. Marble floors, bronze basins, big mirrors, soft lamplight to do your face by. She dried her hands carefully on a towel while she looked at Betsy applying red lipstick, her lips pushed out into a red bud.

'I think the blond one,' said Betsy.

'Siegmund?' exclaimed Daphne, hoping she wasn't giving herself away.

'Yes, I think he's frightfully good-looking – isn't he?'

'Yes, isn't he,' said Daphne, relieved. An image of Otto's face swam into her mind, and stayed there.

'I like Otto too, of course, but he hasn't got It, has he?' Betsy continued, snapping her powder compact shut and dropping it into her handbag. She pouted in the mirror. 'He thinks that Germany is heading in the wrong direction, but Siegmund seems to be saying just the same as Daddy, that actually, England and Germany are natural allies, and actually, England could learn a lot from Germany, how it's put itself back on its feet.'

'I suppose so,' said Daphne. She didn't know what to think, much. It was clever of Betsy to have got all that out of Siegmund, and to have understood what he was saying enough to repeat it.

They walked back together to their table across the red and gold carpet, through a sea of walnut and velvet, of Biedermeier and napery, of silvery cutlery and white-coated waiters dancing attendance. By the grand piano, two conjoined couples were waltzing, eyes locked on the middle distance.

It was cosy and safe and old-fashioned in the Vier Jahreszeiten, with its lit sconces, brass railings and mahogany-panelled walls. The Fatherland was hosting the Olympic Games, the band would play on, and two handsome young German boys were taking them out to tea.

Betsy and Daphne walked behind Otto and Siegmund as they left the hotel. Betsy was chirruping about some drinks they were all going to at the British ambassador's residence after they'd returned from the Alps.

The skiing plan was therefore already set, in concrete, by Betsy and Siegmund.

'I hope it's on Valentine's Day!' she kept saying,

making cow-eyes at Siegmund and suddenly darting forward to grab his arm. 'What on earth am I going to wear? Daphne, what are we going to wear?' she said, as she skipped.

'You can always wear my dirndl,' Daphne offered. 'It's about all I've got.'

'An excellent suggestion,' declared Siegmund, with heartiness. 'There's nothing I like more than seeing a pretty girl in a dirndl.' Then he laughed loudly, as he looked at Betsy's breasts. Sometimes, it had to be said, Siegmund sounded a duff note, Daphne thought. But it was probably because English was his second language. Still, the cousins' English was a million times better than the girls' German, thanks to their shared English grandmother and five years at a freezing prep school on the Sussex Downs.

By now, Otto had fallen back to pair Daphne. Both boys were tall, but Siegmund was taller, and carried with him an air of forests and lakes and wind on bare legs.

They passed the lit glass front of a bookshop. 'Aha,' said Siegmund. 'Just a minute.' The girls stood politely near the counter with Otto, inhaling the delicious smell of foolscap and notebooks, stationery and newsprint, while Siegmund darted along the shelves, looking for something. He came back with a couple of books in his hand, took them up to the counter, took out his billfold, and paid. Then he presented Betsy with a guide to Munich, and a paperback book in English, called *Passing Through Germany*. 'Both have only just been published,' he said. 'I do hope you find them useful, Betsy.'

Suddenly Daphne's leather-bound burgundy Baedeker seemed heavy and worn in her hand. And when she'd unfolded the city map insert over tea in the Four Seasons, so Siegmund could show her where they were in relation to her house on Königin-Luise Strasse, and the consulate on Pranner Strasse, the English Garden and the Museums and the Opera, she had torn a great rip in it, and felt like crying. The Baedeker had belonged to her father – his name was inked on the onion-skin paper flyleaf – and he'd lent it to her.

He'd looked after it for years, and then she'd gone and ripped it the first time she used it.

They started threading their way south the short distance from the hotel on Maximilian Strasse, with a couple of hours to kill before they had to present themselves for duty at the *Gräfin*'s. Siegmund was clearly in charge.

'We could do a circular drive, but they don't start until April,' Siegmund said crisply. 'Annoyingly, the Alpine Museum at Praterinsel, it closes I think at five.' It was four thirty. A difficult time of day, at a difficult time of year, but Siegmund still had plans. He led the way down Maximilian Strasse, and darted into the traffic to cross the road.

They cut down a side-street off the main drag, and then the streets got smaller. They spent the next minutes scrambling over cobbles, crossing the main square of Marienplatz, eyes drawn to the medieval towers of the vast town hall looming over the area from its north corner. 'Don't stop now,' commanded Siegmund as the girls paused at the vaulted ground floor of the building, from which the thump of the oompah bands could be heard pumping out from the undercroft. 'We are saving the *Neues Rathaus* and the *Ratskeller* for tomorrow's programme.'

The girls realized that Siegmund had probably done this before, showing English girls around Munich, many times.

Siegmund plucked Betsy's arm and then the two of them stepped together. They tried to cut a swathe as much as they could, through the crowds of sightseers and shoppers, and fought their way through the open-air food market, filled with wicker-basket-wielding women with determined expressions. It was a cross between Harrod's food hall and a game fair: stalls with gaily striped green and white awnings selling red fruits and green vegetables, stalls with groaning displays of yellow-rinded and white cheeses and salamis, stalls selling beer and sausage called a *Schwein-Imbiss*, stalls selling wet fish. There were long queues at each, as at every purchase the glistening fresh produce was discussed, weighed, coddled in paper as if it was a precious object and stowed away safely for supper. 'The people of Munich love their victual market and will never go hungry,' said Siegmund.

Whenever an officer loomed, Sieggy dragged them into the gutter so they never had to deviate so much as a side-step from their course, and it was odd and alarming to see how old ladies and bowed gentlemen scuttled out of their way, eyes cast down. There was something in the expressions in the faces of the old – not the young, who seemed invigorated by the sight of uniforms – that made a question form in Daphne's subconscious: will it all happen again?

It wouldn't; Pa had sworn it wouldn't.

The place was swarming with soldiers. They lorded it over the pavements and they commandeered the streets. It was as if the whole of Munich belonged to swaggering men in gleaming boots, and through the streets sharked black shiny Mercedes with red leather seats, driven by sneering-faced officers in peaked caps, red armbands, wearing those flappy jodhpurs, like Eric's, that caught in thick folds between their thighs.

Daphne was wearing the right sort of shoes for tea in a smart hotel but the wrong sort of shoes for a long walk over cobbles. Finally, after passing countless snuggeries of beer drinkers and sausage eaters, they turned a corner and were in a small square, the footprint of which was taken up almost entirely by a vast edifice. 'Look up,' ordered Siegmund. They dutifully looked up: a sheer, blank red façade of plain brick, each side peaking in two tall towers finished with spindly green Renaissance domes.

'The Frauenkirche, the last resting place of the Wittelbachs,' announced Siegmund. 'Our Lady.' Siegmund pronounced. They entered the cathedral.

'I'm not going to make everyone climb the towers,' Siegmund said in a jokey voice. 'Well, I am,' said Otto. They all followed him, in single file, up and up, and they all stopped talking after 100 steps, and Betsy stopped counting after 180.

Otto led, followed by Daphne, who admired his long legs and straight posture. After Daphne came Siegmund and, finally, Betsy. The tower was narrow. It was a curiously intimate climb. The only sound on the staircase, apart from the tympanic beat of leather soles slapping against stone, was of their breathing. Daphne laid her hot hand against the cool, damp walls of the tower as she climbed.

Finally, out of breath, they debouched into a hexagonal-shaped room with sixteen arched windows. Munich lay spread before them, the mountains beyond. Daphne felt dizzy, but Siegmund had already started lecturing, so she pretended she was fine and went to the parapet.

'See, the Marienplatz, the tower of the town hall, where we were just a few minutes ago, Betsy? And the tower of the Peterskirche on the right?' He searched Betsy's face to make sure she was locking on to the right targets as he pointed them out – the State Library, the Ludwigskirche, the flat oblong of the Deutsches Museum to the right in the far distance. To Daphne, it all looked a bit of a muddle, especially in the fading light: she could make out the wide boulevards, a tangle of lesser streets, bushy, green open spaces, Gothic arches, Renaissance domes, brutal new buildings like huge radiators made of concrete, which they would no doubt be marched around tomorrow, but it all competed hopelessly for attention with the sublime grandeur of the Alps, a backdrop in the distance.

'We're on top of the world,' said Siegmund, in a loud voice, still a little out of puff. 'This city is a hundred times better than Berlin.' He whirled around the parapet, windmilling his arms.

Otto took Daphne aside. 'I am afraid my cousin gets a little carried away,' he said.

'Don't worry, Otto, I'm sure he's terribly sweet,' said Daphne uncertainly. 'Underneath.'

Then Otto did something. He leant in close, and made Daphne even giddier than she was already. He moved some locks of hair away so his lips were near her ear, and she could almost feel them move against her skin. 'You must remember something,' he whispered, as Daphne's cheek flamed and her breath caught in her throat. She'd never been this close to a boy before. Apart from Kaspar, in Oberammergau – they'd barely touched thighs and she had still felt it, for weeks after.

'You must remember. Siegmund isn't really German. Siegmund is *Bavarian*.' As he spoke, Daphne gazed ahead, fighting the instinct to bury her head in his shoulder. His lips were on her ear again. 'And therefore one of Nature's true fascists.'

He sighed in her ear and, in that instant, the very air between them changed, and it was as if, for Daphne, it became not air, but fizzing particles of light. Siegmund returned from doing a tour of the clocktower with Betsy. She looked flushed, in her belted coat. He whirled her round the tower, spinning her, as if they were on a dance floor. He had overheard what his cousin had said.

'And you are a priggish Prussian!' Siegmund had closed in on them from behind, making them start apart.

'I do wish you weren't such an ass, Siegmund,' said

Otto, breaking away and moving to the parapet. He looked back at Daphne, and her wide eyes asked him: what happened just now?

'And if you weren't my cousin, I'd send you to Dachau,' replied Siegmund, squinting over the city, and pointing north. 'For an *Urlaub*.'

'What's Dachau?' and 'What's an *Urlaub*?' said Daphne and Betsy, in turn.

'It's a holiday,' said Siegmund. Then he laughed and clapped Otto on the shoulder.

'And what about Dachau?'

'A sort of lovely, holiday . . . camp,' said Siegmund. 'It's close by, a short train journey away. It's open to the public, actually. There's a day trip you can do. It really is impressive. Very . . . efficient.'

'What fun,' cried Betsy. 'I think Mummy and Daddy are going there, when they come over for the rally. We should all go!'

Daphne looked at Otto, who was glaring at Siegmund as he elaborated the attractions of this place.

She felt transfigured. She knew she would never feel the same again. But Otto looked exactly the same, and the question formed in her mind. Had he felt it too, what she had felt, the way Otto had made her feel, when his lips grazed her ear?

All she wanted to do was feel it, again and again and again.

6

Central London / Little Venice
February 2006

Francie stared at her screen.

Should she send Nathan a text, or an email? A text was more intimate and direct. Yet they were in the office . . . and his name was auto-completing already as she typed the capital 'n' followed by the 'a'.

'Hi Nathan, just back from Bavaria (!!)' she tapped quickly before her better judgement kicked in. 'You up for a drink tonight after wk? Something I'd like to discuss.'

This sounded a bit needy and demanding, which wasn't good. It read as if she wanted to have one of those whinges all bosses dread.

So Francie added. 'Have a surprise for you (not a new dirndl).' Then she realized that this sounded as if she wanted him to picture her in a bosom-cupping dress, so she deleted that sentence. She stared at the email again, added the word 'quick' in front of drink, so it looked like she had to rush off after, and pressed send.

A minute later, her phone rang on her desk. One ring meant it was an internal call. Two rings meant an external. She smiled.

'Hey, boss, so where do you want to go?' she said brightly, picking up.

'Hey, it's Miranda,' came a soft voice. 'When did you get back?' Her voice sounded light, happy. As if she was sitting in a hotel in the South of France, looking out over a sparkling azure sea with a cooling drink in her hand. Not in a grungy office off New Bond Street with stained mushroom-coloured carpet-tiles, less than thirty yards away from Francie.

'I wondered if you wanted to come with me next week? Got a spare, for Burberry. The catwalk show.'

Francie considered this. She checked her email, but nothing so far from Nathan, though she knew from his PA, Georgie, that he was in.

'What time?' asked Francie. She hadn't even realized it was Fashion Week.

She'd been to Burberry's Prorsum show the previous year. There'd been scrums of paparazzi waiting for the hand-picked movie or tennis stars; everyone who was anyone in fashion, from Mario Testino to Suzy Menkes to Anna Wintour.

It had been a nightmare getting in, past mountainous black bouncers, hysterical junior fashion writers and teenage bloggers. It had been a nightmare once you were inside the show, too, as you had to wait for hours on a tiny seat while the A-listers claimed their places in the front row and folded and unfolded their coltish legs for the cameras. And then it was over in ten headachey minutes.

So, in other words, in glossy-magazine terms, it was a

completely unmissable event. Tickets to the Burberry Prorsum catwalk show were as sought after as tickets to the Wimbledon Men's doubles final. They were biked to selected offices on the day, little metal oblong numbered cards inside boxes the smoky colour of the Burberry classic trench mac, so they couldn't be flipped, or even eBayed.

'Sure,' she said, anyway. 'Well, maybe. If you can't find someone more fashion-forward, I'd love to.'

One hour later, she was in the Ladies. She brushed her teeth, applied a second coat of mascara, and had changed into the high heels she kept in her desk drawer. 'Foxy,' Miranda had said, as she watched Francie's eye-lashes turn black-spidery. 'So, who you having a drink with?'

'No one special,' lied Francie, gargling with the blue Listerine she kept in her bottom drawer. 'Some ghastly PR.'

Nathan and Francie sat at a small table in an upstairs room at his club, which was, of course, Soho House. As she'd planned this drink in advance, Francie was wearing clothes that could, as the magazines had it, 'transition' – as if implicated in a change of administration – from work to dinner without breaking sweat. She was wearing a tight stretchy bandage dress, bought in the DVF sale. It was bright orange. Nathan, being in magazines, would get it. Gus, in advertising, also got it. It was an advantage both living and working with proper metrosexuals sometimes.

So far, they were alone at a small wooden table for two, apart from the waitress, nipping about in a short tight black skirt and an apron. Nathan's eyes were on the girl's bottom peeking out beneath its bow as he hurled black-peppered cashews into his mouth. He carried on eating the nuts, his eyes on the waitress, while he talked. It should have been disgusting – if anyone else had done this Francie would have been repulsed – but as it was Nathan, she wasn't.

'So . . . I'm glad we're having this drink,' he said. He didn't look at her; he was looking elsewhere. But she couldn't take her eyes off him. There was something about him. It wasn't a boss thing. It was something else.

She felt her stomach twist. There was no way she could eat a bowl of peppered cashews, she doubted she could eat anything ever again, something about him made her feel . . . *beyond eating*.

Nathan crooked a finger at the waitresss and she teleported herself from the bar to his side. Francie found her chest tight. She was jealous of the waitress. She was jealous of any woman who came near him. She knew she was being ridiculous.

She sipped her drink and forced herself to look away from the seductive sight of Nathan in a white shirt, very dark blue suit and orange tie ordering a bottle of Pinot Grigio, 'the buffalo mozzarella, and some Serrano ham. And some olives, please, and plenty of bread.'

'We match,' she heard herself saying, when the bottle of wine appeared and their glasses were full.

'What?' Nathan's eyes flicked from the waitress to her.

'My dress, your tie,' she said, glugging her wine. Oh fuck! Why did Nathan seem to cause women to stoop to folly so . . . so effortlessly? He was separated from his wife. He 'wasn't seeing' Douchka, his most recent girlfriend, and 'hadn't for ages'. Francie only knew this because he shared with Miranda – as much as men ever properly shared – and Miranda had passed on the headlines to Francie.

Douchka was almost half his age; they'd met on the Eurostar. Everyone had assumed she was an East European hooker until she came into the office. As it turned out, she was ravishing and spoke English, her fourth language, in paragraphs. Far from being one of Nathan's 'Jaguar blondes' (that was the type the office had identified – a glossy girl with long legs ending in heels, the breed you saw only in expensive car adverts), Douchka turned out to be ridiculously talented and beautiful and, as everyone agreed, far too good for Nathan.

'I've got something to show you,' Francie said, getting in first before they got on to Nathan's agenda: he had said, after all, he was 'glad' they were 'having this drink'.

She'd printed off the picture at work – the picture editor had, anyway. She had it in an envelope in her Mulberry satchel. She leant down, grabbed her bag before Nathan lost interest and looked around to see if there was anyone better in Soho House than her, or started picking up the waitresses. She handed it to Nathan.

'What's this?' he said. He wiped his hands on a large white napkin, took out the print and gave it a quick look. 'Hey.'

'Who do you think they are?' said Francie, with excitement.

'Well, I recognize the guy, but the two chicks?' he asked.

'Well, the one on the left is Betsy Barton-Hill, but that's not the point,' Francie said, sipping her Pinot Grigio, and thinking, this is good, very good. I am showing him my hinterland. He will take me off bridal beauty rituals and commission me to do a special investigation into my own past, and I will deliver a cracking, long-form piece of writing that *Vanity Fair* will wish they'd had. Or even the *New Yorker*. And then, of course, Nathan will realize what a versatile, highly textured person I am and put me in charge of the whole of Travel Features and probably appoint me the most coveted gig on the whole mag – Reportage Editor – but by that stage I will be most likely have been poached by –

'And the other one?' said Nathan, jabbing towards the picture with a salty, greasy finger. He licked the finger absently, while Francie watched.

'And that's my grandmother, Daphne Fitzsimon. Daphne Linden, she was then.'

'Cool,' said Nathan. He handed her back the picture. 'Back in the thirties the English couldn't get enough of the Nazis, could they? Didn't think there was any problem with the whole Aryan nation idea. It was only after the war that anyone fully realized. Extraordinary.'

The waitress returned and they made room for the nibbles on the table: the ham, the bread, the olives. Francie tried to steer the conversation back to the picture, but her editor clearly had said his piece on Hitler's Germany 1939–45, the Third Reich and the Anglo-German love-in in the thirties. He had a running order he was clearly intending to stick to, and Francie's heart began to sink.

'So, as I said, it's good we're having this drink,' Nathan said. He gave her a direct look. His eyes seemed suddenly very blue. He batted his dark, curly eyelashes. He glanced down at the table, but he'd already eaten the focaccia, the olives, the nuts, and he sort of hurried it up. So dinner *à deux* was off the cards, Francie thought glumly.

And she'd already warned Gus she'd be late.

They were still alone in the room, apart from the intermittent waitress, for whom Nathan kept a roving and watchful eye.

'Listen. There's no point beating round the bush,' he said, rolling up some Serrano ham into a cigarette and popping it into his mouth. He continued in a slightly muffled voice. 'All the editors in the group, and that includes me and *Event*, are having to cut down on staff costs by 25 per cent.'

Francie didn't understand why he was bringing this up with her. She'd had a staff job at *Event* for three years. She'd been there longer than he had (he'd come to *Event* from the glossy supplement of a many-sectioned Saturday newspaper). She'd left the bloody *Telegraph* to come to *Event*. As Nathan well knew.

'As you travel so much anyway . . . and Gus has a good job – not that what your husband does has any bearing on decision-making of course,' he added hastily. 'Well, I was going to ask you, actually, if you'd *prefer* to go on a freelance contract.' He paused and popped some ciabatta in his mouth. 'What do you think?' he said. He didn't make it sound like a question. 'It shouldn't make that much difference.'

Francie stared at him.

'And not immediately either.' He refilled both their glasses. Francie glugged half hers in shock, then pouted at him. They stared hard at each other. He swallowed. 'I'd like you to think about it.'

And then something happened.

Nathan Galsworthy, editor of *Event*, leant in, across the table, and brushed his lips softly on the corner of her mouth. What's he doing? Francie thought. Then she felt the shock of a thousand volts at the contact.

'I don't want to lose you,' he whispered.

Like a baby reaching for the nipple, she turned her head so her lips met his and they started kissing, without caring whether the waitress or anyone else could see them. Francie, obviously, never wanted it to stop, but when it did she wanted to cry out, and when she tried to remember what it felt like, later, all she could think was the opening credits of a Disney cartoon when the fairy castle explodes with fireworks and cascading showers of light. If she had to describe it to anyone – and so annoying that she couldn't, not even to Miranda – that was how it felt.

His mobile rang. He glanced at the screen, saw the caller ID, but didn't answer it. Francie tried to read it too, but couldn't quite make out the letters. He saw her looking, sent a quick text, jabbing at the keys with his forefinger rather than two thumbs, and slid his mobile into a pocket. He scribbled in the air, signed for their drinks then added something suddenly under his signature as an afterthought.

'I've got to go,' he muttered, and he put his head down this time towards her ear, and sort of nuzzled her. 'I'm sorry, but Mandy's on a double yellow. She's taking me on . . . to a work thing.'

Mandy, born Andy, was Nathan's driver, and Nathan, and IMAG, had supported him throughout his transition from Andy to Mandy. Even though *Event* didn't make a ton of money, IMAG was famously good to its editors, and they repaid the investment by behaving like despots in Third World countries. Treating its editors well extended, in Nathan's case, to a shiny black Porsche Cayenne with DVD players for his kids in the seat backs, and the services of Mandy, Monday to Friday, whenever she was needed.

Mandy. Miranda and Francie often joked that there was one significant other in Nathan's life, and that it was she.

'And hey,' he said, getting to his feet, leaving Francie in a scrim of ciabatta crumbs and confusion. He put a hand on her shoulder. It burned through the orange dress. There was a final kiss-off to come.

'Why don't you do a piece: the story of the picture? Why *was* your grannie in Germany with the *Führer*, Francie? It might make a good feature. Obviously, for your freelance stuff I'll make sure you get a decent lineage rate, to make up for the fact that you . . .' He couldn't say it. He couldn't say he was kicking her *off staff*.

He grabbed his jacket. He looked disgustingly handsome. Francie couldn't take her eyes off him. What the *fuck* had just happened? Did he or did he not leave his mobile number for that waitress? Had she been fired, or pulled?

'Take your time with it,' he said. 'You've got three months till . . . you know. Hey, that was great. Really good. I'm so glad we did that – had that drink. See you later.' He handed the bill to the waitress, who was also watching him go, and clattered downstairs.

At least, Francie thought, he had the decency not to wink. At either of them.

Two days later, Francie entered into a mêlée of people wheeling bikes, staring at overhead displays, trotting along with paper cups and mobiles clamped to their ears, checking emails on BlackBerries, or filling a few spare minutes by browsing in Monsoon or Accessorize, sitting at the sushi carousel at Yo! Sushi, or getting their hit of sugar and fats at Krispy Kreme. She plunged into Costa.

As she waited for her latte, Francie perked up, even though she was worried about seeing Grannie after her stroke. And worried about her job. She loved Paddington.

Everywhere you looked, everyone was consuming something – information, caffeine, clothes, food, news, chat, transfats, celebrity gossip, messages. Even couples marching in lockstep were talking into their mobiles, apart from one elderly man with a beard and a trilby and an overcoat and scarf on a bench near the hissing, belching Penzance train, outside W. H. Smith. He had an expression on his face which said, I don't like being old. I don't like the horrible modern world. I'm only putting up with it because it won't be long now. He was probably a war hero, with a string of medals and decorations to his name, but now he slumped on a bench, like an under-stuffed guy waiting to be slung on a bonfire.

She got on the Oxford train, found a seat – brilliant, as trains at all times of day now were rammed – took her magazine out, put her tray down, placed her coffee cup on it, but then, total disaster.

She'd just removed the lid from her coffee when she spotted the girl in the seat across from her, wearing a bright-pink velour sub-Juicy Couture-style tracksuit. She had a large pack of Cheesy Wotsits in her lap and was slotting them into her mouth while talking into a mobile.

'And I was like, and he was like, then I was like . . . *crunch crunch* . . . and I was sat there and he was like . . . and then he was all, I'll ring you later, and I was like, OK, but what do you think he meant when he said "later" . . .?' Francie considered the meaning of 'later', as used by men to girls they'd slept with, wondered again what Nathan had meant when he said, 'I'm so glad we did this,' and by 'See you later,' and her fellow passenger was off again.

Crunch, crunch. 'But then he didn't ring, didn't text, and

I'm like, what's all that about – if you're gonna blow me off, don't like say you'll call later, right?'

The girl finished one pack of Wotsits, folded up the packet into squares, tucked it between the seats, and then – to Francie's horror – removed a Big Eat lime-green bag of pickled-onion-flavour Walker crisps and opened it one-handed with a practised movement. This was too much to bear. Francie got up and moved down the carriage to a man who'd already opened his laptop and was deep in a spreadsheet, with an *FT* and a Burberry safely bagging the seat alongside. To her relief, the man's only oral comforter was a plastic bottle of Evian mineral water with a nipple.

'Grannie?' she said, an hour later, holding a small bunch of snowdrops she'd picked in the garden of the home. She plonked them in her grandmother's water glass. They splayed out untidily. She filled the glass from a sink in the corner, and sat on the wingback armchair, the one from Hendridge.

After Grandpa Jeremy had died, Grannie had sold Hendridge and moved to semi-sheltered housing in Headington. Grandpa had been a kind, gentle man, with perfect English manners, who'd made Francie a doll's house of Hendridge for her eighth birthday, complete with a duck pond made of tin foil and little wooden models of all the chocolate Labs and her pony, Crump. After ten or so years in her flat in Headington, she'd downsized again, to a single room in a residential care home in Faringdon.

On the dressing table, next to the perky white snow-drops, rested the meagre mementos of an ampler life: a photograph of Grandpa Jeremy taking silk, wearing buckled shoes and a wig; Grannie's various pills in daily dispensers; an old-fashioned leather fold-up travelling alarm clock, ticking; a stem vase containing a single daffodil; her tortoiseshell reading glasses in a battered case.

Daphne didn't open her eyes. She was breathing faintly though, so Francie knew she was definitely alive. 'Grannie?' Francie said again, slightly louder. 'It's Frances. How are you? Are you better?'

Apparently, Grannie was sleeping a lot, but it wasn't clear whether she'd had a stroke.

'You were asking for me. Sorry I took so long to come. I've been away. In Germany. It was very interesting actually.'

She wondered when and whether to produce the photo.

As Daphne stirred, Francie began to anticipate the narrative. Grannie would wake up, see Francie. Francie would reassure her that she was there, that Daphne was loved, that everything was all right. Then her grandmother would tell her the thing, to do with Hitler. It would be a shameful family secret that had been kept hidden for decades.

Well, Francie hoped it would be – she was braced for anything. Nothing could shock her. Her father had died when she was four in a plane accident. So she knew, more than most people, that terrible things could happen in life, because one terrible thing already had.

Daphne did not speak of the death of her oldest son – Andrew, Francie's father – very much. She was of a generation that hardly ever spoke of money or health. Jeremy refused to talk about the war. Daphne didn't talk about the time she spent in Germany at all. All this meant that mealtimes, at Hendridge, could – it had to be admitted – be quite perfunctory affairs, sometimes accompanied by the wireless, tuned to what her grandparents insisted on calling the Home Service.

But still. Francie was here now, and she had to change all that. She had a commission, to write about all this. Grannie had to share. Francie looked at her sleeping face, the downturned mouth, and heard her soft breathing, and wondered why had Grannie chosen her, Francie, of all her surviving children and grandchildren to tell, and not Uncle Francis, or Aunties Jill or Sally.

'Grannie's been asking for you,' said Gus, when she was in Germany. 'This woman called. So you've got to get to Faringdon as soon as you're back from your Nazi spa.'

Francie knew that whatever Grannie had to say, would – stood to reason – be about her. She had always been extra-special to Grannie, because of Daddy dying young and handsome in a glamorous plane crash and Mummy buggering off with big-game hunter Geoff and Francie's semi-orphan status. Francie had all the cuttings from the *Daily Mail*.

She leant over the bed. Here she was, the dutiful granddaughter, the receptacle – no, the *chalice* – for the family secret.

'Grannie?' she said again. She gently took Daphne's hand. She looked at it, the white, elegant fingers, the blue raised veins, the large emerald engagement ring, set in a circle of diamonds. She stroked the back of it with her own thumb.

'I was in Germany – like you were – and Gus, he called.' She was pleased she had raised the subject already. 'He said you were asking for me. That's what Gus said. Gus told me. So here I am, Grannie. I'm here. I want to know all about it.'

She gazed at Grannie hopefully, willing her to wake up. She glanced at her watch. She'd been there only seven minutes.

At that moment, a woman came in, walked over to the curtains and twitched them fully open. The view was of a lawn, muddy in parts, with sprinkles of snowdrops and crocuses spearing through the turf. A robin hopped on the branch of the tree outside the window. As views went, it wasn't too bad.

'Hello, are you Frances?' said the woman, who was intelligent-looking, in her thirties, with a beaky nose.

'Yes I am,' Francie said, wondering whether she should rise to her feet.

'I'm Milly Goddard, I'm in charge here. I think I might have spoken to your husband. Mrs Fitzsimon was asking for you. I found your number in the book. You were abroad?'

Francie inhaled the smell of disinfectant and noted the hand sanitizer mounted on the wall. There was something omnicompetent about Goddard; she had a manner that suggested she had seen and performed duties for her elderly charges that Francie could not even begin to imagine. 'Yes. I'm her granddaughter.'

'I know,' she said. 'It's a shame Mrs Fitzsimon isn't brighter. She's sort of faded again, hasn't she?' Goddard smiled down at Grannie fondly. 'It's happened before.'

'Yes, but how is she?' Francie asked. 'You said she was asking for me. You called my husband, er, Gus . . .' She trailed off, guilty that, in truth, she had only come because Grannie had asked for *her*, and not for her sister Demeter in New York, Uncle Francis who lived in Leeds, and not Jill or Sally. Jill lived in Suffolk and Sally in Cornwall, which meant that the one person who could be bedside within the hour was Francie.

She went over and stood by the bed and twitched at the sheets, straightening them and smoothing them, to show the other woman that she could do hospital corners, too.

'No, it's good you're here,' said Milly Goddard. 'When people reach your grandmother's age,' she went on, 'it's important to listen. Sometimes they say things. Things they've never said before.'

Francie was so relieved that Goddard had used the formulation 'your grandmother' rather than 'Gran' or, horrors, 'Nan', that she didn't pick up the loaded implication of Milly Goddard's little speech. 'When they're coming near to Their Time,' Goddard continued, somewhat ecclesiastically, 'they're like the last leaves in winter.' She looked directly at Francie. 'You have to catch them before they fall.'

Francie wondered whether the woman had said this before to other relatives, or whether she had reserved this chill little blast about the End of Days just for her.

Goddard went to the cupboard in the corner. It had drawers at the bottom and a hanging bit above. There seemed to be so little in there – the dressing-gown was on the back of the door; Francie could see a couple of cardigans, a navy dress, two white blouses, a Liberty-print blouse and a navy jacket. Francie went to the cupboard and inhaled a smell. Grannie's smell: Calèche, by Hermès. She drew out a box.

'She wanted you to have this,' she said, handing it over. Francie hoped desperately that Grannie would wake. But still, a box. This was a start.

Francie loved a quest. On long plane journeys, she had very much enjoyed reading more than one lady novelist's moving account of uncovering dark family secrets. She'd even read an entire book about a woman who found an anonymous letter written by a mother to a dead son in a bottle on a beach in Normandy and spent the next six months of her life trying to find out who'd written it, and what had happened to the son ... and failed. She'd also, more recently, read the memoir of a daughter who had called up every single person she'd found listed in her late mother's Filofax. Francie'd really enjoyed it, even though the mother was only a Pilates teacher in New Jersey.

Francie loved this sort of thing, being of the generation who truly believed that life was all about a journey of discovery to the dark heart of oneself, and for whom even serious programmes on Radio Four/the Home Service were now series of interviews with people in which they discussed themselves in the third person, with titles like 'Meeting Myself', and so on. She peered into the box: bits of paper, postcards, letters, menus, trinkets, something white and fluffy like an egg cosy, what looked like a dried rose . . . She took out a little flat blue leather box, a few inches long.

Inside, there was some tissue paper, on top of which nestled a bronze coin. Francie took out the coin from where it had been sitting indented in its bed of tissue. It was satisfyingly heavy to hold in the palm, a bronze disc, five or so centimetres across and a chunky, near half-centimetre thick.

Francie gave it a quick nip between her teeth, not caring that Goddard's eyes were on her. Then she studied it more carefully. On the back, in the upper half, there was a chariot pulled by three horses soaring over a triumphal arch composed of four rays. The Goddess of Victory – Nike – sat on the chariot holding a laurel crown.

She turned over the coin slowly. On the other side, there was a bas-relief illustration of winter sports equipment – a hockey stick, some skates. Around the rim was the inscription GARMISCH-PARTENKIRCHEN and a date, 1936, across the horizon of the coin. In the middle rose an Alp, its peak bisecting the inscription:

IV Olympischewinterspiele
Garmisch-Partenkirchen

Even Francie, who had limited German, knew that *Winterspiele* meant Winter Games.

She put it back, and took out a couple of faded photos. One was of Grannie and another girl. She looked hard. Francie was sure it was the same girl as in the picture with Hitler.

Curls bobbing, wasp-waisted, in a hand-stitched blouse, Daphne Fitzsimon was sitting at a café table on a cobbled street stirring her coffee, eyes half closed against the sunlight, smiling merrily towards whoever was taking the picture. Next to her, a creamy blonde pouted in a tight sweater, as English as a cornfield painted by Constable. Both girls were absolute stunners. When Francie had told Grannie how pretty she was – as a teenager, she was glowing with health and happiness with wind-whipped cheeks – Grannie would say, 'Every dog has his day, dear.'

The other was of two boys, one dark, one blond, in pleated trousers, Norfolk jacket and woollen mittens, on wooden skis. They were snapped standing on the top of a mountain, with further ranges crumpling whitely into the far distance. There were other things that she would look at later.

Francie sat holding the box by the bed, wondering whether she should leave or wait for Grannie to wake. It seemed like a wasted journey, but at least she had the picture and the coin and stuff.

'Don't worry about hanging around to keep her company,' said Milly Goddard, as she cracked open the window and fresh air flooded the room. Francie pulled her coat around her. Just then, a tiny Sri Lankan nurse in a blue uniform pushed a trolley past the open door. 'Tea?' she asked, poking her head into Grannie's room. 'Today custard cream.'

'No, thank you.' Francie shook her head, and the trolley trundled past to the next room. She flipped over the photographs. There were no names, no dates on the back. Francie sighed.

If she left now, she could be back in London in under ninety minutes.

Or she could stay for a custard cream, and see if Grannie woke up. She glanced at her watch.

It was only when she was on the train, riffling through the box again, that she found the envelope at the bottom with the words 'Andrew's Birth Certificate' on it in a hand she didn't recognize.

Inside, folded up, was her father's birth certificate. The date was 30 October 1936. His mother was Daphne Hero Linden. Francie knew both those things already.

What she found strange was that Andrew's birth wasn't registered by a Linden, or a Fitzsimon, but by a woman called Janet Cuthbertson. What was even stranger still was that, when she looked for the dear name of her grandfather, 'Jeremy Fitzsimon', in the space allotted for the name of her father's father, there was nothing but a neat, clerical dash.

At that, her heart skipped a beat.

7

Garmisch-Partenkirchen, Bavaria
February 1936

Chalet Huber was set on the slope above town on the Partenkirchen side of the resort, and was, Betsy and Daphne agreed the moment they saw it, heavenly pretty: red gingham curtains at windows with peephole-hearted shutters, low-ceilinged bedrooms containing huge mahogany beds piled high with crisp, plump white-cotton eiderdowns. There were cosy cushions on the beds, benches and armchairs, there were even cushions lining the window-seats. It was comfort piled upon comfort. In the bedrooms there were crucifixes and samplers embroidered with pieties on the walls, but in Daphne's room, the one above her bed said '*Lachen ist die beste Medizin.*' Laughter is the best medicine.

The Hubers had greeted them in the hall, a dachshund, Rudi, at their heels, and then a maid had shown the girls down some wooden stairs to their rooms, both on the lower-ground floor. Daphne peeped out of her shuttered window and looked out at a steeply rising bank. Logs were stacked with Mayan precision in a pile to the right of her window, under the wide awning of the chalet.

Daphne and Betsy had their own bedroom each, but shared a bathroom, which had a tall bath made of copper which spouted endless piping-hot water, and soft white towels. It was all so clean. And toastily warm, too. They were so happy to be here, it was lovely to be in a house with a dog again, said Betsy, and the *Gräfin* seemed only too relieved to be shot of two English girls for a whole week and hand them over to the Hubers.

After they had both unpacked their frocks and skirts and hung them in pine-scented cupboards, and piled their vests, underclothes, sweaters and shirts in the paper-lined drawers scattered with lavender, and bundled their heavy ski clothes, gaberdine trousers and silk leggings and windproof blousons into the biggest drawer at the bottom, Betsy rushed into Daphne's room. 'Your room's bigger than mine, the bed's bigger,' she said, and bounced on it. Then she turned and sat facing the pillow and looked at the sampler above the bed. 'Can we swap? I don't like mine, it's next to the kitchen. What does this one say?' Betsy asked, pointing at the sampler above a mahogany chest of drawers.

Daphne flumped on to the bed face first and lay next to her friend. She read the embroidered message, carefully stitched in coloured threads on a cream background, the work of many hours. So typical that Betsy wanted her room. Even though she had everything, and Daphne had practically nothing, Betsy always wanted what she had.

'What it says is, "Never forget you're a German,"' she said.

For some reason, they found this terribly funny.

'Betsy, we're guests, someone will come, please try to behave,' said Daphne, as Betsy tried to muffle her giggles in the billowing bedclothes. But it was too late.

Sieggy appeared at the door. He looked at the two girls lying on the rumpled bed, their skirts hoicked to their thighs, their hair mussed, and something flashed in his eyes. They both lay on the bed and looked back at him. Daphne pulled her skirt back towards her knees, but Betsy simply turned on to her side and regarded Siegmund, her head resting on her elbow.

Siegmund may have been annoying in many ways, but he looked so handsome in uniform, and this week he had most certainly come up trumps, with the chalet, the skiing, and the Winter Olympics to boot. Both girls now rewarded him with direct stares.

'Is everything all right?' he said. 'I heard a scream.' He somehow looked more noble, master in his own house, wearing his frogged Loden jacket with gold buttons. 'Don't worry, Siegmund,' replied Daphne, who was feeling fluttery about seeing Otto again. 'We're just powdering our noses. We'll be up in two shakes of a duck's tail.'

Sieggy clicked his heels together. His English was good – his prep school on the Downs had seen to that – but sometimes, he had a blank expression that was difficult to read. He gave the girls a courteous nod. 'Tea is served on the sun terrace, when you're ready,' he said.

Ten minutes later, a more composed Daphne and Betsy joined Otto and Siegmund on the sun terrace, which had an uninterrupted vista over to a jaggedly impressive mountain. Daphne simply stared at Otto when she saw him and felt faint, and couldn't think what to say, so it was good that Betsy never stopped talking and Siegmund always had a timetable.

'Well, this makes a change,' Betsy sighed, as they settled in chairs dressed with navy-linen cushions and looked forward to tea together. The air was crisp but not cold. 'Not that Munich hasn't been lovely, so far.'

'So,' said Siegmund, picking up a newspaper he had folded in a special way, as if he'd been waiting for this moment. 'Now you're here, let me read to you what the *Reich Sports Journal* has to say about this occasion,' he said.

'*Gott in Himmel!*' exclaimed Otto. 'Do you have to, old boy?'

'Jolly good,' said Betsy. 'Does it mention my cousin?' She kept mentioning Celia, their entrée to the winter games.

'Not so far,' said Siegmund. He began reading. '"How much goodwill, how much time, hard work and personal sacrifice on the part of thousands of Germans and friends of the German people have been necessary in the past year to – yes, to fight the battle"' – Siegmund's voice rose – '"that we now have behind us and to prepare for the coming decisive warfare of the new year."'

Luckily, the housekeeper arrived with the tea, because everyone was beginning to realize the reading could go on for some time.

Siegmund leapt to his feet and made sure everyone

had everything: tea, milk, lemon, cinnamon cake, sugar. There were little biscuits shaped like crescents that were a bit like powdery shortbread. They all relaxed back in their chairs, their faces turned towards the sun, sipping tea and nibbling cake.

Otto picked up his copy of *Buddenbrooks*, which Daphne found disappointing. He hadn't really said anything, let alone to her, since they'd arrived at Chalet Huber, or even eaten any of the delicious *Kipferl* biscuits, but as she looked at him and noticed how long his eyelashes were as he devoured each page, Daphne remembered something Meg Dunton-Downer had said as she stood in front of the fire, statuesque and blond like a caryatid painted with heavy make-up, at the *Gräfin*'s. 'You're in my old bedroom, I expect,' she said. 'Do watch out, won't you?'

'Who for?' said Daphne. 'Otto?' she said, her heart beating. Just saying his name, talking about him, made her feel dizzy. 'Not Otto Koenig? Why?'

Meg had become evasive. 'He's not *necessarily* one of us, if you get my drift.' Everyone laughed, as if they rather did get Meg's drift, only too well. Then Meg had made a point of admiring Daphne's blue dress from Debenham & Freebody, so of course Daphne started liking her tremendously after that, but not as much as Betsy, who had decided that, when it came to Meg, it was a definite pash.

What had Meg meant about Otto not being one of us? When Daphne looked at Otto, she felt an ache of longing in her stomach, and all she wanted to do was carry on staring at him. Sometimes he stared back at her, their gaze met, and she felt giddy, and didn't know whether to carry on looking at him, or to stop. She thought of bringing up Meg and finding out what they all thought of *her*, but at that moment Betsy rose from her chair.

Her friend walked over to the balcony and leant over, picturesquely, so her own curves were silhouetted against the sky.

'Is that the Matterhorn then?' asked Betsy, with a sideways glance at the boys. She knew she looked sensational. Her cherry-red sweater had shrunk after she'd deliberately hand-washed it in very hot water and dried it on the towel rail in the nursery bathroom at Tiddington. Now it clung to her bosom and she insisted on wearing it, on the basis that, if her mother and Daphne both discouraged her, it must be most becoming.

'No, my little noodle, it is not the Matterhorn. It is the Wank,' said Siegmund, with pride, and he dragged his gaze from Betsy and pointed to the highest peak in the range. He climbed mountains in his spare time, like most German boys.

'Isn't it lovely, there's not a cloud in the sky,' said Betsy gaily, red and cheeky against the bright-blue sky. The air was clear and pinging and the mountains seemed to press in on them. This seemed to plunge Siegmund, however, into gloom.

'I know, don't remind me,' he said. 'The *Föhn*. I know.'

'What?' said Betsy, as if she didn't know how awful it was, about the weather.

'The *Föhn* is a warm wind in our part of the Alps. It often arrives, this time of year.'

The girls digested this. They'd come for the winter games, along with the world's press, and its leaders, and now, it appeared, the event had the makings of a historic humiliation for the Fatherland, whatever it said in the *Sports Journal*.

'But it is all under control,' he said, with a decisive nod. 'The ski-jump will go ahead as planned in a few days, we've packed a large mass of snow at the Olympia Ski-Stadion in ammonia as a precaution. The speed skating, the figure skating, the bobsleigh races' – he checked them off on his hands like a scout-master – 'these are all taking place on the new artificial rink.'

The girls gazed at the sad brown sides of the mountain, patched with greying slush. Apparently, even the world-famous bobsleigh run was in very poor nick.

'Well, if this whadchacallit wind always arrives, this time of year, in this area, then why on earth did everyone insist on holding the Winter Olympics here, and in February?' asked Daphne, closing her eyes and basking in the sun. 'It seems a bit daft, to be honest.'

Siegmund didn't answer. One would think it was obvious. Berlin had beaten all-comers to hold the games – not just the athletics, but the Winter Games too – and therefore the contest had to be here, where the highest mountain was. The Zugspitze. The stadia had been built, with seating for 10,000 in the ice-stadium and 15,000 at the ski-jump; the competitors were on their way; the international press and picture agencies had descended *en masse* on Garmisch, a town that had been conjoined with its neighbour, Partenkirchen, for the occasion. There was only one thing missing.

Snow.

'The *Föhn* is blowing for longer this year,' said Sieggy. 'But never mind! The snow will come. And tomorrow, we will take the Wank-Bahn.' His eyes flashed. The girls smiled back, to show their host they were content, however adverse the climatic conditions. Mr and Mrs Huber, or rather Herr and Frau Huber (not even Betsy would have risked using their Christian names, which were Norbert and Waltraud), seemed charming, and the chalet couldn't have been more welcoming either, especially with Rudi, the sweetest dachshund. The girls kept their wooden skis and poles with the rest of the family's, in a little side-room by the wood-store, all heated by a small stove. They had cosy bedrooms, endless food and, best of all, the constant attention of the cousins to enjoy. It was all absolutely perfect, apart of course from the lack of snow, but as English girls, Betsy and Daphne were hardened to the weather never quite coming up trumps.

After breakfast the next day, the plan had been to take the cable car to the higher slopes, as they were quite ski-able, according to Siegmund. Daphne would have been quite happy sitting in the sun reading *The Great Gatsby*, but the truth was, the weather had closed in, so they strolled down the hill into the village, their stout shoes making a clopping sound on the dry cobbled road.

First they went down Frühling Strasse in Garmisch, two abreast, and then Ludwig Strasse in Partenkirchen.

Siegmund monitored their faces for evidence that they found the Bavarian painted houses, geraniums spilling from window-boxes, *Hausfrau*s cleaning stoops with buckets of hot sudsy water, pretzels piled up in windows, steeples piercing the sky, as entrancing as he did.

It was difficult to move at the cracking pace Sieggy liked to set. There were simply so many people in town, with every single hotel room taken, and all the Pensions full to bursting. New arrivals had to knock on doors and ask housewives if they had a bed. The streets were fluttering with bunting, crawling with hansom cabs bringing thousands of spectators, journalists, participants, contestants. A gala atmosphere was building by the minute.

It was Otto who saw the sign. They were heading towards the Talstadion when it jumped out at them. Even Betsy could have been in no doubt as to what it meant.

JUDEN ZUTRITT VERBOTEN.

'You see,' Otto said, grabbing Siegmund's arm. 'What did I tell you? And look over there.'

Then, as they stood at one end of the main street, he pointed. They all looked down the street, at the flags fluttering from second-floor windows. Interspersed between the Olympic flag, with its interlocking rings, was the swastika.

'So pretty!' cried Betsy, throwing up her hands.

All the flags, and the bunting, made the charming, tumbly streets of the modest Bavarian town look like something out of Grimm's fairy tales. The painted houses, shuttered windows and carved balconies, cosily timbered tea houses, bakeries and dairies, appeared to the girls like a stage set for some *opera buffo*.

Otto gave Betsy a scornful look. 'No, this is not pretty, not pretty at all,' he said. 'What it is is a pathetic, brazen attempt to persuade the world that the aims of Germany and those of the Olympics are the same. How can anyone be taken in?' His eyes burned, and Betsy blushed.

When he spoke like that Daphne suddenly understood. Now she knew why Meg had said that Otto was not 'one of us'.

Otto stormed openly at his cousin as they stood in the street.

'How much more evidence do you need that these are pantomime games!' Otto dashed Sieggy's copy of the *Reich Sport Journal* on to the pavement.

Siegmund looked away, as if his cousin was nothing to do with him, or if he was, he was providing a moment of temporary unpleasantness that would soon pass. Betsy and Daphne looked at each other; they didn't know whom to support. They'd all been having such fun up to now. It seemed such a shame, to spoil things, over a silly little flag.

Sieggy was studying the sky again for any hopeful signs of snow.

Other passers-by edged away. No one wanted even to hear the sort of indiscretion that could only too easily land them with months in a work camp.

'How can anyone pretend that this nation isn't

successfully duping the whole world?' Otto then said in an even louder voice. By now they were outside a bakery but within earshot of uniformed guards, who shuffled and twitched and kept him in their sights, like cows when ramblers with dogs cross a field.

Sieggy placed a warning arm on his cousin, but Otto went on.

'These Olympics are indeed a game – a game of evil. If anyone should doubt it, tell me why, in that case, the swastika is still fluttering from every balcony, window and flagpole in the whole town?'

Of course, the girls felt frightfully sorry for Sieggy, after this. He'd put so much into this. So much. He had arranged for them all to stay, to attend the opening ceremony; they had everything they wanted, he was the most attentive host, and guide.

Now, they wanted it to be all right, if just for Siegmund. After all, he minded so much.

8

Little Venice/ Oxford
February 2006

Francie flicked on the kettle, sat down at the zinc-topped Conran table and opened her emails. Gus sat at the other end. They had matching MacBooks, so formed a sort of mirror image of each other – a portrait of the state of contemporary marriage – as they sat, contentedly surfing and tapping away.

Amid all the messages from Net-à-Porter and Amazon to tell her that her goods had been dispatched, or to invite her to rate her order, she was pleased to find three from real people she actually knew in real life as opposed to online.

After leaving the nursing home, the first thing she'd done was to email all her aunts and uncles, to see what they knew of her grandmother's – their mother's – time in Germany. She obviously couldn't ask them, not by email, who her grandfather was, if it wasn't Jeremy Fitz-simon, because that was a biggie.

But she could ask about Daphne in Germany. Everyone knew she'd been there in the mid-thirties. And Grannie had been *hot*. And now it turned out, she'd met *Hitler*. Did the others know? The questions now seemed to be: Who else had she met, and what had she done? And, above all, why, why, was there a blank in the space for Andrew's father where Jeremy's name should be?

It was all so . . . *tumultuous*, compared to now. Daphne's children and grandchildren lived in plodding peace-time. The high points of their history had been the fall of the Berlin Wall, Thatcher resigning, the death of Diana, and 9/11, events Francie and Gus had mainly watched from the comfort of their Roche Bobois sofa, glugging Pinot Grigio. She couldn't wait to find out more about Grannie but saved the email from Uncle Francis (after whom she'd been named) until she'd glanced at the one from her neighbour downstairs, Meriel.

'Hey guys,' Meriel wrote. 'Just to let you know, first, that I'm putting the flat on the market and, second, I've actually taken the plunge! Crispin and I are finally making the move at last. Hove here we come!' Crispin was not her husband, or even partner. Meriel's constant companion was a black and white cat with facial markings and luxuriant white eyebrows that made him look like former chancellor Norman Lamont.

Meriel's email included a link. When Francie clicked on it, hoping it wouldn't take her to a YouTube video of a cat doing something funny, it took her to a property page featuring a first-floor apartment in a 'truly unique Grade I listed property on Hove seafront'. There was also a link to Meriel's current flat, now on the market: the ground and lower-ground-floor maisonette in Clifton Villas.

Without thinking, Francie forwarded the whole thing in a rush of warm-spiritedness to Miranda, who had always said she adored Little Venice, and added a few lines at the top. 'Hey, honey, see this! The flat below White Cube is for sale. You could do a private deal with Meriel, and we'd be neighbours. Total result! See you Monday . . .'

As she did so, she said out loud, over the zinc table-top, 'Meriel and Norman Lamont are moving to Hove. Selling the flat. I'm telling Miranda. Maybe she can buy it.'

Gus grunted.

Miranda lived in a flat at the top of a Victorian block near the Portobello Road and was having a dysfunctional relationship with a fiftyish music producer who lived in the flat below her (enabling Francie, Gus and everyone else to joke that the relationship was 'wrong on more than one level').

Jim had been big in the sixties in Laurel Canyon but didn't cut a swathe now. In Jim's view, this was because he'd never bothered to make – in his words – 'serious dough' and 'had never been enough of a breadhead'. In other people's opinion, it was because Jim was – though tall and talkative and full of anecdotes about Carole King and other songbirds he'd dated – a sponger, who always somehow forgot his wallet when it came to paying the bill in Notting Hill restaurants.

So it was all a bit crap for Miranda, who was now given to saying how much she loved the north-west

London vibe of Little Venice, and also how great Gus and Francie's flat aka 'White Cube' was.

Even though Gus had only grunted – he was always somewhere else in his head at the moment – Francie decided it would be amazing having Miranda, almost her best friend, definitely her best work friend, downstairs. Especially when – I mean if – she and Gus ever had a baby, because then they'd have an in-house babysitter on tap! The more she thought about it – jolly Sunday brunches in the garden, drinks on the terrace in the summer – the more excited she felt.

She clicked open Francis's email next. He worked in music recording rights, which everyone was careful not to ask about in case he actually told them what he did in any detail. But Francie'd always loved him – partly because she was named after him.

Dearest Francie,

Thanks for your email. I'm not surprised you want to find out about your grandmother. She is an amazing woman, and has no doubt an amazing past . . . of which I know next to nothing. I was criminally incurious when young. If we did ask, she was adamantine in her wish never to talk about that period in her life. And then, all too soon, it was too late, for Pa at least. Still, as you are asking: I do remember a tone, though, of melancholy and regret. She was in love with a German student.

Francie leant towards her screen. This was great. She was finally getting somewhere.

Like countless others, he was a Nazi. A medic? In Munich? His parents disapproved. It all went wrong. An abortion? They broke it off? She broke down? Whatever happened needn't've been all about politics or Germany. Even in 1936, if I'm right about the date. Life for most people chugged on as it does. If old Granpop Linden had studied Icelandic scripts, say, Ma could've had her unhappy tryst in Oslo rather than Munich. She was only, what, twenty? If that. Not that it's being Germany was wholly irrelevant. She had some fairly nutty friends, but that was the thirties. Everyone lurched from one extreme to another.

Sorry I can't help more. Your Aunt Jill has the best family memory, though maybe more for dates and places than for crack-ups, and so on. Have you tried Meg Dunton-Downer (if still with us) or that much-married madwoman Betsy something-something, formerly something else? Or Susan Crewe – you know, who came out in 1939 aka The Last Season, who worked with Daphne during the war?

Of course there's always Aunt Dem, your Great-aunt Dem, in upstate New York, not my favourite part of the whole of the United States but not entirely without its charms. I know she's been ill, but she is, apparently, still compos.

Are you all well? What is your news? Why do we so rarely see each other?

You and Gus are dear to us both.
Best love,
Francis.

Gus got up and stretched, his lean belly visible in the gap between his American Apparel T-shirt and grey Lonsdale tracksuit bottoms. To Francie's astonishment, he'd started going to Triyoga twice a week, after work, and now went at least once a week at 7 a.m. too. He'd admitted that he thought Shelly, his instructor, was super-hot. 'Whenever she bends over so we all have to look up her yoni, as she calls it,' he said, laughing, 'she always says, "You've got the great view." Gus had also used the words 'core strength' in conversation, and a box of teabags called 'Pukka Cleanse' had appeared in a cupboard.

'Hungry,' he said. He now had a BlackBerry in his hand. He had started checking it obsessively. He slipped it into a pocket in his track pants, opened the fridge and started reading the date stamps on the yoghurts and cheeses, as if Francie was attempting to murder him with fruit-on-the-bottom Activia yoghurt.

Francie opened the third email. It was from an address she didn't recognize. She was cc'd into it, as were, she saw, all her aunts and uncles, including Francis, from whom she'd just heard. It was catchlined 'sad news'.

She wondered why she hadn't opened it first but supposed it was that the name Jared Masters, the sender, did not ring any immediate bells.

'Just to let the English family know that Demeter died last night suddenly in her sleep at home in Tarrytown,' the email said. 'We know this will come as a shock to you all, even if not entirely unexpected. She was only 83. Funeral and memorial arrangements to follow. Do of course circulate this among her friends and family. We have, of course, contacted Daphne, but we were not sure she took it in when we phoned . . .'

Francie closed her laptop and pulled the box towards her. Jared Masters was Demeter's daughter's son. She'd only met him once, and Demeter only a few times. She opened the box and took out one of the little white booties. She stuck it on her index finger. The booties had been in the box too. On the lid, it said 'Germany'.

'Shit,' she said out loud, not even to Gus. 'Great-aunt Dem died. I just don't believe it. And before I got a chance to really to talk to her about Grannie's Munich crisis.'

She popped the bootie back in the box, alongside the rest of the stuff, which included a battered copy of *The Great Gatsby* with the words 'Daphne Linden, 12 Park Town, 1935' inscribed in a schoolgirl hand.

'God, how awful, but also inconvenient,' said Gus. 'Weren't you going to call her? Does that kill the Quest?'

This was how they referred to Francie's delving into Grannie's hopefully dark past.

'But you're still going to push on? Doesn't that dick-head editor want a piece? Can't believe he's taken you off staff! If I were you, I'd do it for a serious magazine. Like *Vanity Fair*. Or the *Telegraph*. Or even the *Guardian*. They love that sort of stuff. Can't get enough of it. Surely anything's better than that PR rag, *Non-Event*, you work for?'

Francie thought it was sweet of Gus to say this, but he really had no idea how impossible it was to get commissioned. She didn't have a high enough profile. She couldn't begin to pitch the story – now minus Demeter's input – to a more prestigious publication, and, anyway, the mere thought of having no contact whatsoever with Nathan turned her stomach to ice.

Since the snog in Soho House, to her shame, she thought of almost nothing else. He'd sent her some texts, and of course work emails, and every time she saw his name in print . . . sometimes, even a name beginning with 'N' could set her off thinking about him. Once she'd seen a Porsche Cayenne parked in Clifton Villas and she'd almost vomited. She had three months more in the office, near him . . . then she would have to free-lance from home.

'Frankly, Franz –' Francie looked at her husband. Gus had left the table and was standing up, spreading red-pepper hummus from a tub on to an Emmenthal & Sunflower Seed Spelt Dr Karg cracker that looked and tasted like MDF. His teeth splintered into the snack, making a noise like a firing squad. The cream door of the Smeg fridge was open and Francie could see his oblong cartons of coconut water lined up like building blocks at the back. 'So far as I can see, whatever happened in Germany, Grannie Daphne has only ever lived a life of blameless domesticity, and you'll hit a blank wall. OK. Change of subject. My turn,' he said, still crunching. 'The beer tastes like shit of course, so the slogan should be "Piss in one End, Piss out the Other", but how 'bout "Half the alcohol. Twice the taste"?'

Gus was working on a new campaign for a Korean

company that was launching a low-alcohol lager in an eco-friendly biodegradable can in less than six months. Village was doing really well.

'How about "Small beer, big taste"?' Francie tried.

'Not bad,' said Gus. 'But not great.'

'What shall we have for supper?' Francie asked. What she meant was, What will you make me for supper? Gus always cooked. 'Well, I was thinking of doing the salad we had at Ottolenghi the other day,' said Gus. 'The one with Carmargue rice, pistachios and apricots.' He started fiddling with his new toy.

Francie did know. The Ottolenghi thing was one of her favourites, and took at least two hours to make (including getting the dozens of ingredients; luckily, they were near not one but two chichi delis that always had things like shelled pistachios, verjuice and preserved lemons).

She peered into the German memory box again, as Gus started opening long boxes in which caplets of different coffee beans nestled.

'I think Java, grand cru, full strength,' said Gus, as he popped a hermetically sealed capsule into the strange new machine he'd brought back from the office the day before. Then he filled the tank at the back with – Francie noted with alarm – neat Volvic. 'Forget Starbucks now, Frankie baby. This is the future.'

The machine started hissing and a dark stream of golden black fluid shot into the heavy-rimmed cup he'd ordered online at some expense from Italy.

'What the hell is it?' asked Francie.

'It's called a Nespresso machine,' said Gus. 'We've got

the account. I think we should get a bloke to do it. Some-one smooth, dark, handsome. And with 100 per cent recognition. And straight.'

'How about George Clooney?' said Francie.

The next day, Francie sat at her desk at work. Five p.m. She usually left between five thirty and six. She was star-ing at the screen. She dealt with a succession of dementing emails from PRs asking her if she wanted to meet the CEOs of luxury hotels for breakfast, or when pieces were scheduled to appear, or if she wanted to go on river cruises up the Danube, while trying to work out how to start her Berchtesgaden piece.

Ah.

Email from Miranda Lewes.

'Have found someone to go to Burberry with so you're off the hook.'

Ten minutes later.

Email from Nathan Galsworthy.

In her haste to open the email, Francie sent it to trash. So she had to open the trash and send it back to herself.

'Hey, F. Off to look at a maisonette in Clifton Villas. Isn't that where you live? Are you guys moving?'

'No. 61?' she wrote back. 'Garden flat?'

'The very one,' came back from Nathan. 'Going there now. Lift?'

They both sat in the back of the car. Mandy stared ahead as they ploughed up St James's. It was as if she had been trained.

The air between them clotted as they navigated Piccadilly. Francie turned to stare at Nathan meaningfully, but he was looking straight ahead.

She couldn't believe Nathan was going to look at the flat. How, and why, had he found out about it?

Without looking at her, he pushed up the black leather armrest between them and reached for her left hand. Her heart started thumping. She started stroking his hand with her right. 'You started this,' she said.

'Started what?' he said. Then he gave a tug on her arm, and pulled her towards him. She almost fell on him in her anxiety to taste his mouth again, to smell him, and soon they were kissing, without a thought for Mandy. The back of her ears were perhaps slightly redder, but she didn't even glance in the rear-view mirror.

Nathan had clearly done this before.

He pulled at her top and stuck his hand down her front as she was flung slightly against him as they whirled round Hyde Park Corner in the outside lane. He pulled down her bra so her left breast poked free. Francie yelped. 'It's OK,' said Nathan. 'The windows are tinted.'

As if in confirmation of his supremacy, his mouth bent down to her nipple and he placed her hand in his crotch.

As she unzipped his fly, her only certainty was that 1. he would have a big one and 2. it would all end badly, partly but not exclusively because of 1. She'd always thought it was very unfair that women's secondary sexual characteristics were – the top half anyway – pretty obvious. A woman, on the other hand, had to get past the point of no return with a possible mate before the great (or more often not-so-great) reveal. And now she was past the point of no return as her hand closed on a hot cosh suited in Paul Smith grey flannel with a very faint green pinstripe.

The chances were, she was doomed. Not only was he her boss. Not only did he have form. And baggage. No – Francie had read enough magazine articles in her lifetime, had written some of them even – the likelihood was, that afterwards, she would be another tick in the box, like Sam, and Elinor, and Ingrid, and all the other girls at *Event* he'd been linked with, before he moved on to the next. Her hand closed around the head of his gratifyingly large penis, burning through the thin fabric of his suit. He made a little noise – a bit like the sound Nigella makes when she spoons cream pie into her mouth in front of the cameras.

'How's your travel piece going?' he asked, his eyes shut.

'Be quiet,' she replied.

The next day, after a swift bowl of gluten-free toasted muesli with buckwheat and a cappuccino made by Gus (he got the milk right after several attempts with an ejaculating nozzle that gave her terrible flashbacks of the previous evening's activity), Francie took the train to Oxford but, this time, she stayed in the city, and didn't go to Faringdon.

Even though Oxford was always two degrees clammier than London, she walked, in her outfit cleverly pitched halfway between student and professional female: belted mac she'd bought in a little boutique in Paris with Gus over flat-fronted tweed trousers from Toast; crisp white shirt doing all the right things under a V-necked merino sweater; black-leather Converse. Leaving the station, she passed by the bike park on her right, a football-pitch-sized area of twisted, locked steel, and wondered where all their owners were.

Oxford was a graveyard of ghost bikes, where Raleighs, Sturmey Archers and even rugged Ridgebacks and Cannondales came to die. She strolled past the Saïd business school, where clever clogs were learning how to run internet start-ups and invest in the greening of China. She could glimpse them at flat-screen computers, no doubt inputting data into spreadsheets on the economic consequences of peak oil. The minimalist structure loomed over an unfashionable *quartier* of the university town, but somehow sucked the life from the crumblier medieval foundations. She wound her way behind the high street, resisting the siren pull of the coffee shops and Whistles, till she clopped across the cobbles to enter the porter's lodge at Merton College.

She gazed at the notices. All the flyers seemed to be about nightclubs, and helplines, as if partying necessarily led to talking therapy. There was surprisingly little about poetry readings or discussion groups. Being here, at Oxford, was a lot of work, was the message of this Wailing Wall of a noticeboard.

The porter sat behind a glass screen surrounded by keys on hooks and cubbyholes so he could monitor traffic, in front of telephones, which flashed rather than rang.

Francie wondered who the 'archivist' was – the email had been signed W. M. C. Cresswell. She had already pulled together a mental picture of a man in a baggy hand-knit brown cardigan, half-moon glasses and Hush Puppies smelling of pipe smoke, but the man who manifested under the arch and made his way towards the lodge was her age. She didn't say, 'I expected you'd be older,' because when she last said that to a man she'd interviewed – about non-invasive plastic surgery – he'd said, 'And I thought you'd be younger.'

Cresswell seemed pleased and excited to meet the great-granddaughter of the distinguished Fellow and professor, Jacob Linden, late of this college.

'*Salve*, I'm Bill Cresswell,' he said. 'Shall we wander up to the SCR?'

Francie presumed he was greeting her in Latin because her great-grandfather had been a specialist in Roman law. 'Er, *salve*,' she said in reply.

'We've got a smart new coffee machine. Come and see.'

He pelted through a cloister, as if in a rush, twisting in and out of flagstoned passages and bounding up little flights of wooden stairs. Finally, they made landfall on carpet, before a heavy oak door with the words 'Senior Tutor' and 'Senior Common Room' painted in gold leaf. This he held open in a courtly way for Francie, so she could enter the SCR first. It was a large room, with deep-set windows giving over a quad with a sundial in the middle. The day's newspapers were spread about, and there were beardy odours of wool and don.

Francie looked at the coffee machine he'd said he wanted to show her. It looked very bog standard. But Cresswell was pointing not to the Kona coffee machine but to a bronze bust in a nook.

'There he is.'

'Who?' Francie said stupidly, looking around at the various elderly chaps with hair sticking out from their heads at all angles, deep in periodicals called things like 'Experimental Prosody.'

'No, him,' said Cresswell. He pointed to a face that glowered from an alcove. It was powerful and jutting in a chill, Mount Rushmore-ish way. 'That's your great-grandfather.'

The eyes of Jacob Linden, boreholes in the black over a hooked nose, seemed to drill into her. 'I thought you'd want to see him before we went down,' he said, giving the bronze prof a fond pat on the head.

Cresswell squirted some brackish fluid into a plastic cup and took a thimble of plastic milk. Francie glanced down at *The Times*. There was a huge photograph on the front page. She picked it up.

'Stars out at Burberry yesterday evening,' the caption said.

The photo showed those in a section of the front row at Burberry, with heads all turned towards the cat-walk and flashlights bouncing off gleaming curtains of centre-parted swishy hair: Gwyneth Paltrow; that new Russian model that was discovered selling turnips in the street; the editors of *Vogue* in London, Paris, New York; Jerry Hall, Jade Jagger . . . usual suspects . . .

She saw him immediately. She would recognize him, now, by the tip of his ear, or a lock of his hair that curled over his ears. Nathan was in Row C, two rows behind Gwynnie, looking bored. Nathan was the reason *Event* still got asked to everything – as she'd once joked to Gus, Nathan was the prettiest thing in the *Event* office, by far. But, she realized, with a thud that left her feeling sick, both Nathan and Miranda had had the opportunity to tell her they were going to Burberry together, and neither of them had taken it.

She dropped the paper back on to the low table, and made a deliberate effort to refocus on the job in hand . . . Cresswell was looking at her, enquiringly. 'Maybe I will have a cup of your delicious coffee after all,' she said.

'As you know,' said Cresswell, as he handed her a plastic cup, 'the bust is by Epstein. Your grandmother gave it to the college; I think when she was moving house.'

'Yes, I think she did.' Now Cresswell mentioned it, she remembered seeing the bust in a passage at Hendridge. She had had no idea it was an Epstein. She didn't really care. All she cared about was how Nathan had managed to fit her, and Little Venice, and three orgasms, then Miranda, at Burberry, into only a few hours.

The answer, of course, was *Mandy*.

'The other one's in Princeton – but we'll come to that anon,' said Cresswell. He rubbed his hands together. 'Shall we?'

They left the SCR and pushed on, down staircases,

the names of dons and undergraduates written in white on little black boards at the foot of each, marched along passages and exited on to yet another quad. Cresswell paused outside an unmarked door, and then took out a key.

Penetrating the archive was like entering a tomb.

'The temperature is kept at between 13 and 19 degrees, but more important is the humidity, which is 60 per cent,' Cresswell explained, as Francie shivered. She wondered whether there was anything here. Any clues. Bound not to be. It was all a wild-goose chase, a displacement activity from writing up her piece about safari honeymoons, the Nazi resort, her agony over Nathan, or having to think about having a baby with Gus.

Seeing the Burberry show pic in *The Times* had, she had to admit, freaked her out.

She tried to work it out in her head. They'd got to 61 Clifton Villas at, say, 5.40 p.m. Francie and Nathan had disentangled themselves, Francie had straightened her dress and slipped her feet back into her shoes, and Nathan had retucked his shirt. He peered up at the stuccoed front, appeared unmoved that he was gazing at Francie's actual house and glanced at his watch.

He and Francie had got out.

'How long will you be, boss?' Mandy had asked.

'I'm not sure, Mand,' said Nathan. 'Not long, I expect.' Mandy nodded. It was clear that her job was not so much driving, but waiting.

Without either of them saying anything, it seemed a plan had already formed. Nathan spent three and a half minutes viewing Meriel's garden flat, and then came up to the maisonette. It was six o'clock. Gus, in theory, was at a two-hour session at Triyoga and would not be back until eightish at the earliest. But Nathan didn't even ask where Francie's husband was. It was as if, to him, husbands were no object.

They sat on the Conran sofa, the atmosphere thick between them, and looked at a Taschen book about Frank Lloyd Wright for one minute and twenty seconds before Francie heard herself saying, as she turned a page showing a lake house based on equilateral triangles, just one word.

'Bed?'

She loved Gus. She wanted to remain married to him. But she was glazed – stupefied – by lust. She hadn't had sex with Gus for a month. And now she was risking her husband, her marriage and dwindling career on *Event* for . . . for what?

For what Nathan would regard as a quick shag.

This did not stop her tipping the book off her lap, taking Nathan's hand and leading the way into her and Gus's bedroom, an all-white cocoon containing a huge white double bed on which she had only, ever, slept with Gus, and Gus had only, ever, slept with her.

As they'd been getting undressed, and he hurled his designer suit casually on to the same chair as Gus did, she thought of warning him that she hadn't done this before – 'this' being extramarital sex – but didn't; she also thought of warning him that, once, Gus had suggested they had 'sex lessons'; but again, she didn't. She had no idea what being 'good in bed' meant. Surely it was about how the other person made you feel, not tricks and experimental techniques? She glanced at him as he hopped from one leg to the other, trying to take his socks and shoes off without sitting down, and slid on to the duvet, and watched him. Even in socks, she found Nathan irresistible. And she wouldn't resist him. She knew that as soon as he'd kissed her in Soho House.

Inside the Merton College archival vault, there were stacks around the walls and a desk, with a green-shaded library lamp over it. She inhaled the smell of leather, vellum, ink, must, and thought for the fortieth time since yesterday evening of the way Nathan had gripped her by the hips as she sat astride him and pumped her up and down until she came.

One shelf held huge leather-bound ledgers. Francie went in close to examine them. They dated from 1521, she saw, as, in her mind's eye, she and Nathan lay side by side and she stroked his face, and then trailed her hand from his face, down his arm, to his hip and then further down, and found he was hard again.

'So, here are the college records from its foundation,' Cresswell was saying, as she struggled to concentrate. 'Accounts, register of conveyance of property, staff lists, staff records, leases, minutes of the meetings of the governing bodies, are in these wooden filing cabinets. The Muniments Room' – he gestured to an iron door – 'has all the college's documents and deeds.'

This didn't sound promising *at all*. Like she cared about deeds in the Muniments Room! She'd written to Cresswell, an email, specifying exactly what she wanted. Which was anything about the Lindens – Jacob, Winifred Daphne or Demeter.

She had come *three times* in *one hour*, she wondered to herself. Nathan smelt . . . wonderful. He smelt right. She couldn't explain. And his cock was . . . oh GOD she loved his cock.

As she stood in the dark room with Cresswell, she regretted that she hadn't stolen something from Nathan – a shirt, a handkerchief – so she could have him with her, smell him, at all times. She tried to look alert. But it was terrible. Since she'd woken up that morning, in Gus's arms (she and Gus had made love that night; it was a bit like that joke about buses: she'd waited for ages then two lovers came at once), it was as if she could only see life through a fuzzy Nathan filter.

Cresswell took down a thick leather-bound book picked at random from a bookcase and opened it to reveal an illustrated manuscript, its reds and blues and greens as bright as the day they were inked by some monk in a garret. It was called 'Meditations on the Life of Christ' by St Boniface and was probably worth millions of pounds and she was lucky to be in the same room as it, but this was not what Francie was after, which was some explanation of why, and with whom, her grandmother had been in Germany in 1936, and what happened to the Lindens thereafter.

She was going through the box systematically. She'd done the coin, which suggested Daphne'd been in the Alps for the Winter Games. That was clue number one. Dead end. There were tons of coins like it; they were sold like Smarties as souvenirs, according to a site she'd found that flogged all manner of Olympic memorabilia on the web. Then there was the postcard from Merton College, and this relic threatened to lead somewhere, for which she had Gus to thank – he'd said that the college probably had a historian, and they'd turned out not merely to have an archivist but a cache of Linden letters, which she was about to get her hands on. As for the dessicated grey-green rosebud and the white booties – well, that was sheer maternal sentimentality.

Francie thought of Grannie, silent in Faringdon nursing home, which had 'rebranded' as Faringdon Lodge in 2004. This digging about was surely what Grannie wanted. That was why Milly Goddard had handed her all the mementos, presumably. Ergo, she couldn't deny her grandmother what could be . . . her *last request*.

As Cresswell told her about the difference between pigskin, calfskin and reverse calfskin, Francie's mind wandered. Nathan hadn't called, hadn't even sent her a text. She felt cold. A terrible thought. Maybe he just wasn't that into her *already*?

The archivist pulled out a Boat Club record dating from 1858 (Francie tried not to groan out loud) and crooked it in two triangular foam wedges so Francie could examine its pages, propped open for her viewing pleasure. She began to feel a little desperate but tried to look thrilled when he pointed out the name of Robert Bridges, a former poet laureate, and Captain of Boats.

'So do you keep a lot of Fellows' letters?' she asked, nudging Cresswell back to the reason she'd come all the way from London.

He looked surprised. 'No, we don't – as you can see, we don't have room.' He gestured round the Aladdin's cave of published material precious only, really, to Merton College, Oxford. 'We only have space to retain a selection of important letters that Fellows generated while they were in the college and, only then if the letters have been left to us. The rule of thumb is, we'll only keep a letter written to a Fellow if it is deemed of historical importance.' He sat down at his desk. He pulled down an Anglepoise lamp so it shone on to a box. The box had been placed there in advance.

Francie liked that. It showed commitment. She cheered up. Nathan was probably busy. It was Fashion Week, after all. In fact, when she got out of this subterranean cave with the archive anorak, she'd probably find a text from him, if not two.

'You can photocopy what you need,' he said. 'It's 10 pence per sheet of A4, 20 pence for A3. I'm afraid our copier doesn't give change.'

She'd shown Nathan out wearing one of Gus's shirts and nothing else. He'd kissed her on the nose.

Francie sat down at the desk in the archive, and looked at the first letter.

Dear Ma and Fa and Dem,

All well in Munich. Last night there was a little cocktail party
here to show us new girls off I think – I wore my blue dress ~~not
that there was much choice in that department~~. I couldn't think
what to say at first, there were so many people. The Gräfin was
circling, saying, 'And have you met the Countess Mallortie?',
and giving me little pushes in the direction of people. I met
Nicky Miles of the Times. He was what Sir Bache would call a
~~contemptible~~ deformation and he had a pink scarf round his
neck throughout the evening. I asked him, when it says from
Our Munich Correspondent, was that him, or was he A
Correspondent In Munich, and are they the same person? He
did explain, but I've forgotten, like when Laurence Lowther
talks about CMG and KCMG, it's in one ear. There was
another man, Teddy Cullen, a diplomat ~~who says his main job
is to pick up the pieces when English girls go off the rails~~ . . .

Now I've met Nicky, I will definitely start taking the Times;
you can buy it at the station. If I buy one copy, all of us here
can read it.

There was also a dread musical interlude. This old woman,
~~who must have been~~ at least 40, with shingled dark hair and in
a turquoise trouser-suit howled ~~and sobbed~~ in German while
another woman with short grey hair played the piano. You
know when the person performing's gaze locks on to only one
unlucky member of the audience quite by chance? Of course,
I was the one. I didn't know where to look. I did magnificently,

though I say so myself. ~~After all, Fa, if you've given your~~ ~~daughters an education in anything, it's how to look as if one is~~ ~~enjoying something when one isn't.~~ My big news is that Betsy and I are going to Garmisch, week after next, to the Winter Olympic Games, with some cousins, approved by the Gräfin, of course, who have a chalet there. They're called Huber. But I think you will still have to pay the Gräfin though, for our rooms when we're gone. She's quite fierce about that sort of thing.

How is term going, Dem? Do write back. Stroke Antigone from me.

Best love,
Big D

Francie replaced the letter. 'Wow,' she said. 'Blimey. They wrote proper handwritten letters in those days, didn't they? Now it's all voice text and emoticons.'

As she said this, she felt another pang that she hadn't heard from Nathan.

'Actually, I'm not sure why we kept that one,' said Cresswell. 'I don't know how it slipped in, but I thought you'd want to see it anyway.'

Francie was scrawling names – Teddy Cullen, the consular chap; Nicky Miles, *The Times*, into her notebook.

They looked at each other across the piles of paperwork.

'You might be interested in a couple of other letters I've tabbed,' he went on. 'They're written to another Fellow of the college, in the, er, freshness of events. Note the date – and the postscripts.'

He handed over a slim sheaf.

My dear Garfield,

*It is months since we have been in touch, & many more months
since we sat down to play together. I hope all has gone well with you
& yours. There is a kind of poison in the world-atmosphere which
makes natural breathing difficult. One isn't oneself. We are all
trying to whistle to keep up our courage. That explains why I
didn't sit down to write you a long letter full of news about
Princeton, the Institute, the US of A & my family in particular. I
don't know how much you know – I do hope Lowther is satisfied
with the turn of events. Man kommt nicht in die Stimmung –
voilà tout. Still, my elder daughter Daphne has been in Germany,
as you know. She met everyone, from the Führer downwards, after
which she wrote, there can't be a war – 'Why would he want to
have all his fine new buildings and roads bombed?'*

Then there was stuff about Linden's latest book, his
hopes to resume teaching, details of his seminars, which
Francie skimmed, then it was back to domestic arrangements, which was a bit disappointing: without ever
meeting him, she'd built up a mental image of a man of
bronze, undisturbed by thoughts of comfort. And then –
after the riders about his meals, at last something personal:

*We have a nice furnished house in Princeton but life is very
expensive. Mrs Linden is much recovered.*

Recovered from what? She bent her head back over
the spidery writing.

*She has found some charming people here, but her interests lie
with the literary set in New York, and she is busy, and has
started writing, which affords her some comfort, after all that
happened in Oxford. It has proved to be quite a release for her.
Thomas Mann is coming for a lecture tour in February – poor
man. We hope to get him here, if he has a moment's time, &
get Einstein to come too for luncheon. I see quite a little of him,
& I like him very much. We take walks. His view of life is
that of the unperturbed sage: nothing surprises him. What is
happening in Germany is, Einstein says, tragic for the
Germans – but as for my race, he says, 'the Jews are used to
persecution.' Only a man au-dessus de la mêlée, can think
like that.*

*Yours as ever
J.E.L*

'That's quite cool, actually,' said Francie. 'He was in
Princeton at the same time as Einstein. Incredible! I've
got friends who sit their newborns in front of Baby
Einstein DVDs. So my great-grandfather actually knew
him. Einstein himself.' Francie preened. 'And Thomas
Mann.

'It's weird, though, he only mentions my grandmother
once. Now you can't shut up parents from droning on
and on, endlessly, about their children. Then, they barely
merited a footnote. He seems more interested in who was
going to make his lunch every day *than in his own family*.'

'Yes. Well, I suppose parents were adults then, they
didn't try to be their children's best friends,' Bill twinkled,

and Francie found herself wondering whether he was married, or had children. She wondered if she had any single friends he might do for – possibly Miranda? – as she turned to the next letter.

The Institute for Advanced Study
School of Humanistic Studies
Princeton, New Jersey
14.ii.38

My dear Garfield,

It was most kind of you to take time and trouble to see Mynors on my behalf, quamvis indignus. I have had word from a Fellow of Balliol: the College will do its best, though they fear the best is poor. For my purposes, it would be most convenient & I have written to that effect. Do not speak of it, yet, as I have as yet had no kind of official confirmation.

'Sorry,' said Francie, looking up at the archivist. 'Why is he suddenly talking about going to Balliol? I thought he was a Fellow here, at Merton.'

'I think this is Linden plotting his return to his University, which was ultimately scuppered by the outbreak of war in September 1939,' said Cresswell. 'Don't forget these letters are dated 1938. It was not at all clear at that point that war between England and Germany was inevitable. He was writing from the east coast of the United States to Oxford at a time when Czechoslovakia was a faraway country and so on and appeasement proper hadn't even begun.'

Francie did not say, 'Thank you for the history lesson, it is quite unnecessary,' because if she was being honest, she was always a little hazy about the Munich crisis and what country Hitler invaded first. She bent over the letter, with its slanted writing quivering with intellectual horsepower.

> *No contact of course from Lowther. I was delighted to hear of the progress the Durham publication was making. Ludwig Traube did not live in vain. His soul marches on; his ideals are being pursued in England and in America. I wish you had a first-rate-man who would be reading to make Roman Law his major interest. Such a man could succeed me at the Institute, not a bad place considering its distance from war-distracted Europe, and quite apart from that, Princeton is a sweet place to live in. There are a number of interesting people, and NY and Philadelphia are only an hour away.*
>
> *It will be a joy to see you again, and of course we'll take a good long walk.*
>
> *J. E. Linden*

'Read the postscript along the side,' said Cresswell, 'on the first page.'
Francie read out loud:

> *I heard Einstein say the other day, on a walk: 'Anti-Semitism is good for the Jews, but they're overdoing it just now,' and we all laughed heartily. I can't measure him as a physicist, but I know a saint & a sage when I see one.*

'Oh yes, Princeton,' said Francie, waking up to the obvious. 'The letterhead says, "The Institute for Advanced Study, School of Humanistic Studies" – whatever they are – "Princeton".'

So . . . the Lindens had left Oxford in a hurry – had there been some sort of disgrace? – and gone to Princeton, and were there in 1938, without Daphne, and Winifred had some sort of *crise* . . . someone called Lowther was being unhelpful about Jacob's plotted return . . . but still, precious little to go on. Francie looked at Cresswell for help.

'Indeed,' Bill Cresswell said, blinking at her. 'Your great-grandfather moved to the US in early 1937, I think it was, with his wife, Winifred, and his daughter Demeter, who still lives there, I believe.' Francie did not correct him. Auntie Dem had indeed lived in upstate New York. But the fact was, Cresswell hadn't explained why Linden couldn't return to Merton. And he'd mentioned not two daughters, but only one.

'But what had happened to Daphne? Why hadn't she emigrated with Demeter and Winifred too, to the New World before the war? she asked.

Cresswell didn't meet her gaze this time. He didn't seem very keen to go into this.

'All I know is in the letters,' he said. 'That's what you asked for. We have other files, of course, citing other actors in the events of the time. But I'd need to know which ones before I brought them out. And why you want to see them. This isn't the National Archive, you know. There's no thirty-year rule or anything, but this concerns the inner workings of the College. The private lives, in some cases, of our most respected Emeritus Fellows. Not to mention the Warden, Laurence Lowther. This is all private, and some of it remains, despite the passage of years, still very personal.'

He removed the Boat Club record from its foam cradle as if the session must, regretfully, come to an end.

Francie got up. 'Is that the photocopier?' she said. She took copies of the letters and fished in her wallet for change, in order to satisfy the archivist that what he had dug out were of interest, more than anything else.

She waited for Cresswell to wave away her proffered pound coins, as if they were on some sort of date, but he didn't and she dropped them into a tin.

'Well, I hope you thought that was *vaut le voyage*,' said Cresswell, as the coins rattled.

Francie suddenly wondered whether Nathan had had such a cataclysmic time as she had, and worried he hadn't. He'd come once, inside her, right at the end . . .

Had she been *vaut le voyage* for Nathan?

As she walked out of Merton, she turned on her Nokia again. 'When you're done Miss-Marpling, call me,' texted Gus. 'I have news.'

But she barely took it in.

There was still no text from Nathan.

9

When Daphne woke up the next morning, she glanced at the square shuttered window, high up the wall, but it was hard to tell what the time was. But when she looked, the window wasn't in the same place as usual – it was to the left of the bed, not the right, the morning light seemed softer, and there was a yellowish aura around the window she hadn't noticed before.

Then she remembered.

She was in Betsy's room. With rising dread, she recalled the events of the previous evening and night.

They'd eaten in the dining room, where the walls, and floor, and ceiling, were wood-planked, and there were wooden sideboards. It was rather like eating in a very hot woodshed. They had cauliflower soup, followed by boar's head with a sauce made with capers, boiled eggs and mustard. The mountain air had made Daphne hungry, and it all tasted better than it looked and sounded, even if the names of the dishes alone would have made Demeter faint. Sieggy's mother, Waltraud, whom he called *Mutti*, explained that the secret of the spicy cabbage was caraway seed and vinegar. The Hubers had a cook, as well as a housekeeper; during the afternoon, as the four were lounging again on the sun terrace, they'd heard Frau Huber shouting, '*Rotkohl, nicht Weisskohl!*'

'Ah, it is then red cabbage tonight,' Siegmund had said, rubbing his hands. 'One of my favourites.'

After dinner, they'd played cards, and then the girls had glanced at each other, and agreed to retire. Otto and Siegmund were on the terrace, smoking little cigars.

Daphne was undressing in her room, and hanging her skirt in the pine-scented cupboard, thinking of Otto, and hoping he might knock on her door to say goodnight and then . . . she didn't know. She did not have a clear picture in her mind of what might happen next.

She was standing in vest and drawers and debating whether to have a strip-wash or hop straight into bed when Betsy burst in without knocking.

'Please swap rooms, mine pongs – bloody *Rotkohl*, I'm already feeling sick. Be a brick, Daph. Just for tonight, why not?' She shivered theatrically, clapped her arms over her chest as if she was cold, and hopped from foot to foot.

Daphne sighed. There was no point in resisting Betsy. She slipped her nightgown over her head and crossed the passage into Betsy's room, which did smell, it was true, of boiled cabbage. She tried reading *Gatsby* but, after a few minutes, turned off the light, and fell asleep.

And now, in the dark room, only the shuttered window framed by morning light, Daphne squeezed her eyes shut in the hope that, when she opened them again, she would wake up.

She opened them again, and it was all just the same. It had not been a dream. Two things had happened, in the night.

She stared at the carved wooden ceiling. For several seconds, seconds she did not know would be among the last, truly peaceful seconds of her life, she lay still. Then her hand went to the place her mother called 'between her legs'. Her hand met with stickiness, and it felt sore. When she withdrew her hand, it was tacky with blood. It also smelt metallic. She brought her hand to her nose – metallic; and – she sniffed again – something else.

She padded her nightdress between her legs, turned over on to her side and squeezed her eyes shut. She remembered being asleep, heavy with sleep after the fresh air, and trudging the slushy streets, and the heavy cooked food, and the cards, and the wine. She remembered dressing for dinner, dinner, and going to bed, and reading a few pages of *Gatsby*. It all came back.

Her room was pitch-black, so she could see only in outline the figure in her room. She lay very still on the bed. The presence came over. He had lifted the heavy eiderdown and slipped in beside her. He was naked.

After the initial, tearing bit he had stayed very still on top of her, and then, he'd begun to move, slowly, but surely, with a skill and confidence that advertised that he had done this before and took whatever it was he was doing very seriously indeed. He approached the business at hand with absolute concentration. He listened to her breath, he kissed her breasts and shoulders, and he whispered in her ear that he was sorry, at a point when it was already too late for her to resist.

She remembered how the feelings, even as she fought him off, had turned into something else, into something she didn't want him to stop, even as she tried to push him off, and even though he smelt of cigar, and had hurt her until she cried out with pleasure. And she had clung to him at the end, slick with sweat. Then, in the darkness, he had apologized.

'I am sorry,' said Siegmund, again. 'You shouldn't be so . . . provocative, my little Betsy.'

Daphne froze. She felt her body turn to ice, and she lay back on her billowing white bed as chill and motionless as an effigy in a crypt.

She had not said a word. He let himself, silently, out of her room, and in the half-light cast by the opening of the door she saw the shape of his head, the terrier-yellow hair, as he bowed his head in her direction, and – as a reflex, almost – raised himself on his toes and clicked his heels.

She lay there.

She turned on her side, put a pillow over her head, too undone by events to slip into a hot bath, and see the copper taps cloud up with steam, and wash herself with a flannel, slide down into the hot piney depths . . . and then wrap herself with a soft white towel that smelt of meadows, and innocence, and pretend nothing had happened. She couldn't. Instead, she slept.

*

Two hours later, on the morning of 6 February 1936, the Huber family, accompanied by Daphne Linden, Betsy Barton-Hill (who was scanning the crowd at the entrance to the stadium to see if any of her cousins were about) and the Huber cousin, Otto Koenig, stood in coats, fur hats and stout, buttoned boots. They were clutching their precious tickets that granted them admission to the VIP seating area in the stands. It was ten o'clock, and a wind was slicing through the happy, exultant crowd.

For the other thing that had happened in the night was snow, and it would continue to snow, someone said, for thirty hours.

Siegmund was in a particularly good mood. He had pronounced this random piece of climatic luck a miracle, which didn't seem, under the circumstances, an understatement. 'The Winter Games are saved,' he kept saying, as the flakes settled on the fur hats, shoulders, the eyelashes of the spectators as they waited for the Fourth Winter Olympic Games in Garmisch-Partenkirchen in Bavaria, the first time both the winter and summer games were held in the same country in the same year.

It sounded, at first, like a distant rumble of thunder. Daphne turned her face to the grey sky, to see a storm gathering above the peaks that were lost in the clouds, but all that happened was that snow went into her eyes. She wiped them with her sleeve. The rumble was getting louder, closer.

SIEG HEIL!
SIEG HEIL!

The sound was rising up the valley, as the motor-omnibuses operated by the Reich Post Office continued to arrive and people flowed off them towards the massive sculpted entrance towers of the stadium, despite the crowds already pressing to get in. The Hubers allowed no room for doubt in anything they did, but Daphne felt doubt as she saw the bundled masses making their way on foot, on field-paths, from the centre of town. Snow was falling, there was snow on their clothes, snow landing white and feathery and then melting into inkblots on their shoulders, hats, feet. They stamped their boots as they crowded together, and the snow landed on their eyebrows, their eyelashes.

Betsy's pupils were dilated, and she panted and laughed as she kept sticking out her pink tongue for snowflakes. Betsy was staying very close to Siegmund. 'Thanks for swapping rooms with me last night,' she said to Daphne, her face turned up to the falling snow. Daphne didn't dare look at Siegmund, with his sunny morning face. Just the two words 'last night' made her want to die.

The crowd was chanting hypnotically and saluting; even the upper limbs of an American couple to their left were given to jerky spasms. Betsy's arm, ending in her green sheepskin glove, was lofted skywards too. 'Come on, *Mäuschen*,' said Sieggy to Betsy. He had not yet spoken more than a few words to Daphne, but here he was, calling Betsy his *Little Mouse* . . . there was no doubting his worshipful tone with Bets today. Did that mean that Siegmund still thought . . .? But she couldn't exactly ask Betsy. And to ask Siegmund whether he thought he had been in bed not with her but with her best friend was unendurably embarrassing.

'I know, let's go to the station and see him arrive,' Siegmund was saying, grabbing Betsy's arm as if they were the greatest of chums. He smiled down into her face. 'It's not far. You will not forget this, I promise, *Mäuschen*. We'll be back soon.'

The pair melted into the crowd, as the Huber parents smiled at their backs and shook their heads slightly, as if Siegmund was a scamp who must always be humoured.

Otto and Daphne watched Betsy's blue beret bobbing into the crowd in the direction of the train station, the special one the Hubers had pointed out had been built, like so much else, in record time for the Winter Games. Then they lost sight of the pair.

I never want to see him again, was the thought that formed in Daphne's mind, with conviction.

All at once, the doors to the stadium were opened and the Huber party was swept forward as the crowd, like a milk pan boiling over, surged towards the entrance, waving their tickets. Otto put a protective arm around Daphne, for which she was so grateful that she felt tears start to prick behind her eyelids. They shuffled forward bit by bit, handed their tickets to the guards, and then they were in the stadium. Almost everyone was made to squeeze on to concentric concrete benches like those in the Colosseum, apart from important people, who were shown towards reserved seating in front of the Olympiahaus, a sort of three-storey chalet with a covered balcony, decorated with looping swags of foliage, which was now hung festively with snow, like in a Christmas card.

Betsy and Siegmund made it back only just in time, and pushed their way up to the Huber seats as the band thumped out '*Deutschland über Alles*'. They were sitting about ten rows back from the front of the central stand, facing the pine-clad Gudiberg mountain, with its two Olympic jumps on its lower slopes. In front of them, at the sides of the enclosure, every foot of space had someone standing in it. The stadium had filled to the brim in double-quick time.

'He's here, I saw him,' Betsy panted, as Siegmund dragged her behind him into their row, and she plonked herself down next to them on the hard benches of the amphitheatre.

'He's coming any second. I saw him, I swear. He's wearing a tatty old coat and no hat and –'

The crowd erupted, leapt to its feet as one, arms poking skywards. Daphne struggled to her feet. She didn't want to get anything else wrong, now, ever again. If she did everything right from now on, maybe last night . . . *wouldn't count*. Otto remained where he was. She looked down at him with an enquiring look. 'They can't throw me in jail for sitting still,' he said briefly.

After only one verse of the '*Deutschlandlied*', the band abruptly struck up the National Socialist anthem and everyone craned their necks towards the western entrance.

'Whatever it is, it's catchy,' cried Betsy. She started to sway to the tune's lilt as a slight, feverish-looking man who looked as if he should be in a mental asylum strode into the arena and struck a pose in front of the cheering crowd. He was bareheaded, his black hair gleaming with oil, his coat, with large, almost theatrical lapels, tightly belted high on the waist.

The 'Heil''s grew in a crescendo, and then swung into song. Daphne glanced up, and saw that even the lower slopes, outside the stadium, were black with crowds. It was as if the mountains were singing.

The man strutted on to the balcony of the Olympiahaus and stood for a moment in front of the crowd, acknowledging their hysterical cries of worship. Then he curtailed the deafening sound of a crowd that numbered hundreds of thousands in full voice with one chopping movement of his left hand.

The stirring strains of song subsided, but then the cheers began anew as the Greek team, clad in white, entered the stadium holding the torch and its national flag. As the team passed in front of the Olympiahaus, they dipped the flag and, in response, the leader's hand flew up in salute, and a gun salute was fired. It was eleven o' clock.

First Greece, then the nations from Australia, to the United States, in alphabetical order. Each team, headed by its national flag, strode proudly around the enclosure to cheers, then passed before the *Führer*, saluting.

The German team, as hosts, brought up the rear, and

goose-stepped in front of the balcony, to wild applause. Even Daphne felt her eyelids pricking with emotion. Then the man next to Hitler started shouting to the crowd. Otto translated.

'What Göring is saying is, "We want to show you,"' Otto said in a loud voice, "that Germany has spared no efforts to make a reality, um, to realize the *Führer*'s orders, of making these festivals – games I mean – which symbolize peace and understanding before all nations."'

Then he muttered, 'What nonsense.'

And then Hitler had stood up in his shabby overcoat. 'I hereby declare the Fourth Winter Olympic Games in Garmisch-Partenkirchen open!' he screamed. At his screech, a flapping white flag, with five interlocking coloured rings, was hoisted on one side of the ski-jump and a huge brazier of pitch surmounting a high Doric column was set alight. A field gun boomed in the valley. As black clouds and leaping orange flame mingled, the twenty-eight teams marched out, the Germans last, goose-stepping.

It was now a few minutes after eleven o'clock. They had started on time, the gods had snowed to order. The Winter Games of February 1936, as Siegmund had foretold, could already be counted a triumph.

When they returned, cold, wet and exhausted, to the chalet, Daphne found that her stained bedlinen had been changed.

She searched through the pine-scented drawers to see if her nightgown, which she had bunched and hidden under her pillow, had been washed and returned. She discovered that her diary (in which the events of the previous night remained unrecorded) lay where she'd left it, with her underclothes, but her soiled white cotton gown, with a broderie anglaise collar, had been removed.

10

Little Venice
March 2006

They were lying in bed trying to decide where to have brunch: the Expensive Place, or the Beyond Expensive Place. As it was Saturday, both would be chocker with couples who'd been house-hunting, i.e. about to drop several million pounds of borrowed money on a property they assumed would double in value in a couple of years. Either that, or one of them worked for a US investment bank, in which case one of them could simply mop up his (or her) end-of-year bonus with a large house.

The merely expensive place – a café that had leapt to chichi deli status after Gwyneth Paltrow was photographed outside with a top-of-the-line off-road buggy and clutching a soya latte – was on Clifton Road. A minuscule and indifferent round of tomatoes on toast – aka 'the sourdough *bruschetta* with first-pressing olive oil and hand-picked organic cherry tomatoes on the vine from Puglia' – weighed in at eight quid. 'At least they're not trying to flog us "lost varieties" tomatoes,' Gus had said, having seen 'lost varieties' on a particularly pretentious menu, 'as if they had to send in Harrison Ford, guns blazing, to bring them to us.'

But, here, the poncy-word premium applied: anything 'pan-fried' or 'artisanal' attracted at least a £5 surcharge. At the crowded Clifton Road café – where the queue just for coffee at weekends rivalled even the pre-Christmas turkey-pick-up queue at Lidgate's in Holland Park – the Emmental was invariably 'cave-aged' and, most tiresome of all, the apples 'tree-ripened'. Not that anyone seemed to mind paying extra, or waiting for hours. Most of the customers worked in financial services. They were now earning millions when, in the eighties, they would have earned £40k for doing exactly the same work, but they thought – no, they knew – that the reason they were so obscenely well paid was because they were worth it.

So the bankers and brokers and fund-managers in their button-down Brooks Brother shirts and chinos, Type As who thought that relaxing meant 1. not wearing socks on Sundays 2. reading the Life and Arts section in the *FT Weekend* as well as Companies and Markets and 3. looking at modular Italian designer sofas, never minded paying, whatever the mark-up. It was as if giving away more of other people's money made them feel better about having helped themselves to so much of it.

Their largesse extended to their trophy wives – gym bunnies nibbling on a crumb of gluten-free pecan brownie between Pilates and their child's tennis lesson – or their nubile girlfriends. In fact, as with most things these days – car, house, clothes, spa breaks, Caribbean holidays, private education, *crostini* in the place on Clifton Road – the more the customer paid, the happier the customer seemed to be.

The beyond expensive place was in the West End, and was more of a trek – more of a place for see-and-be-seen dining than neighbourhood grazing over the Sunday papers. In theory, at least, the restaurant was the capital's homage to the egalitarian, bustling, pillared brasseries of Paris, Vienna and Budapest, where railroad men slurped borscht and scoffed schnitzel alongside diamond merchants, or bejewelled powdered old ladies sat alone, feeding tidbits to lapdogs.

In practice, of course, the restaurant symbolized the new divisions in society: forget the aristocracy (titles no longer counted when making a booking), this place had a formal Weberian hierarchy that assigned tables according to strict principles of money, status, power and, above all, fame.

So the restaurant – which was wildly overbooked months ahead – had a central reservation known as 'The Horseshoe' for celebrities, the super-rich, starry media-creatives, actors, artists, honoured regulars and, more and more, people who appeared on reality TV. There was one telephone number for shiny people, or bold-faced names. Then there was the number that appeared on the website for everyone else. If you called this number and dared to hope for a table in two weeks' time, there would be a pregnant pause, during which the sound of tapping on the keyboard was audible, the same dry sound as rats' feet over broken glass in *The Waste Land*, as your name was Googled and deemed table-worthy, or not.

'I have 11.30 a.m. or 3 p.m. for lunch on that Tuesday,' you might be told. The restaurant kept twenty-six brands of Champagne and was rude to all but a tiny handful of its customers, which was, naturally, why it was so popular. It nourished the egos of the rich and famous with the smothering solicitude of the Jewish mama, and it kept everyone else hungry for inclusion.

'Don't let's go there,' said Francie, as she skimmed a piece about a celebrity's shock weight loss, before turning to a piece that purported to be about a downshifting couple. She was trying to be normal around Gus. But she'd forgotten what normal felt like. As she read, she thought, as ever, about Nathan. Things hadn't been going that well.

He hadn't called once this week, for example.

The endless spread was illustrated by pictures, so many pictures: there was the attractive extended family showing Jack and Christabel amid three generations of gorgeousness camping in a bluebell wood, complete with vintage Union Jack bunting draped between trees and over the mandatory battered Land-Rover with a canvas roof, fairy lights, an old army tent, a kettle whistling over a fire. There was the money shot – the gracious outlines of a large house behind a ha-ha, and the headline, 'Live your dream – this family sold their successful storage-solutions business and decamped with their four children to a peachy Georgian rectory in Wiltshire.'

Francie flipped the glossy pages, took in the details:

there was the MILF, Christabel, the pair of blond bare-foot daughters, matched by two rumpled sons in plaid shirts with unruly hair – check; with cool names like Spike and Tallulah – check; there were the photographs of the kitchen garden, the walled garden, the games room, the media room, and the pigs – check check check check.

It's such a con, thought Francie, when the papers combine country-house porn with lifestyle envy, and wondered what Nathan was up to. She'd texted him, but he hadn't answered; not yet, anyway. She hated waiting for the answering text. It was like being in limbo.

She'd done these interviews, been to these houses, looked into the eyes of people . . . whose lives were so fucking fabulous that all they really, really lacked was to have their fabulousness laid out over six pages in a colour supp for millions of people with less money and no taste to drool over.

Francie knew that the only reason it worked was because – far from downscaling – this was the set-up: Jack – fill in name of high-rolling hubby – was still a boutique hedge-funder with an office in Mayfair and had installed a media hub at his home in a converted barn with several screens so he could watch the markets in the Far East and New York. This was the new deal: hubby was still pulling down seven figures a year, was still banging his secretary while his wife turned a blind eye and devoted herself to Marie-Antoinetting on her hobby farm, hunting, four kids and inevitable Gloucestershire Old Spots.

'Let's not go all the way to central London,' Francie repeated. 'I'm meeting Miranda for coffee, so I'll see you in the Expensive Place at two-ish. You can go to the gym. Or yoga, or whatever.'

It was incredible, Gus's new appetite for yoga. He'd even started doing his teacher Shelly's own 'liquid asana' DVD, 'based on the fluid dance of vinyasa flow'... *before work*.

'But we could go to the Royal Academy after,' said Gus, who had discarded every other section of every other newspaper except the Business Section of *The Times*. 'We could ring the Fletchers, see if they want to join us.' The Fletchers were their official best friends, despite being exponentially richer.

The Fletchers had met in rehab, after they both laughed out loud at the same joke (not really a joke joke, just that, when they met, James asked Saskia whether she was 'seeing someone'. Saskia thought James meant a shrink, rather than a date, which was funny at the time).

Francie and Gus realized that the Fletchers had pulled into the fast lane financially about five years ago. James was in private equity. Francie didn't know what this was, but, whatever it was, it had allowed James to endow the new science wing at his old school while insisting he remain anonymous on the list of donors in the *Old Boys' News*, which meant that the technical term for how much money he had was 'fuck-off rich'.

James and Saskia had also bought not just one villa in Val d'Orcia, one of the most beautiful valleys in Tuscany, but two. So while merely rich people might have his and hers sinks in the master bathroom if they were lucky, the Fletchers had his and hers villas. With pools, loggias, shaded terraces and endless uninterrupted vistas over cypress-spiked misty green hills and rolling vineyards. Even more distressingly, both residences came complete with their own housekeepers, who made fresh pasta, rolling it out by hand over marble-topped tables in cool kitchens hung with bunches of lavender and ropes of garlic, and pressed their own olive oil.

It was almost enough to ruin their friendship, but Gus was quite cool enough – grounded and centred, especially now with his buff new yoga bod – to cope.

Francie knew Gus was trying to connect with her, to say stuff they could do together. But it was no good. They were just not on the same page at the moment. They were in two very different places and, once again, it was all her fault.

She lay back on the white bed, staring into space, wondering if she had time to masturbate while Gus was in the shower. Without thinking, she reached out for her mobile to check yet again if Nathan had texted her back. It was dementing. She'd counted the number of texts she'd sent him, and he'd sent her, and then, in a frenzy of worry, counted the number of emails they'd sent each other, and it was all too telling. Hers to him outnumbered his to her by a ratio of 3:2, and he owed her a call.

Ten minutes later, she was sitting at the Expensive Place gazing into a screen saying 'no new messages'. She was waiting to order coffee until Miranda arrived. When she looked up from her mobile, Miranda was plumping down in the chair opposite, looking freshly showered, pink and pretty.

'You look well,' said Francie. For some reason, her tone sounded suspicious. There was a merry light in Miranda's eye she hadn't seen for ages. Not since the time Bryan Ferry actually came into the office when they were doing the Roxy Music CD cover-mount and cover-shoot.

'I am well,' Miranda said, with a secret smile. 'Very well.'

'Oh yes?' said Francie, in a leading way. She was pleased. Miranda shouldn't be single, at forty. She looked amazing, for her age. She had a willowy figure, and lovely dark hair, and the ethereal colouring of a woodland elf: dark eyes and brows, and very pale skin.

'Who is it?' said Francie. 'Actually, before you tell me, I've got something to tell you.' She raised her eyebrows and widened her eyes, to signal there was plenty to come. She paused as their cappuccinos arrived. They'd forgotten to order skinny ones, so they started spooning the creamy froth scattered with chocolate powder into their mouths and studying each other's faces for clues. Suddenly, Francie knew she was going to tell Miranda about Nathan. Not name him, of course. One, he was quite carey-sharey with Miranda. Two, he'd shagged half the office, if you believed the gossip, which they mostly did. And three, four, five, he was their *boss*, as neither of them needed reminding.

Francie wiped her mouth, laid her heavy cup down on its saucer, wondered if she should order another – perhaps with one of the crunchy explosive almond *biscotti* on the side.

'Well,' she said. Miranda looked up. 'I've met someone,' she said, pleased with the formulation, as it ruled out Nathan. She saw Nathan every day, so she couldn't exactly have suddenly met him, could she?

'What?' said Miranda. 'Are you serious? But what do you mean? Met someone? How could you – what about . . .? Ohmigod, well so *have I*. This is ridiculous. But you go first.'

Francie launched in, not saying that much. She said she wasn't in love with him (she said 'in lurve'), but the awful truth was – not that she could say this out loud, to anyone – she was crazily in lust and had started to find the lyrics of top-ten pop songs profound.

'Have you been to bed with him?' asked Miranda. Miranda gave Francie her patented, irresistible 'You can tell me anything' look, which worked so well with office juniors in the Ladies at *Event*; a look that was usually followed by the 'I'll be there for you, day and night' promise.

Francie had no intention of admitting she had been unfaithful to her husband. 'Yes,' she found herself saying, anyway. 'I don't know what the fuck to do.'

'Well, do you want to leave Gus?' asked Miranda, dropping a nubbly pale-brown sugar lump into her cup. She was so good at this stuff. She always seemed to be interested in everything, the tiniest detail, as well as the seismic shifts.

'NO!' said Francie, vehemently. 'Of course not!' It was clear that Nathan had never even discussed the fact they'd been to bed; she didn't expect him to! But she knew that if Nathan so much as crooked his little finger at her, she'd be tempted to come running, so she hoped he wouldn't. All she could do was pray it would pass, this feeling. It was addictively nightmarish, as if she'd been possessed by a malign toddler.

Then Francie told Miranda a lot more about their physical connection and how great the sex was and how she felt alive again and couldn't think about anything else and counted the hours, the minutes even, till she saw him, even though she knew he was a tool. Only she didn't use the word 'tool', because that was one of their words for Nathan.

'And does the, um, man you've, er, met want you to leave Gus?' was Miranda's follow-up.

'No,' said Francie in a smaller voice. He hadn't said anything about 'them' at all. Francie knew it could take long years before most English men even admitted they were in a *relationship*.

She hoped no one they knew was within earshot; the café was crowded with families and men in chinos, as usual, plus the odd Hampstead type reading the *TLS*, on their own. Suddenly she felt miserable. She wished she hadn't said anything.

'So come on, what about your chap?' Francie said. But then Miranda went all coy and wouldn't offer much in return. Apparently there was a man. He called her All The Time. He thought she was the sexiest thing he'd ever seen. He was mad about her. He asked her out every night. But Miranda was holding out and playing the Long Game.

Francie felt like crying. Miranda always got things right. She would never, ever, have sex with someone who had less to lose than her, or shag her boss. She gazed into her empty cup. Miranda seized the moment to say her piece.

'Well, I think you know where this is going, I'm afraid, my love,' said Miranda, in a consoling voice. 'Which is nowhere.' Her face had taken on a private, self-satisfied look, as if others couldn't be expected to have her luck when it came to the affairs of the heart.

'I know,' said Francie. She couldn't believe she felt miserable, already. They'd only been to bed, as in bed bed, once.

The second coffee had made her even janglier than she was already. Then her mobile started vibrating. Even though she knew Nathan wouldn't call her at a weekend she allowed her heart to skip a beat. Then she saw from the caller ID that it was an 01865 number, and she knew.

'Oh. Hello. Frances?' said a voice she recognized. Milly Goddard, from Faringdon Lodge.

Francie herself had a while ago reached an easy accommodation with the guilt that lingered during her visits to Faringdon. Grannie always wanted her to stay longer than she did. After only half an hour, Francie would find herself twitching about trains and deadlines and taxis, while Grannie was hoping ('Do you have to go, darling?' she'd say. 'So soon?') that tea might elide into a drink. But now things were different. Any call could be a new lead in the quest.

'Hello, yes, it's Frances,' she said. 'What's up?' Miranda

raised her eyebrows. Francie hadn't told her about the German stuff at all yet. 'Has Grannie taken it in about her sister, the one in upstate New York? Does she know that Dem has died?'

'Yes, she has. Very sad. She's spoken to the nephew. I'm sorry. But listen, I've found something else you might be interested in. I could post it, but good news. Your grandmother's a little brighter today, and it would be such a shame if it got lost, after all this time. It's a bit delicate to put in the post . . . and I wondered . . .'

'Of course, Milly,' she said. 'But what is it, though?' Francie sat bolt upright. Grannie was brighter. She could, therefore, begin asking her questions.

'It's her scrapbook from the thirties,' said Milly Goddard. 'And it's got photographs stuck in the pages too. And all these dried flowers!' Even though the café was noisy, Francie could hear a dry, scuffling sound, as if Goddard was leafing through it as she spoke. 'They keep falling all over the place.'

Francie's heart leapt again. This was great. Now, whatever happened with Nathan, at *Event*, didn't matter so much. She could already see it unfurling: the semi-autobiographical novel . . . the film rights . . . the interviews in the Review section of the *Observer* accompanied by pensive portrait shot of her in black and white by Jane Bown, with her chin resting on her hand.

Miranda's mobile had also rung while Goddard was talking. She'd taken the call.

'You again,' she was saying. 'I told you not to call because I was having coffee with Francie,' she said,

Cheshire-cat smile playing about her lips, and then she added, quickly, 'You know, Frances Fitzsimon? The friend at work I was telling you about . . .'

As Francie was walking to Paddington yet again, she realized that she hadn't said anything about Miranda taking Nathan to Burberry, but no matter. And Miranda had offered nothing, either, about her having gone with Nathan to Burberry, even though this was the sort of thing they would debrief each other fully about in sneaky sessions in Costa Coffee.

Never mind, thought Francie. She was bound to hear all about it on Monday.

11

Munich, Bavaria
Late February 1936

Daphne was running as fast as she could down a side street, rushing to meet Otto, and she was late.

Her feet kept sliding on the greasy cobbles, as she was running in the street, rather than on the pavement, because the pavements belonged to men in uniform. A light rain was falling, shrouding the street lamps with a fuzzy golden halo, and the cathedral was tolling the hour. She ran past the sheer red façade of Our Lady, the cathedral where she'd climbed to the bell tower her first week in Munich, where it had all started. She knew if she didn't get to Otto on the steps of the opera house, he would leave, and she would never see him again.

Then she slipped and was in the arms of an officer. He was tall and white-faced – Eric's face loomed above her. Eric! Eric, the *Gräfin*'s son, who opened doors, held out coats, was icily polite and played the piano but who also couldn't conceal his disgust that his own mother, a countess, had been reduced to the status of landlady by the unfairness of Versailles.

In the dream, Eric grabbed Daphne by the arms and pushed her up against the wall. She could smell the rain on the wool of his jacket, and his lapel caught against the brooch on her coat, the brooch that her mother had given her on her sixteenth birthday, from Tiffany, a lovely thing in the shape of a heavy, glittering glass star, so it came away and fell into a puddle. He held her there easily with one hand, and towered above her.

'You English girls, who come here, and live off us, you are all the same.' His wet, bloodless lips were moving against her ear. Then he hissed one word that Daphne could not but know the dreadful meaning of.

'*Huren.*'

Otto and Daphne were sitting together in the drawing room in Königin-Luise Strasse, and she wondered if the dream – and she'd had it more than once, she felt sure – meant anything.

Otto had made a fire, which didn't seem to give out any heat, but, for once, the house was quite warm. Daphne fingered the brooch on her dress, checking the clasp was secure. It would be awful if the dream – well, more of a nightmare – came true and she lost it. She would be running to meet Otto, sometimes at the opera house, sometimes across the grass of the English Garden, but she never got to him. In the dream, she and Otto had a plan but, somehow, the plan never happened.

But now they were alone, and together, which was all she had hoped for. She sat on the hard moiré sofa. She wished she hadn't chosen it: it was so slippery she had to sit still and upright and press down hard on the floor in her shoes so as not to slide towards the floor. Otto sat in a chair opposite, in a dark suit and white shirt, looking serious as he studied the cover of the record, which he had been doing as Daphne spoke, as what she wanted to say to him was so difficult.

She had considered taking him upstairs, to talk there, in the twin-bedded room she shared with Betsy at the finishing school that overlooked the courtyard, but felt shy, even though the others were all out.

Daphne had been taught she should never be in a room on her own with a young man, especially one with a bed in it. She knew that when she went to Somerville, if she had a male visitor, she would have to push her cot on its castors out of the door into the corridor. And keep the door open, and one foot on the floor at all times, and be out before the gong rang for Hall at seven.

When she and Betsy met up in London at the Barton-Hill residence in Park Lane they weren't even allowed to go to Harrods, which was terribly unfair because Diana – who lived in Tite Street, which was at least two stops away on the bus – was allowed to go to Peter Jones, and Diana was a whole year younger than Daphne and Betsy. Betsy's mother, Esmé, had explained more than once that if the girls did go to Harrods or Lyons Corner House or the cinema on their own they would be kidnapped by white slave traders and end up in Buenos Aires and they would only have themselves to blame.

Daphne had made two tisanes for them in the kitchen. She'd found the tea-set high up in the cupboard, and now the tisanes sat cooling in delicate porcelain tea cups on the sofa table behind them. She'd drawn the curtains.

The house was still and quiet; everyone else – Meg, Eric, the countess, Betsy – was out.

They sat in silence, Daphne with her hands folded, digging her heels into the rug so she remained reasonably upright despite the silk sliding under her skirt.

'Otto,' she said, 'I wanted to see you because I need to tell you something. It's about Siegmund. Well, about me and Siegmund.'

She was glad she hadn't tried to have this conversation earlier. They'd finally gone to the Koenig *Stammtisch* – where his family always sat, for years and years – in the *Hofbräuhaus* that afternoon. They had been back from the Alps exactly two weeks. They sat close together on a bench, watching whole tables of strangers rocking with merry laughter and the men slapping their spreading thighs, while Otto explained the concept of *zusammen*, which meant, so far as Daphne could work out, that Germans did German things together.

Daphne had sipped from her *Stein*. 'Are you hungry?' Otto had asked politely, his eyes burning dark in his face. Daphne was never hungry when she was with Otto; her stomach shrank from the prospect of food. There was only meat on the menu anyway, and meat all over the table, on platters: there were great knuckles of pig, white bone and shiny pink flesh, and orange frankfurters curving obscenely out of sloppy pale tangles of sauerkraut. 'No,' she said, putting down her beer, so it spilled and a little pooled into a dark puddle on the pale surface of the scrubbed wooden table. She looked at him. He didn't seem hungry either.

She could not say it here: 'Siegmund came to my room when we were in the mountains.' But she had to say it. She had to tell someone.

They were in a flagstoned hall big enough to raise an army devoted to the consumption of cool blond tankards of beer and hot pink knuckles of meat. Their companions at the table ate and drank and talked and ate and drank and talked ceaselessly, looking lost and sad when, for only a few minutes, there was nothing to fill their gullets, until the reappearance of the dirndl'd, red-armed waitresses bearing yet more flesh and beer to fill their bottomless stomachs and hollow legs, and their empty pewter and grey china tankards were whisked away to be rinsed in copper sinks lining the sides of the room.

'Come back to the *Gräfin*'s?' she murmured.

'Yes,' said Otto, simply, as if the rest of their lives was now arranged.

A waitress pushed past him carrying five *Steins* in one hand and slopping beer on the stone floor as she passed. Otto stood up, as if relieved Daphne did not have to witness for a second longer these scenes of unbridled carnality in the *Hofbräuhaus*. The regime had set fire to synagogues, blown up churches, shut down Catholic schools, pillaged art galleries, dynamited entire blocks of residential housing to erect monuments to Fascism, but it would never touch the beer halls. 'Hitler, a vegetarian who doesn't drink himself, at all, floated to power on a tide of beer,' Otto said, as a Bavarian brass band struck up a tune and its deafening crashes chased them out.

They spilled out into the Platzl, and walked in silence back to Königin-Luise Strasse, dodging puddles. Daphne had held her breath till they were safely back at the place she called home.

'So?' Otto said. He moved to squat on a tiny footstool embroidered with the *Gräfin*'s husband's family coat of arms, so his legs were almost in his chin. He'd made the fire without being asked and when Daphne watched him nursing the little flame, and blowing on it, and saw it flicker into life and begin to burn eagerly, she felt the splinter in her heart that had lain there since Garmisch melt a little.

Daphne was silent at first. She reached behind the sofa for her tea, and took a sip, then she placed it back.

'Siegmund,' she said. 'When we were in the mountains, last week. The night before the Winter Games . . .' She looked down at her feet in her pumps. This was harder than she thought. It was going to sound awful. They'd had such a lovely week skiing after, and she'd said nothing, as if everything was all right.

'He came to my room and got into my bed. It was a mistake –'

Even now it hurt.

'What do you mean, a mistake? Is that what he said to you?' Otto was sitting at her feet. The little fire was smoking, and the room felt colder. 'I am going to strangle him, put my two hands round his neck' – Otto held out his elegant white hands, too delicate to crush a grape – 'until he realizes what he has done, and begs your forgiveness. And then I am going to kill him even though he is my cousin, and then I will throw his body in the Isar. Did he hurt you? He's done it before, you know. I need to know. Tell me!' he almost shouted. 'He even tried once, with –' Then Otto stopped himself. He made a disgusted sound at the back of his throat. 'Forget it. Compared to what that animal did to you . . .' He plucked at the tasselled edge of the rug, laid over parquet. He poked the fire, then looked up, straight into her eyes. He dropped his gaze, shuffled logs about and then directly looked at her again, his eyes glowing like black coals.

'It was the night that it snowed,' said Daphne, putting her hands on her knees and squeezing her eyes shut. She couldn't look at Otto, or even into the fire, she just looked into the depths of her shame.

He grasped her ankle in sympathy. 'Let's stay here,' said Otto. 'Don't let's go to join the others.' He kept hold of her ankle. Then he started stroking it with his thumb. At the touch, Daphne thought her heart would burst. Otto didn't mind what Siegmund had done. Siegmund certainly didn't mind about what Siegmund had done; it was as if he gave it not another thought.

When they'd returned from the Alps, the only thing that had changed, officially at any rate, was that Siegmund had joined the elite corps – the *Totenkopf*. He proudly wore his new hat with a silver skull set above the peak. He took it off to look at it, would polish it lovingly, as if it was a precious scarab.

Daphne burst into tears, and told Otto almost everything. She didn't explain about swapping rooms with Betsy. The tears flowed hot and fast.

As she finished her brief account of the night before the Winter Games, she realized Otto's head was in her lap, and she was playing with his dark curls, and twisting them in her fingers. They were supposed to be meeting Betsy and Siegmund at ten that night in the Marienplatz for a concert, for which the *Gräfin* had mysteriously produced tickets. Six tickets! Somehow, for all her complaints of short-handedness, the *Gräfin* knew all the right people.

But it was ten o'clock now.

She took Otto's hands in hers. The mere touch of his skin set off little pulses of electricity between them. She stroked his long fingers and slipped her own up and down his, dipping between his fingers and gently caressing his palm.

There was no one in the house; they were alone. She knew what she wanted to do; after all, she had done it before.

Otto went to the record player. He found the 1931 recording of *Tristan und Isolde* in Bayreuth that the *Gräfin* had been playing earlier while contemplating her widowed state, and by some miracle found Act III Scene III. Soon the strains of the orchestra were joined by a pure soprano and desire started throbbing through the room. 'Nanny Larsén-Todsen,' Otto said. 'A Swedish soprano, a Brünnhilde and Isolde of the first rank,' he continued, with a serious expression. Wagner was one of the things that the Germans never joked about. Like lederhosen. They simply didn't see the funny side of fat men in leather shorts, or of a well-upholstered blonde with plaits wearing a helmet shaped like a swan nesting on her head, which is what Nanny looked like on the album cover.

'Just listen,' Otto said.

The violins came in below the soprano's sobbing voice, building exquisite cadences that never quite finished, then ebbing away and building up again, to a higher plane, before ebbing back. They listened to the aria, almost unable to breathe as resolution deferred, and then deferred again, the violins coming in like the little waves that break on the shore, retreating further every time, building up, ebbing back, but becoming louder and more insistent until at last a big wave, a huge symphonic breaker, towered, trembled at its apex and toppled then broke.

They gazed at each other, and Daphne realized she'd been holding her breath. She exhaled, and shivered, as if the ghost of Siegmund was in the room.

Otto stood up. He was leaving. Of course he was. She had disgraced herself, and brought shame on his whole family. Why else did Eric call her a *Hure*, even if it only was in the dream?

But he held a hand to her, as she sat on the sofa, still. He was not smiling. 'Let's go upstairs, to your room.' She tilted her face, and he looked down into it.

'Are you sure?' she asked. He laid a hand on the top of her head, as if giving a child at the altar-rail a blessing. At the touch of his hand she felt her doubt melt, and that she could trust him: he was what Betsy's father called a good egg, even if he was a filthy Hun.

'Yes,' he said. 'I'm sure.' He hauled her off the moiré sofa and into his arms. After a few moments, leaving the tea cooling in the cups, and the smoking, fitful fire, she led him upstairs.

I 2

Portmeirion, North Wales
March 2006

Nicky Miles's kitchen in his house, Plas Deudraeth, was a crooked little affair. After a quick tour, Francie shepherded her host back to the kitchen, which was dominated by an oak table covered by a white cloth with washed-out, pinky-brown red-wine stains.

Compared to their kitchen in Little Venice, with its gleaming Bulthaup surfaces, its top-of-the-range appliances, every artefact in the Welsh cottage spoke of a life well lived, as opposed to well spent: there was so much going *on*, in every single inch of it. The dresser was crowded with chipped blue and white china, eggcups, mugs. Postcards from Italian galleries showing marble-buttocked boys, writhing Bernini sculptures, Rembrandt portraits, receipts, invoices, notes from the cleaner, were stuck in at all angles or propped in front of plates. Keys to lost suitcases and junked cars dangled from cup hooks, all the flotsam and jetsam and detritus of many decades jostled on this one piece of brown furniture. Next to the chipped butler's sink, with a red-gingham-curtained underside, sat a two-oven cream Aga the

Arran-sweater shade of English teeth. She narrowed her eyes, framing the scene as if through a lens.

Actually, if you regarded the whole kitchen as a sort of *installation*, she could sort of see it in *House & Garden* or *World of Interiors*: 'The Bohemian World of Nicky Miles – Old Etonian, Journalist, Nazi, Communist, War Hero, Homosexual'. Nicky Miles was a cat, with at least nine separate lives, a man who'd packed more experience into one lifetime than Francie's peer group had managed in a generation.

The table was already laid out for four with port wine glasses, glaucous from going in the dishwasher, blue checkered napkins, wildflowers stuck in a lustreware jug. As it was only 10 a.m., there seemed to be two explanations: either Nicky kept hospital hours, or there was some super-efficient housekeeper who'd come in and done it all the day before.

Little oils and framed black and white photographs of famous-looking people covered the lacquered yellow walls, and torn chintz curtains were held back to reveal a sea view through French windows. Unfortunately, it was raining and the north Welsh coast was not looking its best; it was, in fact, invisible.

'May I?' Francie asked, as she moved a place setting so she could put her recorder and notebook on the table. Then she attached a mic to the 'V' of Nicky Miles's stained green lambswool jersey. 'I think the audio will be better if it's here,' she said, with a professionalism she did not feel. She realized with a shock that people with proper jobs – obviously that couldn't include her, but did include nurses, doctors, TV cameramen, government ministers, anaesthetists – probably felt this slight panic while being observed in the act of doing their jobs.

She knew a member of the shadow cabinet. He always sounded smooth on air, when being interviewed by John Humphrys about the Tory response to the Budget, or the fact that the housing boom had now been going on unchecked for years, or bankers' pay, or whether or not interest rates should go up.

But one night, over dinner, the member of the shadow cabinet had admitted that, in the car on the way to the studio, in the dark before dawn, far from feeling smug and confident, all he heard was this voice in his head, saying, 'Don't fuck up. Just don't fuck up.'

She reached into her bag, removed the scrapbook she'd driven to Faringdon to fetch and then taken all the way to north Wales to show Nicky Miles, and put it on the table in front of him.

Nicky Miles made a slight 'ah' noise, as if he was interested in what Francie had brought to show him, as if she was a cat with a dead mouse.

She pressed the skip back button and then play, just to check that she was taping. 'In the war,' she heard her voice bleat – gosh, she sounded wet – 'you describe finding a German soldier on the ground and hitting him . . .' Her voice trailed off meaningfully. Then there was a loud *drrinnnggg!* . . .

She pressed stop, relieved it was working. She'd stopped the tape when the oven timer had gone off. The *dring* was the timer for the roast chicken and, at this point in proceedings, Nicky had leapt to his feet to move the chicken down from the roasting to the warming oven and clattered about for a while, spattering hot fat on to clean tea-towels, for his housekeeper no doubt to deal with, and swearing. She'd seized the interruption as a good place to call a halt for a tech check.

Miles was now staring at the scrapbook on the table, as if lost in thought. On the front, it said, 'Bavaria 1935–6'.

'If you're OK to, we can carry on.' She took a sip of the weak Nescafé. She tried to remember as she tasted the liquorice-flavoured brew when she'd last had Nescafé, and decided it wasn't actually that bad, but only if you thought of it as a hot drink entirely separate from coffee.

'I don't ever want to think about it,' said Nicky Miles loudly. 'I closed that box and turned the key, many years ago.' Francie was startled, then remembered: he must be talking about the time he killed the German soldier. Or the entire war period? What was it with this war generation? she wondered. Why did they never want to talk?

The front door was open, bringing in the sea wind through the house. Francie pulled her grey cardigan around her. She was amazed Nicky wasn't cold. Old people had lived through things that baby boomers, sixties hippie chicks, Generation X's and Thatcher's children could read about only with open-mouthed awe. They'd lived through bombings, rationing, starvation, boarding school at six, digging for Britain, the Blitz, Suez, Vietnam and whatnot, but one true fact remained: old people were always freezing. But not Nicky Miles, apparently.

She pressed record. 'So why did you go? To Germany,

I mean? I sort of know why Grannie went, and her friends, because it was what everyone did then, the Germans were like cousins, they were trusted, the country was regarded as respectable, it was safe . . .' She trailed off again.

'Oh goodness,' he said. Then he sort of gathered himself, glanced towards the sea through the open door, and Francie had the feeling that he'd explained it before. 'I was a tourist of the revolution,' he began, 'one of many young men taken in first by Fascism, then by Communism. National Socialism, as is often forgotten, began from the far *left*, not the right.' He looked at Francie, and she nodded as if she knew.

'We all wanted, deep down, much the same thing: a new system, a system that didn't destroy the wheat, while millions of people were starving. The only difference was – who would deliver? Hitler or Stalin? At first, I much preferred the Communists, until they became spies, of course. We queers loved Germany too . . . all those sunburnt boys in shorts . . . but that wasn't the reason I went, well, not the only one, anyway.'

He paused and slurped at his cold coffee. 'I saw unemployment in 1936. On the streets of Gloucester.' Francie visualized dead-eyed men in flat caps holding placards or standing on street corners smoking hopelessly. 'I was horrified by it, horrified. *This* is the very profound reason that I went to Germany.'

Francie noted Miles still used the present tense. 'Tourist of the revolution,' she jotted on her pad. Then she added, 'Gloucester.'

'As a boy, I could see the unemployed standing idly around on the street corners of once great industrial towns.' Francie eyed the recorder, and hoped it was working. This was fantastic! She could already hear it on Radio Four.

'I believed that Hitler had solved unemployment, built roads, was a man of peace. I wanted to meet him, I was a journalist, and so I used a friend' – he paused – 'who knew him, and we went to the osteria, the Osteria Bavaria.'

'God, how fascinating,' said Francie, hoping that the oven timer wouldn't go off again or the telephone ring and spoil the audio clip. 'So you met Hitler.'

'I told him how popular he was with the English. I was a terrible toady really,' said Miles, who was now doing something frightful with his teeth. Francie tried not to look: he was sucking them in and out as he spoke. She checked the red light. Still recording. 'I wrote letters home. "Dear Daddy, I'm just off to see a labour camp." "Dear Daddy, the *Parteittag* at Nuremberg was simply marvellous, I sat right behind Hitler for all the speeches!"'

He placed his hands together on the table, covered with dark bruise-like age-spots.

'My delusions took several months to leave me. What happened was – so easy to see with hindsight. My objectivity for a time deserted me. I honestly thought . . . he was a good thing. Then. Most people did. It's hard to understand now, I know. But then, you know, things were different.' He sighed. 'He gave me a signed copy of *Mein Kampf*.'

'Wow,' said Francie, wondering whether this was an appropriate response. 'You still have it?'

'Good God no, I lost it immediately,' said Miles, as if losing a signed copy of *Mein Kampf* personally given to him by its author was only natural. 'I lost it, like everything else. Had a Triumph then, two-seater, sweetest thing, but terribly unreliable, I used to use it for weekends, and driving up to Berlin, or to stay in castles, it took a terrible hammering on those dusty Bavarian roads, those humpy hills. My copy fell through a hole in the floor.'

Francie was both transfixed and frustrated. She loved the image of *Mein Kampf* tumbling through the dusty chassis on to a twisty mountain road as Miles bombed from Munich to a *Schloß*, possibly with a golden boy in shorts riding shotgun. It was a good image. She was sure there was some symbolism there. The world knew about the advance of extremism in the thirties, the enthusiasm of the intellectual class for Marxism, Fascism, any type of extremism really. Francie knew a bit about it already. So she wanted to know not about cabaret and cream cakes with the *Führer* – one sensed Miles had done that story to death – she wanted to know about her grandmother, and her set.

They'd known each other. They were English, in Munich between the wars. They must have known each other *well*. And she knew that Miles would be able to tell her who Andrew's father was, and fill in the blank on the birth certificate. There was no way she could drive all this way and not find out, that just wouldn't be fair. A granddaughter deserved to know.

'Nicky,' she said. 'Do you remember why I'm here?' Nicky Miles's life may have spanned the whole of twentieth-century history, but – she glanced at the spine of a book by Duff Cooper on a shelf above the Aga whose title reminded her – Old Men Forget.

The scrapbook lay between them. Francie took it in her hands, gently, so all the little bits of petal and stamen – it was so old the flowers had crumbled to papery brown tissue – didn't cascade on to the table-cloth. She opened it to the black page.

```
Garmisch-Partenkirchen,
      Chalet Huber,
  February 5-13th 1936
```

The captions were written in some sort of white crayon, and there was a series of black and white snaps with rick-rack edges showing two young women: a smiling chestnut-haired girl, and a pouty blonde with a Zeppelin bust wearing a tight jersey.

He nodded. 'Daphne, and Betsy,' he said. 'That ghastly countess with the even more ghastly son.'

'I know this might sound like the biggest cliché, but did something happen in Germany, something you might be able to help explain? Did Grannie have a boy-friend who was, you know, more than a boyfriend? Is there something I don't know about? My father, Andrew, died in a plane crash when I was tiny; I never knew him. My mother's in Argentina and she's useless. Grannie took care of me. But Grannie – Daphne Linden – isn't really saying much. Otherwise, I might never. Find out. Whatever it is. I've got that missing-piece-of-the-jigsaw feeling, about who his – I mean Andrew's, my father's – father was, if that makes sense.'

She produced the birth certificate to make things crystal clear and pointed to the telltale dash. Nicky Miles studied it, and sighed. Then he made the clicking noise again with his false teeth.

'Do you see, what this means is, I don't really know who I am. Does that sound silly?'

Francie looked at him with brimming eyes. It really sounded quite dramatic, put like that. She tried not to milk the fact that she was fatherless too much – she saved it for special occasions. But now she was officially grand-fatherless too, so she felt she could bring it on a bit.

His sticky eyes, veiled with glaucoma, looked at her. She could tell he hated being old. 'The Otto boy,' he suddenly said. 'Otto something. Can't remember now. Came from a good family, if you know what I mean. Brave. She saw a lot of him; they went to the *Winterspiele* together, I'm pretty sure they did, and skied. We all did. That would be February, 1936. The Games were in August in Berlin, but she didn't come to them, I remember now. She'd gone by then. I last saw her in Nuremberg, or was it Regensburg?, at some Godawful rally, either farmers, or Hitler Youth, or youthful Nazi farmers – goodness knows, it was so long ago. Seventy years? She left Germany without even saying goodbye.'

He started examining the album. 'My, how very good-looking the Swiss bobsleigh team were, in their tight white jerseys,' he said with approval.

Nicky Miles was looking at a yellowing press cutting which indeed showed the Swiss bobsleigh team, draped all over the bobsleigh. They were clad in heavy cream wool roll-necks, emblazoned with a square enclosing the neat little red cross of Helvetica. The men were all square-jawed, slim, with their jerseys tucked into high-waisted tweed breeks. Fedora hats with white braid around the brim sat on their gleaming, Brylcreemed heads at jaunty angles as they gave crooked smiles to the camera. The one in front had placed his arm casually on the black-spoked steering wheel of the bobsleigh, and on the white steering column 'Garmisch-1936' above the Olympic rings was clearly visible.

'What about this one?' Francie said, pointing with one of her manicured fingers to a photo of her teenage grandmother with a girl, and two boys.

'My goodness,' said Nicky Miles. 'That's him – Otto – the one I was telling you about. And there's Siegmund. An enthusiastic member of the Hitler Youth. Big, blue-eyed – a bit like Boris Becker in his prime. Very keen, he was. Keen in every way. My my. Betsy. And Daphne. My goodness,' he repeated. 'The girls weren't yet twenty. Yet don't they look old?'

It was true. They looked very stately, and formal, with helmet-like hair, and side partings, in their wool and gaberdine and tweed – and they were barely out of their teens. Francie couldn't help noticing, also, how naturally thin everyone was then.

He took the diary and a fern fluttered to the floor, and a little cutting from *The Lady* – a recipe called 'Delicious Roly-Poly Pudding' made with flour, golden syrup and suet.

'Do you know which one was Daphne's boyfriend?' asked Francie. 'Did she have any sort of *walk-out* with either of them?' She was sure that was the expression of the time.

'Not Teddy Cullen, that's for sure. That's him, in a suit,' he pointed. 'He was far too up his own arse. Gave me a hard time. Every time I saw him, he'd say, "Nicky, old boy, what do you know?" I'd tell him about some thundering party I'd been to the night before given by the Ruritanian ambassador. As it turned out, the *Times* correspondent in Munich – yours truly – like everyone else, didn't know an awful lot.'

Now Miles was looking at a photograph of a woman in a long, white fur coat, arms linked with a man clutching a Hasselblad box camera in gloved hands. 'Ah,' he said, with a faint sigh. 'And there, of course, is Leni. She always looked splendid. Did Daphne have an affair with either of them? With Otto, or Siegmund? Well, put it this way, dear: I'd be awfully surprised if she didn't.' He pressed a forefinger on the blond one so it covered his face.

'This handsome young blond. Siegmund Huber. It was well nigh impossible not to have some sort of . . . tussle with him. I remember him very clearly. Anyone was fair game.'

'Goodness, golly, gosh,' said Franci, in a shocked voice. She realized she was starting to talk like a cut-glass thirties starlet. She dreaded listening back to the tape.

'Oh yes, this is Betsy Barton-Hill. Silly, but such fun. Rather a goer in her day, as I recall. Fucked like a ferret, apparently. Of no interest whatsoever to me, but you'd better go to see her.'

His wrinkled finger remained on the charcoal-black page, poised, as he dredged his memory for ancient gossip.

'Who became Betsy Jarvis, then Lady Stockbridge . . . *und so weiter, und so weiter* . . . I remember her well. Betsy. Very well. Is she still alive?'

'Well, actually, I'm seeing her this week,' said Francie. 'My Uncle Francis supplied the name. I think she's, you know, a bit vague these days, but I'm hoping she might say something.'

'Well, I'm sure she'll have plenty to say,' said Miles, grinning. 'Do ask her about the time I took her to that nightclub in Berlin. It got her into such hot water with the dreaded *Gräfin*.

'And this is Otto – Koenig. That was his name. I've always wondered what happened to him. He was brave, you know. Didn't go along with things. Daphne loved him, I think. He's your man, Francie,' said Nicky Miles, with authority.

'If anything happened in Germany with Daphne Linden, and a chap,' he confirmed, 'it would have been with Otto.'

*

'It's going OK,' she said, after her mobile had finally recovered a signal. She was now sitting in a café in the little seaside village of Portmeirion. Retired couples strolled past, and she crumbled her raspberry flapjack as she talked. 'I've seen Nicky Miles and, I think, narrowed it down to two. Number one is an enthusiastic blond rapist called Siegmund.'

'Oh yes,' said Gus.

'Number two is called Otto, and I don't think he's a rapist. I don't know much more about him, except he's dark, and brave, and looks like an El Greco painting. Nicky Miles said that Grannie and he were close. So I'm going off to chat up Grannie's old friend Betsy, who Miles says was a distinguished nymphomaniac, back in the day. The diplomat Teddy Cullen's dead. Demeter's dead, and I can't find Sue Crewe. So far as I know, apart from Miles, Betsy's the only one who's still alive. So she's my only hope. I'm recording her the day after tomorrow. She lives in London.'

'What do you mean, "recording"?' asked Gus.

'I'm taping interviews with them,' said Francie. 'You know, to catch them before they fall, you know. Like autumn leaves.'

There was a silence. Francie thought about Nathan. She now thought about Nathan all the time – her life was like a Joni Mitchell song; he was in her blood like holy wine – and she was only surprised by the pure, refreshing intermissions of the day when she realized she wasn't thinking about him.

A seagull cawed plangently on the wall, as if in hope

of some of Francie's flapjack. 'Where the fuck are you again?' asked Gus.

'Portmeirion,' said Francie, as she looked out over the flat golden sands to the sea, and felt sad she didn't miss Gus more.

'About as far away as I can possibly be.'

13

Munich / Regensburg
April 1936

Sir Bache Barton-Hill did not believe in beating about the bush, but then nor, it turned out, did the *Gräfin*. His thick, tangled eyebrows knotted and unknotted as the hero of Vladivostok was obliged to hear the *Gräfin* out.

'As you pay me only one mark a day to keep your daughter,' she said, standing erect by the fire in the drawing room, lecturing Sir Bache and Lady Barton-Hill as they sat side by side on the moiré sofa, 'I rather think you owe me the courtesy of listening.'

'Well, go on,' said Sir Bache. 'Don't let us hold you up, my dear woman. As I understand it, we have a cocktail party and the opera still to get through this evening.' He glanced at his watch.

Lady Barton-Hill looked down at her lap, in a state of misery. It was unbelievable. Shocking.

Esmé simply couldn't believe that the *Gräfin* – after all, a woman of blood and birth, even if she was only German – had stooped so low as to mention *money*. They'd already heard from Sir Eric Phipps, the British ambassador, about Betsy's little jaunt to the Four Hundred Club in Berlin the week after they'd got back from the Alps. But, as Betsy had protested, she'd behaved with the utmost propriety and Miles was a queer, so they didn't really see why the *Gräfin* was making such a fuss.

Up until now it had been such a relief, Betsy being safely away in Germany. The season had been exhausting. Waiting up until the small hours for balls to finish, wearing a heavy tiara that dug into her scalp, sitting on chairs pushed to the side, making conversation with the other mothers. Lady Barton-Hill had had to stay in the Park Lane house, which she hated, much preferring to leave it under dust-sheets for months at a time.

There were balls and dances and dinners every night. In the end, Esmé was so tired that she'd slip back to Park Lane after dinner and then instruct her lady's maid to wake her at midnight and help her dress all over again. She'd squeeze herself into a long gown, pearls, gloves, tiara – and all so she could go and pick up the little baggage, Betsy, from Spencer House or St James's Square, or somewhere. It was utterly dismal. She'd done it too many times. And now – it did seem as if the countess was sacking Betsy. Something to do with an episode in the chalet in Garmisch during the Games, when both girls were there with the two boys, the cousins? Or was it something to do with Eric? It was all unclear, and Esmé wasn't entirely sure she wanted to know. She glanced towards the angular countess, who was wearing a long skirt and a high-necked blouse, with renewed hope. Surely the ghastly creature and her appalling son depended on the Barton-Hill's blessed mark a day?

But the countess wasn't looking at Esmé. She was the

sort of woman who, if a man was present, addressed herself only to him. Esmé felt tired at the prospect of unpleasantness. She could be back in Suffolk. She went into a reverie as she transported herself back to Tiddington, while the *Gräfin*'s angry voice went on and on.

First, she imagined snowdrops, in February, on either side of the Great Walk, raising the curtain on a colourful pageant of spring flowers, Lent lilies, daffodils of course, aconites, fritillaries. She called forth the box-edged *parterre* and herbaceous borders with their tapestry of bright hues, a riot of colour in May and June. She sighed, thinking of all she was missing in her favourite place: the Elizabethan walled garden, with its crunchy Peter Rabbit rows of lettuce and cucumber frames, its elegant potting sheds and sweet smell of mulch, her little chats with the head gardener and his son. . .

'Frau and Herr Huber were shocked,' the countess was saying, 'to think that this had taken place under their roof. They only discovered, from the maid, on the final day . . .'

It was all right for Bache: he enjoyed travel, rough shooting, and took no interest whatsoever in his home surroundings, or family. If the Germans hadn't asked him as their guest and the *Gräfin* hadn't called and suggested that they should come in person, she'd be on her knees with her trug now, weeding.

Having said that, she'd enjoyed seeing the work camp at Dachau. Very much. It was, as Bache had said, terribly efficient. The kitchens were spacious, and so clean. The prisoners wore clogs – just a piece of wood, with a strip of material on top – and they weren't allowed to wear them indoors. Such a good idea, Esmé thought. If only she could do that to the guns when they came back from the last drive before lunch . . .

'The maid told Frau Huber just before the girls left. She had been into Betsy's room, and she found evidence . . .'

Esmé wasn't really listening. What on earth could the countess be talking about? Betsy had denied anything had taken place in the mountains, and Esmé was inclined to believe her. Thank God, she thought, only one more social function and one more night to endure in Munich at the *Gräfin*'s so-called finishing school; then they were headed for Regensburg. The *Reichsleiter* had a castle by a lake, and had extended a cordial welcome to all the Barton-Hills and also, graciously, to Fräulein Daphne Linden as a prelude to the main event, which was of course Sir Bache's attendance as a guest of honour at the Reich's Farmers' Rally on Tuesday in Nuremberg. Bache had Walter Brüning's letter of invitation in his pocket.

'There has always been a strong connection between the free farmer and the soldier,' Walter Brüning wrote. 'The farmer and the people's army are never to be separated; both are impossible outside the community of their people. Thus it is a wonderful symbol of the New Germany . . .' Brüning's letter went on in this vein, and culminated in fervid salutations of Anglo-German kinship and ecstatic expressions of yearning for their imminent meeting.

Esmé opened her eyes, and this time they locked with

those of the mock-countess, who was leaning against the mantelpiece. They gave each other wintry smiles. Why didn't foreigners realize that, if you didn't call attention to something, be it a wasp at a picnic, Sir Bache's thing for Peggy Lumsden, or a rash, it all too often went away of its own accord?

Sir Bache glanced at his watch again. In theory, they were all due at the von Schirachs down the road at Königin-Luise Strasse 31 at six for cocktails before it was curtain-up at the *Staatsoper*, which was bound to be tricky. When Sir Bache went to the opera or the theatre, which was only if he had to, he always took two seats: one for himself, one for his hat and coat.

'Forgive me for what I am about to tell you,' said the *Gräfin*. She assumed a pious expression as Esmé braced herself for the blow.

'Elizabette has not behaved as a young lady should. Let us leave aside the Berlin escapade. What happened in the chalet is of far greater concern. And that is not all. It is clear – and please do not ask me to go into any details – that your daughter has become visibly . . .' she paused, and raised a hand to her forehead delicately while searching for the right euphemism '. . . *affichée* to my son, Eric.' The *Gräfin* had a tendency to lapse into French to underscore key changes in moments of high drama.

Sir Bache goggled at the countess. Esmé did not dare look at her husband. He regarded himself an expert judge of horseflesh and had surmised with one glance that young Eric was a sorry excuse for a chap and not

Betsy's type at all. Betsy was a pretty young thing; and pretty young things, in his long experience, preferred shits. Not defectives, into which category Eric, without a shadow of doubt, fell.

'I'm afraid she'll have to leave, even before you return from Regensburg and the *Appel* in Nuremberg.' She looked suitably moved as she referred to this noble event. 'I simply cannot be responsible for her any longer. Eric, as you know, is working for Herr von Schirach, who has so graciously invited us to his house tonight.'

At this unnecessary reminder of social duty and the piling up of obligation, Sir Bache made a tiny groaning noise that Esmé knew only too well.

'Eric is of course very busy, helping with the *Jungvolk*. It is such a vocation to him. He has high hopes of soon being promoted, to the *Hitler Jugend*. His ancestry is sound and, if he plays his cards correctly, there is no doubt that he could enter the SS, the *Schutzstaffel*. We cannot take any risks. There can be no scandal, no gossip. If this – if any of this – became known in Munich . . .' The countess looked down at them. They stared back with expressions of frozen distaste.

'You understand. It really will not do if this gets out. I am very sorry. Daphne, on the other hand, can stay.' Esmé Barton-Hill gazed out of the window, and could see a smudge of green beyond the garden, and trees silhouetted against the sky at dusk. It was the English Garden. She wondered whether Jacob Linden was also forking out a mark a week for the girls' boiled egg a day, the cheap hard opera seats that flapped up, the thin quilts, and how far that went towards the upkeep of the Montdragons.

Walter Brüning's car arrived for the Barton-Hill party in Munich on the dot of eight. They had all said a fairly chilly goodbye to Eric and his mother the night before, packed, and been up with the lark. To their hostess's credit, the last breakfast was a good one. Two eggs instead of one for each were arrayed on the best gaily embroidered Hungarian tablecloth, and there was a fresh loaf of bread, a large pat of butter, jams and hot milk. Their grips and cases were ready in the hall, and stood neatly on the parquet. The *Gräfin* Montdragon remained upstairs. The Montdragons and Barton-Hills would never see each other again, a fact for which the English family was truly grateful.

The motor signalled its arrival with a throaty roar outside, followed by a polite, almost throat-clearing toot. The girls rushed outside, grabbing their wraps and hats. The maid and Sir Bache followed, burdened with the luggage. Esmé came last. She seemed exhausted.

Betsy squealed when she saw the car, and the driver. Even Sir Bache stroked the bodywork as if it was some prize stallion in the owners' paddock at Ascot. 'The things we army chaps have to do to promote international goodwill and understanding, eh, gels,' he commented with satisfaction. 'Hop in, everyone.'

The Party had sent them a gleaming black, three-axled,

six-wheeled Mercedes with three rows of black leather bench seats. It was simply too splendid for words, as they all said several times.

Once ensconced, they began to feel very at home, and very blasé about travelling in such style. 'The Bentley's going to be a frightful come-down after this,' said Sir Bache. He wasn't remotely cross with Betsy for being sent down; he reserved his fury for the *Gräfin*. As far as he was concerned, a healthy, hearty English girl – a fine daughter of best Barton-Hill stock – could do no wrong. It was all a plot. The *Gräfin* had cooked up some cock-and-bull story, which frankly did her nothing but discredit, to get rid of Betsy. But no matter. He would take Betsy to the lakeside *Schloß*, then the *Appel*, and then she would leave Germany with them, at the end of the week, and be done with the entire shooting match.

As for Daphne Linden, well, she would just have to fend for herself. He'd drop Linden a line. He was an intelligent chap, Oxford don and all that, and Sir Bache had always been fond of Daphne, and didn't blame the countess for keeping her. She was a dear girl, Betsy's friend – lovely chestnut hair and complexion; even though she was racially undesirable, she was rather attractive. It was odd how those two things often went together.

'The cheek of it! Absolutely preposterous!' Sir Bache roared out loud, now they were away from the finishing school. He glanced behind at the girls, as the Mercedes convertible tooled through the outskirts of Munich. Sir B. and Lady B. were in the middle and the girls were lounging against the back. Esmé patted him on the arm. It was too noisy to discuss what had just happened as they motored along.

Low glass windows afforded some screen from the dust rising from the road and the noise, but not much. Soon they were zooming along a wonderfully straight and smooth road, with a clipped grassy reservation serving as a lane divider, and Esmé hoped that silence would fall as they surged north.

'There's no way that Betsy would have given that . . . unutterably feeble . . . *milquetoast* of a son a second look,' Sir Barton-Hill bellowed unstoppably into his wife's ear. 'Nor the other chap, the dark one. Smell of the steppes!' he roared.

The 'smell of the steppes' was short for the 'small of the steppes' either on 'the beard' or 'coat-tails' and was Sir Bache's code for anyone remotely Semitic.

Esmé continued to stare as forests flashed by and clouds passed over mountain ranges and the Mercedes nosed eagerly towards Regensburg. She couldn't think who Sir Bache meant by the dark one, but he was right about Eric.

The roads were lovely and empty, thanks to petrol being so blessedly expensive here. The landscape was getting more beautiful by the minute, but she stared at it without really seeing it, working out how many more nights away there were. She wondered how her artichokes were doing and whether Mary had turned out the linen cupboard. 'But I liked the fair-haired chap we met at that ghastly party last night, he was at least tolerable,' he shouted. 'Siegmund, or something? He seemed to have his head screwed on.'

The girls in the back heard Sir Bache bellow Siegmund's name, and each turned away to look out of the window.

By the time they reached Regensburg, after a picnic lunch by the *Autobahn* of cherries, cheese, bread and meats, followed by a cursory tour of a rather boring castle with a very unimpressive garden, they were all feeling rather peaky. The Mercedes roared on, and Daphne had fallen asleep, her chestnut hair spread out against the black leather banquette, and only woke up as the car turned off the *Autobahn* and started winding into the hills. Soon they turned left at a gatehouse and scrunched up a mile of gravelly lane, until they reached a clearing and a Grimm's fairy-tale castle reared above them, poking out of the forest.

A man clothed in a remarkable costume of green hunting jacket with silver frogging and white sleeves, brown leather shorts, a feathered hat and another feather perking up from a lapel, strode out to greet them, his large brown thighs pumping lustily. He carried a hunting horn in one hand.

'Last time I saw a feller dressed like that, in the War, I shot 'im,' said Sir Bache.

At this point, the girls knew that, despite the awful atmosphere between them over Betsy's unexpected, and quite unfair, sacking, a subject they had not yet thrashed out (and Daphne was not sure they ever could), there was still every chance of their giggling uncontrollably. So the girls dared not look at each other. The driver cut the engine.

The astonishing huge man kept a respectful distance. Then he sort of barked and, as he did so, threw up his right arm suddenly, as if catching a cricket ball at slip, and clicked his heels together. It was a command display of co-ordination.

'At ease, old boy,' murmured Sir Bache, as he levered himself stiffly off the leather seats, having been driven for hours in a foreign country surrounded by females. 'At ease.'

Daphne noticed that their German host was also wearing very curious socks: they were like little woollen cuffs, just covering his ankles and calves. She tried not to stare as they were all introduced, or recoil when Herr Grüning grabbed her hand. She thought he was going to kiss it and rub his moustache on it, but he raised it just short of his mouth, then tilted his head and looked up at her piercingly. She noticed he had very blue eyes. His hand felt very hot and urgent, and held hers for slightly too long.

Servants scurried forth from the castle, took their bags and disappeared back into the *Schloß*. She gazed up at the turreted edifice, silhouetted against a crag bearded with fluffy green fur, and then at the jagged outline of mountains in the distance, like saw-teeth, and wondered how on earth she would ever find her way back to her room, and then realized she was also worrying what Munich would be like on her own ... with no Betsy there. And no Otto. A pang pierced her. Why hadn't he come, that day, to the English Garden? There had been no word since. It was as if he'd vanished. Life already felt strange, and she was homesick, and she hadn't even mentioned to Betsy that –

'Follow me,' Walter Brüning commanded as they strode under a portcullis into a massive flagstoned hall ending in a fireplace surmounted by heads of elk.

'Come in, come in, *wilkommen* to my house! So, Sir Bache,' he said, rubbing his hands, as Sir Bache's eyebrows twitched furiously, 'how did you find the Mercedes? Would you like some tea, or is the sun, as you say, already over the yardarm?' He gestured towards a carved side table covered with white damask where tea in honour of English guests – tea cups, a silver teapot, lemon – had been laid out next to glinting cut-glass decanters and bulging soda siphons half encased in brown leather: just like Walter Grüning, Daphne thought. There was ice melting slowly in a covered bowl, and an array of 'dainties' on platters: mainly more meats and slices of cheese.

As Sir Bache engaged their host in conversation – Daphne could hear him referring to Nazis as 'sensible middle-class men of real intelligence' who had 'freed Germany from Communism and disruption from Oriental squareheads' – she felt able to slip away from the main group, leaving Betsy at her father's side. She crossed the drawing room to the two figures lounging by the fireplace, who, luckily, were Teddy Cullen and Nicky Miles. It was always lovely unexpectedly to meet people one already knew in strange places.

Nicky gave a slight bow, so she went up to them, glad she was wearing her pleated skirt (a little tight now), and the blue blouse the same colour as her eyes. The two men were holding drinks. Nicky had a green and yellow paisley cravat on, Oxford bags, and looked hale for once, his skin browned and sheened with exercise. He had a sweater slung around his narrow shoulders in pale green, and his thick blond hair tumbled over his forehead. He pushed it to the side at her approach, as if trying to make himself presentable. Teddy was wearing a dark suit and tie and had his consular black shoes on.

'What are you two doing here? And what on earth are you drinking?' It was a pink colour.

'Eight holes of golf, swim in the lake, lunch and tea so far,' said Nicky. 'Dinner next, fairly soon I expect. I do like it when all the meals blend seamlessly, don't you? It's like being in a residence somewhere grand, like Rome.'

'I'm keeping an eye on Nicky,' said Teddy, holding out his hand to Daphne. She realized that she suddenly felt cold. Her hand was cold. 'Miss Linden, are you all right? You're white as a sheet.' Teddy was rather sweet in the way he appeared to take personal responsibility for the well-being of all British subjects in Germany, but most especially the English damsels in Munich.

'I'm very well, thank you,' said Daphne, hoping very much that someone might bring her a cup of tea. She felt like sitting down, but everyone in the room was standing up, with Walter Brüning now taking the Barton-Hills on a guided tour of the tapestries, which featured gory hunting scenes with wild boars. The party now included a stately wife with thick brown plaits wound around her head and two other men to whom she had not yet been introduced, so she felt she couldn't collapse on to the sofa, even though she was longing to.

'Mm,' said Nicky, taking another long swallow. 'I say, this slips down a treat.'

He passed the glass to Daphne.

'Here, have a glug of this. It's strawberry punch. Bowle, it's called. It really is top hole.'

Daphne took a cautious sip. It was cold and sweet, fruity. 'Half Rhine, half Moselle, wood strawberries, sugar,' said Nicky. 'Delicious. But probably wouldn't be quite the same back home. Like paintings bought in street markets. Never quite the same back in Blighty.'

They sipped their pink drinks. Daphne wasn't sure what to say, so she listened.

'The worst thing is,' Teddy Cullen was saying to Nicky, 'is that there are people in London who agree with her. MPs. Clergy. Half the House of Lords. They all come out here at the invitation of the regime to marvel at the New Germany and, after being fed and watered and driven around in the shiny Mercedes from opera to rally to a castle out of the Brothers Grimm, they, strangely enough, do find the place rather magnificent. They too start banging on about how our two great Aryan nations should unite, and that the Reich should rule the land and Britannia the waves. My job is a nightmare. And you are not to write anything, for once, Nicky. I'm fed up with reading me in *The Times*. I hope she gives it all a wide berth for once.'

Daphne knew they were talking about Unity Mitford. Everyone always was.

'But I'm *praying* she does come,' said Nicky, in his slightly lisping voice. He held out his glass, and allowed the servant to fill it almost to the brim. Teddy covered his own with his hand. 'They'll probably send a car for her, because they know our Munich correspondent will be there and she always makes frightfully good copy.' He put his hands together as if in prayer and grinned. 'Dear Lord, oh do make Miss Mitford come! I haven't got anything into the paper, not for weeks. My glowing write-up of Dachau was the last thing I had in *The Times*, and that was weeks ago. If I don't pull off a stunt soon, I'll have to get a job with Daddy. And I couldn't bear to leave when things are hotting up and I'm –' he pouted – 'meeting so many super storms.'

He gazed openly at the muscular, hairy brown calves of his host, bulging out from the woollen cuffs. 'Yes, we saw your Dachau piece,' said Teddy shortly. He had already sent a telegram to the Foreign and Commonwealth Office about Nicholas Miles's report on Dachau but, like all his previous despatches for the last few years, he had the feeling of filing them directly into a chasm of indifference. He had visions of them piling up in trays in Registries, all those telegrams marked 'Urgent' and 'Confidential' sitting unread in locked cupboards. Cullen had also issued 479 visas to Jews in the last month, desperate to leave Munich, not that anyone in King Charles Street seemed to notice.

'Oh come on, old chap – just because I gave it the

thumbs-up,' said Nicky. 'Do admit, it's just the place to cart off all the discontented grousers and agitators. The grumblers can grouse at one another in Dachau till they're sick of grousing.'

Nicky was useful to Cullen because he knew who Unity was seeing, and had a boyfriend who told him useful snippets, such as that the *Führer* was receiving the Chinese *chargé d'affaires* in Berchtesgaden; in return, Teddy Cullen would disclose some story designed to appeal to the press back in London, such as that the Duke and Duchess of Kent were due to arrive at the *Hauptbahnhof* incognito on the Orient Express, and when. But Nicky was also a pain in the neck. Stanley Simpson, for example, had been on to the atrocities in the work camps for several years, but nothing he wrote ever ran.

After Nicky's *Times* puff piece about Dachau did, and as a reward for good behaviour, he'd been socked this all-expenses-paid junket to Nuremberg, to stay in the Gestapo-run Württemberger Hof for the rally, the one that the Barton-Hills and so on had all just tipped up for.

No wonder, thought Teddy Cullen, that his own despatches, written over whiskies late at night in his office, warning that Hitler wanted war, only seemed to gather dust. And his dark warnings to the Foreign Office that the leader was bent on world domination had gone unheeded. He'd asked for someone from the FCO to come to this *Appel*, but was told by return that 'no gathering could justify a week's absence of a top diplomat in an obscure provincial town.'

And now Nicky was here, about to coat the proceedings, the tank manoeuvres, the airborne displays, the Zeppelin fields, the shiny boots, the mass hysteria, with his own sinister brand of gloss.

'It's ages till the actual rally, not till September, the *Parteitag* this year, if I'm not mistaken. The Rally of Joy, isn't it, this year, Teddy, old boy? Still. I'm rather depending on tomorrow's knees-up to give old Dawson some fruity copy. Poor old Simpson's stuff about how wretched Dachau is never really hits the spot, so do let's hope Miss Mitford, toast of the tabloids, continues not to disappoint.'

At seven, a bell sounded. They were all back in the drawing room, having been on a guided tour of the grounds, which included a dripping, moss-lined grotto beside a dark-green lake, and then gone up to their various rooms to change.

It was still light outside, with the sun lighting the tops of the mountains, and the pines rustling in the early-evening breeze. The smells of the many-coursed evening meal had been layering thickly throughout the castle as the afternoon bled into evening. At the bell, servants suddenly manifested in black with white pinnies in the drawing room, hair tucked into bonnets, wiping their hands down their sides, to remove the drinks and tea and melting ice. A butler came forward and whispered in their host's ear.

Walter Grüning clapped his hands, and said, 'Aha! Our final guests have arrived! The ambassador, at last. Wonderful, wonderful.' He turned to his wife, who laid aside her embroidery and followed Walter out into the baronial hall to meet the new arrivals.

Daphne and Betsy, the Barton-Hills, Teddy and Nicky all fell in with the plan and pursued them out of the room. Grüning greeted his guests – a tall man with a monocle and his equally rangy wife – with cries of joy. They'd come all the way from Moscow for the rally.

At dinner, they sat at a long table, on which many silver objects, such as dolphins and swans, recently polished, glistened. There were candles, and piles of candied fruit, and cut-glass bowls in which red and pink petals floated prettily. After the first course, a sort of jellied brown soup, the man on Daphne's right finally turned to her. She had been toying with her food, and feeling uncomfortable but also slightly relieved that no one was talking to her.

He had been introduced to her earlier as a count and the ambassador to the Russians. He cordially asked her what she was doing in Germany, and she told him briefly, as she sensed he was only going through the motions, about the boarding school in Marquartstein.

'And then I've been at *Gräfin* Montdragon's in Munich,' Daphne said, her heart turning as she thought of Otto, and what had happened, upstairs in the bedroom, and thought she might have to leave the table, throw herself on her bed, and sob.

'Ah so, in that case you must have come across my nephew,' he told her. Daphne looked at the ambassador. Annoyingly, there were no place-cards on the snowy damask. She didn't know the ambassador's name, but she assumed he must be referring to Eric.

'Eric Montdragon?' she queried. She didn't really feel like it, but she sipped her wine.

'No, no,' said the count. 'My nephew Otto Koenig. He's a medical student.'

'Otto!' said Daphne, as the room darkened around her. She couldn't think what to say. She was trying not to think about him – about either of them.

'Why, yes . . .' And suddenly, she found she was longing to talk about him. 'I know Otto well.'

'Ah! I thought so. May I ask you to repeat your name?' In the mêlée earlier, in the hall, in the excitement of their arrival, he hadn't been introduced to the junior members of the Barton-Hill party.

'It's Daphne,' said Daphne. 'Daphne Linden.'

'Ah so, ah so,' said the count, looking reflective. 'Of course. I know. I am sorry.'

Daphne gazed at him, then looked down the table, as women nodded as men talked at them, and pushed forkfuls of meat into their mouths, and the men swabbed their faces with their large linen napkins edged with broderie anglaise, and waiters hovered behind their chairs, and she knew what the napkins reminded her of, like her nightie, stained, soiled, like her. She felt dizzy. She wondered whether she could leave the table; she needed to lie down.

What did the ambassador know?

'You mustn't blame him, it is difficult for him,' Count

von der Schulenburg continued in an avuncular tone. 'He wants to be a doctor. The Nuremberg Laws, you know. The countess can keep you, for a while, as a guest,' he said, while Daphne thought, I'm not a guest!

Then the ambassador continued, 'But he can take no risks.'

At the head of the table, Walter Grüning was gesticulating as he was describing to Sir Bache the annual ceremony called the '*Viehscheid*' when thousands of cows returned home after grazing the high Alpine pastures all summer, accompanied by the village and oompah bands. He was making a jolly accordion motion with his arms, and inviting the Barton-Hills back to the *Schloß* to see it. The count turned to her.

'You are a Jew,' he said, sweetly, watching her face. Then he put out a hand, and turned her face away from him so he could examine her in profile. 'Not that you look like one. But you know what the Hubers call you?' he said. 'You stayed with them in the Alps, I think?'

'No,' said Daphne, her mind racing. Did they call her whore too, like Eric?

'*Die Jüdin*,' said the ambassador.

'But I'm not!' Daphne exclaimed, so relieved she almost laughed.

Her father was Jewish, but all her father had ever said was that she was *English*.

The other end of the table erupted in laughter at some *bon mot* of Sir Bache's, about cows coming home. Daphne smiled glassily, and wondered whether she could ask exactly what the Nuremberg Laws were (could there really be a law that meant a medical student couldn't see a girl in the English Garden for tea?), but something stopped her.

For what she heard in the laughter rocking the head of the table was the clang of steel.

Later that night, the girls lay quietly in their single beds in a room on the first floor. The room was easy to find, as a coat of armour stood outside it in the passage, and you only had to go up one flight of stairs to glimpse the grey figure guarding the door. Not that they needed protecting: Nicky Miles was a queer, Edward Cullen a gentleman and the rest were old.

The room was large and comfortable. There were ottomans at the end of their beds, and a large kidney-shaped dressing table across which they had strewn their vests and underclothes and hairbrushes. The girls had only a small case each, just one change of day clothes, and evening dress, underwear, stout shoes, and mackintoshes in case it rained. Daphne and Betsy had undressed in silence, hopped into bed and switched off their bedside lights by common agreement. This was to discourage moths, which they both hated. They lay there in the dark, listening to the familiar sound of a bluebottle bashing itself between the curtains and the windows, and the rattle of the sash window. The wind stirred the branches of the trees on the slope, and the scent of pine mingled with Betsy's tin of Yardley Lily of the Valley talc, of which she'd spilt rather a lot after her bath and as they both prepared for bed. The silence between them lengthened.

'Bets, listen . . . I'm sorry you're leaving,' said Daphne finally. She raised herself on one elbow and looked over.

'No, you're not, actually,' said Betsy, half sitting up in bed, a blur in her blue polka-dot pyjamas. 'You're very pleased I'm leaving,' she continued. She snapped on the light, and grabbed her Mason and Pearson hairbrush from her bedside table. 'Why didn't you *tell* the *bloody countess* that it wasn't *me*?'

'Shh,' said Daphne, hoping she wasn't going to throw it at her. 'Herr Grüning will come and make sure we're all right. Keep your voice down. Please.'

'Don't tell me to be quiet! We *swapped rooms*, remember? You're such a goody-two-shoes! You want *Siegmund* to yourself, and you want *me* out of the way.'

Daphne sighed. She was lying on her back. One hand stroked the mound of her tummy, which used to lie so flat between her hipbones. It was all the cream cakes, she supposed. They were always tucking into noodles, dumplings and cakes. The *Leberknoedel* at the Osteria Bavaria . . . savoury, brown balls of liver, breadcrumbs, egg and thyme, in gravy – like so many other German dishes, they sounded foul, but tasted wonderful. The *Dampfnudel* alone – it was like a whole baby's head, submerged in custard.

'Why aren't you saying anything?' Betsy snapped. 'Thanks to *you* I'm not staying in Munich and *you are*! Mother and Father are sending me to the beastly, beastly domestic science college in Aldeburgh, the back of bloody beyond! I've already done the Lucie Bleeding Clayton Charm Academy and *it's all your fault*!' She flumped down on to her pillow and stage-sobbed. Daphne waited till Betsy was merely sniffling with self-pity.

'Because there's nothing to say,' said Daphne. 'You don't believe me. I've told you I never told the *Gräfin* anything. I don't like Siegmund. You know I don't.' Then she felt misery grip her. She lay back on her pillows and shut her eyes, remembering.

Daphne had been rushing out to meet Otto for tea in the English Garden, in hairy brown tweed skirt and Betsy's jersey, and was dashing down the stairs, plimsolls squeaking on the parquet in the hall when, suddenly, she'd heard the *Gräfin*'s voice grating.

She had stood outside, listening.

Daphne knew enough German to join the dots between the words '*verloren*', and '*Schande*'. When she heard the words, her heart almost jumped into her mouth. The *Gräfin* must know what happened, that night in the chalet. She was a fallen woman, she was lost, and would have to leave Munich in disgrace.

And then she heard the word 'Elizabeth'. Or rather, 'Elizabette', which is how the *Gräfin* pronounced Betsy's name. The *Gräfin* was not talking to her parents about her; she panted with relief, and tiptoed towards the front door.

It was Betsy who was in trouble, Betsy who was lost, Betsy who was shamed. It was rotten bad luck on Betsy, but there was nothing that, she, Daphne, could do.

As she opened the door and slipped out into König-Luise Strasse to meet Otto, she let out her breath in a

223

gust that mingled with the damp grassy air that smelt like home.

But he was not there. She had waited by the band-stand until dark.

And now, according to his uncle the ambassador, it had been settled, behind her back.

She would never see him again.

14

Francie pressed send on her travel copy (on the mountain resort, Berchtesgaden – a piece she had managed to finish without mentioning Nazis or skiing, as requested), sent an email saying she'd sent it, then called Gus. She didn't think he'd pick up. But he did.

'It's me.'

'I know it's you. I do have my own wife's number stored in my mobile,' said Gus. 'Why are you calling me?' He was at Village, deep in Soho. Francie imagined the common areas, the leopard-skin beanbags, ping-pong tables, vintage jukebox and freezer full of ice-cream and Polish bison-grass vodka.

Francie could hear the sound of music in the background, a snatch of Franz Ferdinand shouting 'Take Me Out' in the background, then someone stopping the track, and cueing it up again. They must be using it for an ad.

Gus had all the right toys for a trendy ad exec in his large, glass-walled office. He had the table football, the £1,000 Bose set of iPod speakers, the chunky Perspex awards, right down to the ironic orange Space Hopper in the corner. Gus was currently pitching for an account to market a new sort of water infused with vitamins and electrolytes, which was going to retail for several pounds a bottle even though the ingredients added to H_2O would pass unabsorbed via the nation's Victorian underground sewers and treatment plants, straight into the sea, i.e. the product was the usual con.

'Look, I can't hear you very well, but, just to tell you that I'm out tonight,' she said. 'I've recorded *The Sopranos* on the SkyBox. After work, I'm going to Victoria to see Betsy Barton-Hill.'

There was silence.

'Fine,' he said.

'I told her I was coming. I'll probably have to stay for supper,' said Francie, as if she would have no choice in the matter.

She didn't tell Gus what she was really doing. After Victoria, she was meeting Nathan for dinner, and God knows what else. All day, she'd been imagining leaving Quo Vadis in Dean Street at 10 p.m., and hopping into the Porsche Cayenne, chatting easily to Mandy the driver, and then . . .

'So see you later,' she said, wanting to get Gus off the phone, wanting to be cross with him, as it made things easier. 'Don't wait up, OK.'

Francie rang the bell of a small terraced house in Victoria Square, and composed her features into the sort of pleasant expression that would not frighten old people, very young children or non-English-speaking carers.

A young woman in low-slung jeans and dirty Ugg

boots stood there, her tummy squidging out between the hem of her T-shirt and the waistband of her jeans. She looked blank.

'Hello,' Francie said. 'I hope you're expecting me? I called and spoke to someone, a daughter, I think.'

The young woman stared at her.

'My name's Frances, er, Fitzsimon. I've come to see . . .' She paused. She had no idea what Betsy's final surname was – she'd run through so many husbands. One or two she'd even married twice, which was above and beyond the call of duty. So she just said, 'Betsy.' It sounded awfully casual, for a woman in her late eighties, but there it was.

'Come in,' said the girl, in a buoyant Australian voice. 'I'm the carer.' All Francie heard was 'I'm the Keira,' as in Knightley.

'Keira' stomped upstairs, and Francie waited in the kitchen, which was small with a fold-up Formica table in the centre. The oven was an old electric one, with a coating of dust; pictures of gummy-mouthed baby grandchildren covered the fridge. She heard voices, a dull, thudding sound, as when a baby rolls off the bed and hits the bedroom floor and there are a couple of silent, outraged seconds before the room fills with screams. The thudding noise upstairs passed off without consequence.

She gazed out of the not very clean window on to Victoria Square and watched a plane fly towards Westminster, the Houses of Parliament, and wondered whether it was going to hit Big Ben and why on earth they still allowed flights over London, after 9/11.

'Lady Stockbridge is ready if you'd care to go up now,' said the Keira.

Betsy was sitting very upright in a wing chair. The *Spectator* lay across her knees. She grasped a cane in a knuckled hand and looked at Francie with her head cocked, as a bird might regard a juicy worm.

'Dephne's granddaughter,' she said, in her last-days-of-the-Raj tones. 'Well, well. What can I orfer you?'

She pressed a little bell and the Keira manifested.

'Could you be an angel, Chanel, and bring two of my specials?' Betsy ordered.

'Chanel?' queried Francie.

'I know,' said Betsy, with a drawl. 'I have a carer called Chanel. And she has a friend called Chardonnay, would you believe. In my day, children were only called after saints. Now they are called after anything.'

'They're called after brands,' said Francie, joining in the disapproval, as she extracted her little Toshiba recorder. She held up the little mic, from which a wire dangled. 'Would you mind awfully if I recorded this? It's not for anything in particular,' she lied. 'How old are you?' She hoped this didn't sound rude.

'Eighty-six and three-quarters,' Betsy answered.

'And which surname should I use?' Francie continued. After all, she would have to cue her up, if she was on the radio.

'Well, let's see,' said Betsy. 'Born Barton-Hill, then married Gerard Jarvis, of course, then he died, then I rebounded and married his best friend, that didn't last

228

long – I'll have to look up his name. I'm getting a bit vague, don't know whether it's Christmas or Easter.'

She went on through her marriages until they got to Sir Jock Stockbridge, who, it turned out, was the husband Betsy had married not once but twice.

Francie sat, thrilling with anticipation, her little recorder in hand.

Now she'd done a bit of research, it all turned out to be fascinating, the time these ancient old biddies had danced with the devil. They'd partied with the National Socialists in the Dirty Thirties between the two world wars, when total annihilation loomed for the second time in a single generation. Grannie and Betsy had played a walk-on role in one of the great aristo-diplomatic failures of history, when the British upper classes flirted with the jackboot and cosied up to Hitler in a vain and doomed attempt to avert another war. This sort of stuff was radio gold. With the Nicky Miles interview already in the can, she could already hear it on Pick of the Week.

'No, record away, I don't mind, nort remotely,' said Betsy, her blue eyes bright. 'Do you know that when Chanel applied for the position, here' – Betsy gave the name Chanel the full, rolling rue Cambon treatment – 'I saw her form, and orn it, it said, "I have a personal development plan." I keep meaning to ask her,' she said, twinkling. 'What *ken* it mean? And *ken* one still have a personal development plan *at my age*?'

Fucked like a ferret, Francie was thinking.

Chanel returned swiftly, with two drinks in spindly,

conical glasses on a round wooden tray, and a Coke for herself. 'So, darling girl.' As Daphne and Jeremy Fitzsimon's granddaughter, Francie was immediately an intimate. Betsy treated her as one of us. 'Tell me all the news.' She took a sip of the drink and set it down on top of the *Radio Times* and next to a special remote with big buttons for the elderly on the occasional table to her right.

'Well, Grannie's not very well, to be honest,' said Francie. Then she filled Betsy in on the Faringdon nursing home, taking care to give each of her grandmother's various ailments their due. Betsy listened with the solicitude of a contemporary whose own passage towards everyone's final destination was proving easier.

'Well, I *am* sorry,' she said finally, after Francie had delicately hinted that Daphne might be meeting her maker before too long and, therefore, by implication, this was the moment to spill whatever beans there were. 'Apart from my silly hip and dicky heart, I'm going like a train. Aren't I?'

'Yiss, Lady Stockbridge,' came the assertion. Chanel returned to her Coke and *Heat!*

Francie pressed record discreetly.

'Betsy – if it's OK I call you that –' Betsy waved a bony wrist, weighted down by a heavy gold chain, presumably gifted by one of her five husbands – 'can you tell me about the months you spent in Munich? You went out there in 1936, didn't you? Why did you go out, do you remember?'

And then Betsy, who as a teenager could fill a tight sweater like no other, was off. It was like pressing play on a brand-new CD: the entire file was there, uncorrupted.

'Of course, it's clear as a bell,' she said. 'I'm the third of three daughters. By the time it got to me, my parents had pretty much hung up their boots. I came out, of course, but when it came to going to Germany on my own, they couldn't have cared less! My father . . .'

Then she talked for a bit about her father; as far as Francie could gather, and reading between the lines, Sir Bache had had a 'horror of Communism', having 'landed at Vladivostok in 1917' and seen the worst excesses of 'Bolshevik brutality'. After that, Sir Bache had travelled 'a long way in the other direction', if Francie knew what Betsy meant, which she did.

'So, as you might sense, he was rather taken up with politics and the peace movement, and very keen on anyone who was putting Germany back on its feet, so I was given a loose rein in Germany,' she recalled happily.

'In London, I wasn't allowed to go to Peter Jones orn my own, even to the cinema. You must remember' – she sipped thirstily – 'that gels were so innocent, then. We were *terribly* chaperoned. Diana Mitford couldn't walk to Harrods from Rutland Gate orn her own! Imagine that now!'

Francie did try to imagine as Betsy went on. She was awfully good value.

'I only knew two girls before my first wedding who hed the first idea of the facts of life.' She looked at Francie brightly. 'One of them was the Duchess of Northumberland. The other was Diana Mitford. It was she who told me, after I found out rather late in the day, the facts of life – that is, that unmarried girls couldn't get contraception. So I hurried up and married as early and as orften as I could.' She laughed.

Francie looked at her pale, withered face, but with such bright eyes, shining with the memory of men she had loved and been loved by.

'But you want to know about Munich. Well. When Daphne went to Munich, I went too, for a few months. I joined her. She met me at the station. It was quite the done thing, then.'

And so it was. Francie knew a bit about it now, had done her due diligence on the English colony in Munich, and had already prepared a par on it for her piece for Nathan, which would explain it all: while their parents gurgled Ambassador Ribbentrop's Champagne at tiara'd soirées at the German Embassy on Carlton House Terrace, and were active members of the Anglo-German alliance, their teenaged daughters had been sent out not to France, not to Italy, but to *Germany* to be 'finished'. Because it suited everyone.

Betsy picked up her thoughts.

'The Kaiser, after all, was Queen Victoria's grendson! So all the gels went to Munich, and even though Daphne was *de bonne famille* up to a point, she wasn't – really – *smart*, not in the sense that we were smart, when Linden called, and asked Pa if I could go, to keep Daphne company, really. I adored Daphne, so I went, and the *Gräfin* Montdragon was highly respectable, her finishing-school place highly rated – the Cavendish girls all went. I wouldn't have missed it for the world . . . not for the world.'

'Why?' said Francie, pushing the recorder closer to Betsy.

'Oh!' Betsy cried out, and then closed her eyes, as if in reverie. 'It was heady wine, heady wine. Skiing in the morning, opera in the evening, and handsome young men, all day long, in shiny black Mercedes with red-leather seats. After this awful Lucie Clayton place – total waste of time – I went off to Munich, and in no time was kicking up my heels at balls, skiing – we went to the Winter Games, you know – and then I was always scooting off to nightclubs in Berlin.'

'It does sound fun, but I still don't get why Germany?' Francie persisted. 'There'd just been a war . . .'

'Dear girl,' said Betsy. 'Versailles was frightfully hard on the Germans! And all one's people were related! I mean, you could go to Paris, or Florence, but the done thing was to send one's teenaged daughter to Germany. The men, much safer in taxis, of course, and we had blood ties, remember? Our royal family is German. So Pa, and the Anglo-German alliance, they were all desperate to avoid another war. They did everything they could. And we played our part. The regime was thrilled to have us. We all came home full of the joys of spring, chattering about full employment, maternity clinics, and the fast new roads. No one – I mean no one except Churchill – could possibly believe that anyone in their right minds would plunge our two nations into war again.

'You must remember,' she continued, 'the Nazis hadn't reared their ugly heads so far. We went to the rellies; they took us. To Nuremberg. I'll never forget the sound.' She started smacking her hands together rhythmically. *Smack, smack, smack.* 'The sound of their boots on specially metalled roads.' She shivered.

'He went over the top, that was the trouble, thet man, but he did drag the Germans out of the mire. This awful hatred came later. Hitler did a lot of good for Germany, there's no question about it, and it was such fun. I went to that nightclub in Berlin, got caught of course, and then I was yenked home. Had to go to this drear place in Suffolk. Aldeburgh.' She polished off the dregs of her 'special'.

'Then I was given a choice. Have another season, or get married. So I gort married. Then the war came, and he was killed. In 1940. Poor Giles. I barely knew him.'

'So that's why you left Germany?' asked Francie. 'To get married?'

'No, no,' replied Betsy, her voice stronger. Francie hadn't touched her drink – it was clearly strong enough to stun a mammoth. 'I left because I was secked. I've never been back, I want to preserve my marvellous memories. I've always blamed your grandmother.'

'Why? What did she do?' asked Francie, shocked.

'She'll deny it till her dying day, no doubt,' said Betsy. 'But she was in a bit of trouble herself. It was a muddle. She was running around with a young man. Getting up to all sorts. The *Gräfin* got it into her head that, among other things, I'd been carrying on with her son. Eric. The *Gräfin* was a countess – all the Europeans have meaningless titles, one can't possibly be expected to take them seriously – but anyway, she was a nice enough woman, mad on Hitler of course, we had to curtsey – or was it salute? – when we passed the portrait of him that hung in the hall in Königin-Luise Strasse.'

'Did you?' asked Francie, hoping that Betsy would confirm her romantic attachments one way or another.

'Oh yes,' replied Betsy enthusiastically, throwing up the arm that wasn't holding a drink in a salute. 'I always heiled like Billy-oh whenever required.'

Betsy was back in Munich in the thirties, her eyes glistening as she recalled the shiny leather boots, the natty uniforms, the weekends in Bavarian Schloßes, the jolly day trips to work camps.

But Francie wanted to get back to Daphne's love life. 'So who were your boyfriends?' she asked, as if she was a great one for men herself. Betsy clearly struggled to remember. There had been so many since. 'Well, I hed a soft sport for Siegmund, and hedn't the slightest interest in Eric, as I said,' said Betsy. 'But as soon as I was caught in that nightclub in Berlin by the British ambassador, the gig was up, and I was out.'

'It must have been a relief in a way,' said Francie. 'With the Nazis becoming more and more overbearing, life must have been pretty difficult. Especially, of course, for the Jews.'

'Nort at all,' Betsy said firmly. 'Nort. At. All. I didn't know what "Jew" meant. I had no conception of it. How should I? I had never met any Jews.'

'But Grannie was half Jewish . . .' said Francie. 'Her father, Jacob Linden –'

'Everyone said what wonderful things they'd done,' Betsy continued. 'How Hitler put Germany back on its feet. Father was terribly impressed when he went to Munich and some relly – I can't remember which one, it was so awfully *dull*. Everyone was there. The speeches did go orn, and orn. Thet was the thing, really: Nazism could never have rarely taken off here. Not in England. The Party bored from within and without, they would have been booed off the public stage in no time here. That was the thing,' she repeated.

'Everything in Germany seemed to go on for ever. One always longed to leave, halfway through. Not just *rellies*. It was everything. *Parsifal* was at least three and a half hours, and seemed to last even longer on those cheap hard seats the *Gräfin* got us; she was awfully tight with our marks.' She was lost for a moment in memory. 'Yes, everything went on for so long, apart from the Third Reich, which instead of lasting a thousand years, ended in 1945.' Betsy seemed pleased with this insight.

'My first husband – I've had at least three, maybe four, I don't remember now –'

Francie laughed encouragingly. This was great stuff. She nodded at Betsy to continue. She wanted all this on tape.

'After he went up to Cambridge, Raymond, I think it was, he went out to Germany, too. Shortly before he died we were discussing all this, and he made one of the best remarks I've ever heard. He said, "Hitler came to power, he gave the Germans a meal ticket, but they didn't read the small print."' She glanced at the machine's red light, still on record, and came out with her apologia, as Francie knew she eventually would.

Betsy looked at Francie, and tears filled her eyes.

'It was a terrible blow when he did what he did,' she said, as if it was all a personal insult to her, and the English aristocracy who'd sucked up so sedulously to the *Führer*. 'We cheered ourselves silly – you have no idea how awful I feel about it, even now.'

'How did you realize you'd been taken in?'

'Just after the war, I worked for the Red Crorse. It sounds saintly but it was mainly bandage-making and knitting. I was only twenty or so. And the Red Crorse, of course, had all the pictures of the camps. Those days, as I was saying, one hadn't the faintest idea who was or wasn't Jewish – the thought never occurred – why would it? I have never forgotten the horror with which I looked at them. I couldn't believe' – Betsy's voice rose impassionedly – 'that the charming, charming people I spent those *mahvellous* few weeks with could in any way be responsible for this,' she said, waving her arm as if to wave away the nastiness. 'I still can't.'

'So . . . why were you sacked?' pressed Francie.

'The countess gave me the old heave-ho,' continued Betsy. 'I've always thought it was Daphne's fault, as I said. Water under the bridge now, of course.' She sniffed.

Francie thought that whenever people said 'water under the bridge', it meant they still minded something bitterly. She wished Betsy would explain things in the order they happened; the timeline was very confusing.

'Must have been 1936, though I'm terrible with dates. I remember because of the Games. We had a whole week – or was it two? – in Garmisch for the *Winterspiele*.

Skiing . . . I remember, how deshing it was to be with boys, to wear trousers . . . and to ski . . .'

'Tell me about the Winter Games,' said Francie.

'It didn't snow and it didn't snow and then, as if by megic, the day before the Games started, it snowed. My cousin Celia was in the English figure-skating team, she ended up marrying a Canadian, after the war. Those were the days. I remember how handsome Siegmund looked in his uniform. We were young and high-spirited then, and didn't know about Buchenwald. I still wouldn't change any of it.' She looked up, her eyes blazing.

'In fect, I feel very sorry for you lot, y'know. You have nothing in your lives, not even a war. My life started in Germany, and when war came, of course, we all rellied round and fought the Germans. Even my father changed his tune. I thought it was my war, and no one else's. That was how we *all* felt.' She gazed at Francie, gripping her cane, her bony hands veiny and knuckly with arthritis.

'So . . . going back, to the finishing-school place, in Königin-Luise Strasse . . .' said Francie, she hoped with urgency. She was not getting very much out of Betsy, after all; she just went round and round in circles.

'Well, the long and short of it is, I hedn't been carrying on with Eric, the son of the house, as it were, but I was keen on someone else,' she continued happily. 'His name was Siegmund. So hendsome. The kind of chep one always fell for, time after time!' She emitted a girlish giggle.

'He'd been in the Hitler Youth and was totally hipped on the Party. They all were – Eric, Sieggy, all of them.

Except Otto. Otto refused to join the *Hitler Jugend*, studied medicine. Then he had to leave Munich, very suddenly. The family insisted. Forced him to join the Party, like everyone had to. He had curly black hair. Nice-enough-looking young man. Daphne was jealous, of course. I was prettier, you see, and well – I knew how to be around boys. I remember wanting to talk about the difference between German and English boys, and her wailing, "But Betsy, I don't *know* any English boys."

'She lived in Oxford, and only had a sister, poor thing. The only boy died. It was rather' – she struggled to find the word – '*sed*, you see, the Linden household. Linden himself was rather a monster, of course. Yes, all that was rather sed, one felt. Yes, darling, another *soupçon* would be lovely. Thank you, darling,' said Betsy, held out the drained glass to Chanel, and sighed.

'Have you kept anything from your time in Germany?' Francie asked. 'Photos, anything?'

'Oh no,' said Betsy. 'I was only there a few months! When I left, the *Gräfin* kindly gave me a copy of *German Cookery for the English Kitchen* – I think she gave it to all her girls, even the ones she gort rid of. I've still gort it, somewhere.'

There was a pause as the two of them digested the gastronomic car-crash of a cookbook that combined the two worst cuisines of Europe . . . during the thirties.

'Daphne wrote to me from Marquartstein, once or twice, early on,' recalled Betsy. 'Her best friend at the school disappeared. She was quite upset about it; the truth is, we had no real idea what was going *orn*. No one did, least of all English gels, caught up in our own world. Once, when we were in Munich, there was some sort of *Putsch* a few streets away, but again, we were so engrossed in ourselves, we barely noticed. Daddy told me after it was rather like *Kristallnacht*; there'd been carnage only streets away from where we'd been. It was literally as if we were here and there was slaughter going on in St James's Park.'

There was a silence as they both pictured slaughter among the pelicans and nannies.

'So did you fall in love with anybody?'

'Everybody!' said Betsy, with a terrible leer. She smacked her lips.

'But who?' asked Francie. Betsy took a slug of her drink.

'Siegmund, the tall blond one I've mentioned, very Aryan. The one your grandmother and I rather fell out over, though Daphne always denied it. Something happened, but it doesn't matter now. No. She loved the dark one, Otto. The medical student. Then there was Edward Cullen, and Nicholas Miles, but Teddy was much too proper to make a pass, and Nicky was a poof.'

'So, do you know, the war – what happened to Siegmund and Otto?' Francie asked.

'Darling, everyone I knew died,' she said. 'Every single German I met in Munich, gone, in their prime. It was the war. I try not to think about them – all that youth and beauty, smited.'

Betsy looked out of the window, to the view of rooftops in Victoria in a time of peace and plenty, when houses doubled in value every ten years, households threw away as much food as they consumed, and men didn't die for their country, they did Yogacampus or BeautCamp Pilates.

When Chanel let Francie out, a few minutes later, she heard a voice raised in song from an upstairs window, as Betsy lustily sang and the first three verses of the '*Horst Wessel Lied*' wafted out through the open window on to Victoria Square.

Betsy's last words, her answer to her final question, echoed in Francie's ears as she made her way to the Tube:

'But what about Daphne, then? Did she have a romance, too, with Otto? Or Siegmund? A proper one? Did she get into . . . trouble?'

Betsy had given her a bright stare. 'My dear girl,' she said. 'You have nothing in your lives. Not even a war.'

She gestured for another top-up of her lethal 'special' to Keira, who got to her feet with a grin and made towards the sideboard. She ignored the question hovering in the air.

'Our entire time in Germany was one whole romance, from start to finish.'

Francie walked to the Tube and switched on her mobile. She wasn't sure what she had expected Betsy to tell her, but she felt that she hadn't told her the truth. Her mobile beeped. 'You have voicemail,' it said.

She stood in the swirl of commuters at the open mouth of the Tube and listened to the message.

Twenty-five minutes later, as she walked up the road

to Clifton Villas from Warwick Avenue Tube, she had planned everything out.

She would give up Nathan, as he was a jerk and he'd cancelled her for dinner and she didn't believe that he had a 'work thing'. What work thing could be more important than seeing her, followed by sex?

Yes, she would give up Nathan, a lost cause, and would refocus on Gus, her husband, who loved her, and was the only thing that was worth anything in her life.

She felt almost cheerful as she let herself into the flat.

'Gus!' she called. 'I'm home.' She dropped her bag, cursed because she'd forgotten it had her new laptop in it, and put her keys on the shelf. Gus was playing something on the Bose stereo she hadn't heard before, loudly. It was Indian-sounding, with twanging sitars.

She was glad she'd come home, to spend some proper, quality time with him. The voicemail from Nathan – the tool – could not have come sooner.

The low-lights were on in the kitchen, and the fridge had been left slightly open. She took out a Tiger beer (Gus had done the campaign – there was a never-ending supply) and shut it.

She cracked open the bottle, then wandered through to the bedroom. The door was shut.

She opened it and walked in to see the sinuous back of a woman sitting astride her husband, and as the woman rose and then leant forward, her breasts brushing his face and chest, Francie was treated to surprising glimpses of Gus's penis disappearing and reappearing crossly.

'Oh God, Shelly,' Gus was saying, 'Oh God, oh,' as if in pain, which he probably was, as the woman was his yoga teacher, and now Francie knew exactly what was playing on the Bose system: it was the liquid asana DVD 'with Shelly Torben' he'd brought home last week, 'based on the fluid dance of vinyasa flow'.

She knew it was Shelly Torben herself here. Images of the shaggy blonde in unnatural poses and white Lycra, a beatific expression on her taut, tanned face, had been filling the plasma screen in the sitting room as she passed through. This woman on her bed had the exact same hair, the colour of Shredded Wheat, cascading and bouncing down the naked back in her bed. And Gus kept saying, 'Oh God, Shelly, oh, oh,' which left, sadly, little room for doubt that her husband was hurling what his Californian instructor would call his 'yogic javelins of desire' into her loamy loins.

Shit, thought Francie. She thought Gus was a bit more upmarket than that. She knew that lust was no respecter of creative boundaries, but even so . . . he was in advertising, so he must be aware of the living cliché he presented.

Francie left the room before the awful sounds rose to any sort of crescendo, and went to sit in the kitchen. At first she thought she would just wait for them to emerge. She sat on a stool and took a deep pull of the Tiger beer, and waited for the hurt to flatten her like a dump-truck.

But when the pain kicked in, it came not just from the bedroom, but from different places, like honey that is the produce of many countries, and she thought better of the confrontation. It wasn't just Gus and his yogic javelins. It was because Nathan Galsworthy had cancelled dinner in Quo Vadis at the last minute, on top of him sacking her from the payroll. It was something Sam had said to her in the loos at work about an abortion, which had sewn yet another terrible suspicion about her boss in her mind. And so the fact that her husband, meanwhile, was at it like knives with a bendy yoga bunny, was only, if she was being honest, a part of it.

She quietly left the second-floor flat of Clifton Villas, beer in hand, to spend the rest of the evening at Miranda's, so Gus/ Shelly would never know she'd been there at all.

When she got to St Stephen's Gardens in Notting Hill, a Porsche Cayenne was idling in the Royal Borough of Kensington & Chelsea resident's bay outside Miranda's first-floor flat.

She wouldn't have noticed the car at all, had she not, as she passed, seen there was someone in the driver's seat – a stocky female figure, sitting patiently, watching sport on a little screen that rose up, triffid-like, from the dashboard. It was the in-car TV, which didn't play while driving.

Mandy. Francie would recognize the back of her trans-gendered head anywhere.

Mandy was watching a sports quiz in Nathan's company car outside Miranda's flat at 8.40 p.m. This told Francie all she needed to know. Nathan was the man Miranda was talking about, who was crazy about her. And Miranda hadn't the faintest that she, Francie, and

Nathan, had ... what? It reminded her of a pancake restaurant she'd once spotted in Soho '*Crêpe Affaire*'. That's what she and Nathan had had: a non-event, a *crêpe affaire*, and now Miranda was even thinking about buying the flat below White Cube – Francie realized with horror – as a *love-nest* for her and Nathan. All this would make a funny story, one day, perhaps, many years hence – she pictured herself and Miranda chuckling over it in a care home by the sea – but it definitely felt like the purest agony now.

By now, she was level with the car. She tapped on the window. Mandy buzzed it down eight inches or so.

'Hello, Mandy,' she said. She couldn't stop herself. 'Are you waiting for his lordship?' So this was the 'work thing' Nathan had been referring to in his voicemail, which had cancelled his date with *her*, which she had been obsessively looking forward to...

'Oh, hello,' said Mandy, trying to remember, clearly, which one of Nathan's back-seat babes Francie was, and managing to look slightly guilty herself, by association. 'I am indeed.'

Francie had called Miranda from outside White Cube, but it had gone to voicemail.

So, in the end, Francie took herself off to the Expensive Place down the road. It had taken her two glasses (large) of Sauvignon Blanc for her to book flights to Munich, and a hotel.

Two days later, Francie stared at the four-storey villa, set back from the road. All that divided the house and the

English Garden was Königin-Luise Strasse. Lorries thundered by on their way to Austria.

It all felt a bit odd; it was a bit like a *Who Do You Think You Are?* programme, only she was doing it without a TV crew, a slot on BBC1, or an audience.

You're doing this for yourself, Francie had to remind herself, even though Nathan, in theory, was expecting a piece.

The location of the finishing school was not at all what she expected. In front of the villa, there was a small area of brave lawn, struggling against damp and shade, surrounded by shrubs. She stood on the paved bit around the house and peered up. She went round the back: each floor had a little balcony. One or two had plastic picnic chairs on them, for the occupant to sit in and turn their face towards the sun. Francie tried and failed to picture Betsy and Daphne sitting there, after lessons, or before the opera, or writing letters home, or – Christ knows – darning their dirndls, probably a highlight of their day back then. She took a picture with her digital camera of the house where Grannie and Betsy had lived for three months, then took a cab to Möhl Strasse.

The consulate was a large detached villa on a street composed demurely of large detached villas and punctuated by pollarded limes.

A Moneypennyish woman in a taupe cardigan, spectacles on a chain, sat behind the glass screen in reception, a week-old copy of the *Daily Mail* on the counter in front of her. Behind her, there were the mandatory portraits of the queen, in profile in navy cloak; a photograph of Tony Blair grinning, with Cherie; a photo of the British ambo with a white-haired German politician whose face Francie recognized but could not put a name to. She gave her name, but didn't even have to wait in the leather armchairs set around the walls, as in a hospital.

'He's expecting you,' the Moneypenny said, and led her into another office, down a short corridor, to a door marked 'HM Consul-General'.

'*Salvete!*' said the youngish, balding Chris Warren, rising from behind his desk in a small back office, clapping his hands together as if thrilled to see another subject of Her Majesty. He took his glasses off, then put them on again and smoothed down his hair then rubbed his hands on his cords, as if wiping them. Francie guessed: Winchester. Or possibly Westminster. Definitely not Eton – not confident enough.

He seemed pleased about something. A Union Jack flag drooped behind his chair. He opened a deep desk drawer and shoved the copy of the *Week* he'd been reading into it, along with a slim carton of ten Silk Cut, a lighter and, finally, as an afterthought, his coffee cup and the ashtray too.

The room smelt stale, of smoke. 'Sit down. Coffee, tea? Water? Whisky? Ha ha. No? Fine. Well, then. I think I have what you asked for. I hope so, anyway, ha ha. Sit down.'

Francie sat on one of the two chairs lined up opposite his desk. He plucked up a folder and handed it to her.

'Thank you,' she said, taking it. All she could see were

some ancient cuttings from *The Times*. Francie felt short-changed. She was a member of the London Library – a cross between a gentleman's club and a central London office for £400 a year, plus you had the occasional bonus of spotting Hugh Grant or Jeremy Paxman in the stacks. She could have accessed the online archive of *The Times* back to its nineteenth-century early editions from the comfort of the laptop room, or seen originals in the *Times* room in the basement. Then she would never have had to stay at the back end of the Pension Beck on Thierschstrasse 36, 80538, München.

To her relief, she saw that underneath the cuttings there were also some greyish documents headed 'CONFIDENTIAL'.

'The one you want is on top,' said Warren.

It was a two-column news story underneath a grainy photograph which had zoomed in on a line of people standing in a row wearing hats, arms outstretched in salute.

The headline was FÜHRER IN NUREMBERG:

'WAR HERO AT RALLY WITH MISS MITFORD'
From our correspondent in Munich
Nuremberg, 12 April 1936

Herr Hitler arrived in Nuremberg this afternoon and drove through the principal streets of the town on his way to the parade grounds where the Rally for Young Farmers was underway in sunshine.

Large crowds lined the route and cheered the Führer as he passed by in an official car with Count von der Schulenburg, the German Ambassador to Moscow. An official leaflet, hundreds of thousands of copies of which were flung into the streets from motorcars this morning, called on citizens to demonstrate their approval of the occupation of the Rhineland, the introduction of the Deathshead guards at the camps, and other measures to secure the world against ruin and disruption.

At the Zeppelin Field, Herr Hitler, whose arrival was greeted with a salute of 64 guns, addressed a gathering that numbered tens of thousands. Among many British subjects attending against Foreign Office advice were Sir Bache and Lady Barton-Hill of Tiddington Hall, Suffolk, their youngest daughter, Betsy; Miss Daphne Linden, the elder daughter of Professor Jacob Linden of Park Town, Oxford; and Miss Unity Mitford, daughter of Lord Redesdale (all pictured, left to right).

A summary of the Proclamation to the German people and foreign comment, p. 11.

More pictures, p. 16.

'OMG,' said Francie. 'Oh *mein Gott*, I should say. Don't tell me this was in *The Times*? Who wrote it? Was it Nicky Miles? Why didn't you tell me when I sent you the picture?'

Francie had emailed Warren the photograph she had papped in the Documentation Centre at Berchtesgaden.

'Yes, it was the *Times*' man in Munich,' said the consul. 'As you guessed, the one and only Nicky Miles.'

Francie felt a twinge of guilt about her job when he said 'One & Only', which was, to her, the *ne plus ultra* of luxury hotel chains.

'And who's this chinless chap in the natty uniform standing next to Grannie?' She couldn't help noticing how well cut the line of the jacket was before she remembered: Hugo Boss was the Nazi tailor, as she had discovered while researching – though 'Googling' was perhaps the more accurate word – a story Event Fashion was working on (and eventually pulled) called 'Stormtrooper Chic'.

'That's Eric Montdragon von Obernitz. *Gräfin* Montdragon's only son. He worked for that nice man who ran Hitler Youth, Baldur von Schirach.'

'It just keeps getting better,' said Francie, turning to the other papers, which were all official Foreign Office telegrams.

```
Pranner-Str, 11
13 April
The Farmers' Rally


1.a The Times yesterday reported that the Foreign
    and Commonwealth Office had issued advice to
    British subjects regarding their attendance at
    National  Socialist  events.  The  Consulate
    has  never  issued  any  such  advice  formally
    though it remains the position of the Munich
    Consulate that it is unwise for British sub-
    jects openly to support the National Socialist
    regime.

b.  The Consulate is forced to reiterate once more
    its position. The Chancery is now overwhelmed
    with applications from Jews to proceed to Pal-
    estine,  England,  or  any  parts  of  the  British
    Empire. Professional men of the highest stand-
```

ing have consulted this office with regard to
emigration in recent days.

c. In the absence of any guidance or special
    instructions from the FCO, it remains clear
    that neither the Consulate-General here in
    Munich nor the Embassy in Berlin has the author-
    ity to instruct British subjects whether or
    not to consort with a government that openly
    practises a regime of moral and physical per-
    secution against innocent workers and their
    wives.

(sd) Mr Edward Cullen
F.O. 254/21176

She turned to the next one.

Pranner-Str, 11
15 April
Miss Unity Mitford

1.a In response to your telegram of 13.04.1936, in
    reply to mine of April 1, the Consulate-General
    is aware of the potential embarrassment to HMG
    in the activities of Miss Mitford.

b. There is a large English community in Munich
    among which Miss Mitford moves freely, as she
    does among members of the National Socialist
    Party. She is known to see the Fuehrer regu-
    larly, dining with him both in his apartment on
    Prinzregenten Strasse and in the Osteria

Bavaria. She is an open supporter of the regime, as are many British citizens both here and at home.

c. I do not propose any action to be taken at this time.

(sd) Mr Edward Cullen
F.O. 257/21176

Pranner-Str, 11
20 April
Miss Daphne Linden

1.a Following an incident in the Maximilianeum in the early hours of this morning, Daphne Linden, a British girl aged 18, was apprehended by the police in the possible act of causing criminal damage to street furniture.

b. She became unwell in custody and was taken by ambulance to hospital. It was at this point that the police contacted the Consulate's night officer and within the hour I proceeded to the *Stadt Krankenhaus* (State Hospital) where Miss Linden was receiving treatment. I am returning again to the hospital this morning.

c. The Ambassador is a friend of Sir Bache Barton-Hill, with whose daughter Betsy Miss Linden shared a room. The Ambassador has asked me to inform Miss Linden's parents in Oxford of the events of the last twenty-four hours. I have

done so and Professor Linden is on his way from
Oxford to Munich. I will offer him any assis-
tance he needs.

(sd) Mr Edward Cullen
F.O. 259/21176

Francie read this one slowly. She looked over at the
consul, who was now reading telegrams and paying her
no attention.

So. Grannie had been arrested, or apprehended, whatever that meant, and had ended up in hospital. Had she
been beaten up? There was a family rumour, uncon-
firmed by Grannie, about how, as a teenager, she went
around Munich breaking the street-dispensers for *Der
Stürmer*.

'Excuse me,' she said. 'This one, about my grandmother going to hospital. Do you have any more on
that?'

She handed over the page. He glanced at it. 'This one
about Daphne Linden? No. Not really.' Then he looked
at her. 'Is she still alive?'

Francie nodded. 'But she's never given much away
about her Munich period, and then it seemed as if she'd
changed her tune, which is why I'm here – I'm actually
doing a story on it now,' Francie said, suddenly moved
by the possible mystery at the centre of her own cre-
ation. Francie found herself telling Warren about going
to the home, about Grannie's stroke, even about the
birth certificate in the memory box which suggested

she'd had a child by an unnamed father shortly after her spell in Germany.

'Keep asking,' said the consul, opening the desk drawer and removing the Silk Cut. 'This is 2006, for goodness' sake. Whatever happened, happened seventy years ago. You don't want her taking her secrets to the grave or anything silly like that.'

15

Munich, Bavaria
April 1936

Daphne lifted her head from the pillow.

Meg Dunton-Downer rose from the metal chair she'd been sitting on under the high window, and came over to her friend. The room was bare, and dark, lit only by windows set high up the white walls in the ward, in so elevated a position that not even the tallest, most deranged of patients could tip themselves out on to the wet pavements below.

It was so awful for Daphne Meg hardly knew what to say. And she'd only been in Munich, really, a matter of months, and it had all gone so horribly wrong for her. She gazed down at Daphne's chestnut hair, splayed on the pillow, her pale face and pinched mouth.

'I don't know what's going on,' said Daphne in a flat voice, though she knew perfectly well. 'They arrest me. I start bleeding, and they bring me here.'

Her hand checked the pad that the nurse had somehow trussed up between her legs, and came to rest on her belly. It was now, undeniably, mounded. She was lying on her back, but if she lifted the sheet the evidence was before her eyes.

'Do you think that nurse will come back soon? I want to leave before she does. I want to leave before that nurse comes back, and definitely before Cullen comes back,' Daphne almost wailed. 'Oh Meg, why did we think that was a good plan? We were always going to get into trouble. What on earth am I going to do now? What am I going to say?' She covered her eyes with her hand, but Meg could see her mouth widen into a howl.

Teddy Cullen had appeared in the small hours of the morning, in a tweed jacket over an open shirt, his tie spilling out of his trouser pocket and one shoe unlaced. Daphne had just had an injection, during which the doctor took blood; she'd also been examined, her stomach palpated, and thick fingers had probed her vagina as blood had trickled down her thighs and hot tears down her cheeks. Teddy took in the scene with a glance, had a quiet word with the doctor outside and announced he'd be back in the morning.

At seven sharp, Meg – who'd been allowed to stay in a side room – had been ushered in. Daphne was sitting up, sipping some weak tea and nibbling a biscuit, looking pale. Meg had been there ever since.

They both looked up as a new nurse bustled in. This one – a large woman with a severe expression and grey hair escaping from underneath a surgical wimple – came and started tucking in Daphne's undersheet so it was as smooth and white as icing on a Christmas cake.

'*Ach so, du bist schwanger,*' she said conversationally. Then she stood away from the bed, and raised her eyebrows. Then her hands went out, as if smoothing down

256

a smock over a vastly rounded belly. Daphne didn't need to ask what the horrible word meant. She'd understood the night before. She'd understood that in an instant, when the doctor's fat hairy fingers were pushing into the soft flesh above her pubic bone to locate her womb.

It had all been a terrible mistake. Daphne knew from Betsy that it was impossible to start a baby unless it was your time of the month. This was what Sibyl Leslie had told everyone at Betsy's convent. When Sibyl had passed Highers, the whole school had the day off and processed around the garden singing 'Ave Maria' in celebration. She was the expert, in other words. What Sibyl Leslie didn't know about sex wasn't worth knowing! They all knew that.

Daphne groaned.

She recalled her Little Talk when Ma was pregnant, before John was born. Ma didn't say anything then to warn her. And now, it seemed, as a result of a tiny misunderstanding, her life was over. Her ears burned with panic and her stomach heaved. Her breath came in shallow gasps. She clutched at the sheet and the brown woollen blanket, and turned over on her side, to face the wall.

'Are you all right, Daffers?' said Meg from the chair. She looked tired. Meg's view was that this happened quite a lot, and that Daphne had a choice.

'No,' whispered Daphne. 'I haven't the faintest clue what to do next. If only I could kill myself.'

'Don't be a goose,' said Meg. 'You're not the first girl this has happened to. And you won't be the last. There but for the grace of God go us all. There is a way round this, you know. It just depends on you. You have some money, I presume?'

'Some,' said Daphne. 'I haven't been spending much.'

'How much?' said Meg.

'About a hundred or so marks,' said Daphne. 'Why?'

'I think that will be enough,' said Meg. 'I'm going to call Daisy again, so I need to go back to the telephone. You'll have to get dressed – we've got to hurry.' She disappeared into the corridor with its polished floor and bare white walls. The place was like a lunatic asylum, only cleaner. In the distance, behind a door, Daphne heard a woman howling like an animal. When the howling stopped, the swearing started. Even in her distress, Daphne recognized that, when it came to expressing pain and grief, the German language had no equal.

She swung her legs over the bed. She wondered where her clothes were. Last night – well, early this morning – she had been made to undress completely and put them in a cotton bag with a drawstring. She scrabbled at the cabinet by her bed. Her clothes were folded in a heap in the lower section. She grabbed them and put them on, struggling with her Kestos brassiere, which no longer fitted, then hopped back into bed and pulled the sheet up to her neck. Meg slipped back into the room.

'Daisy will be here in half an hour,' she said. Daisy was the countess's favourite. Daisy had countless handsome boyfriends in uniform, a car, was out all night, but Daisy – or 'Day-zee', as the countess called her – could do no wrong. It was one of those things. 'She knows a place in Tutzing, less than an hour's drive away.'

'I've been to Tutzing,' said Daphne, wondering whether this was really happening, or if she'd wake up any minute in the little room she'd once shared with Betsy, with its etching of Mad King Ludwig above the desk, and one bedside light they'd always fought over but now didn't, now she'd gone. Betsy had been sacked. She missed Betsy.

'There's another finishing school on the lake,' said Daphne, 'just up from the main street. Peggy's there – she enjoyed her term so much she's stayed on, to help Frau Schmidt, she's been helping some of the younger ones with –'

'Fine,' cut in Meg. 'Now, listen. I'm going to go out into the corridor and keep watch, in case you're taken away. If I don't come back in half an hour, just get out of bed and cut straight down to the main entrance on the street. Daisy should tip up, in her new car – you've seen it, it's black. Don't look at anyone. Otherwise you might be arrested again. Just remember, you're an English citizen, a subject of the king.'

She looked at Daphne fiercely, willing her to be strong.

'And remember,' she said. 'You've done nothing wrong.'

'Hop in,' said Daisy. She leant over and pulled a silver handle and the door swung open. Daphne gave a look up at the hospital, expecting to see faces at windows, or soldiers. But all she saw was Teddy Cullen going in the main entrance. She wondered if Meg was still there and, if so, what she'd say to him. Her head spun. She didn't know what to do, where to go. So she did as Daisy said. She hopped in.

'Are you still pinting?' she asked.

'What?' Daphne asked, as Daisy put the car in gear.

'*Pinting,*' Daisy said, louder. 'As in *pints* of *gore*?'

'No, I'm not. Though I'm not sure whether that's a good sign or a bad sign,' said Daphne, wishing that Daisy wouldn't shout so. Would losing the baby be good or bad?

'Where are we going?' she asked, tugging the door shut. It clicked expensively, as it should: it was a Humber four-seater. The more badly behaved Daisy was, the more her parents spoilt her. Daisy started driving very fast across the cobbles, so Daphne gripped the leather handle on the passenger door tightly and kept her head down, in case anyone saw her. She hoped very much she would not 'pint' on to the new, cream seats of Daisy's car.

They bowled along until the *Feldherrnhalle*, the sort of temple place where you had to salute the officers and the flag or you got duffed up. Otto, on principle, used the little cut-through behind called Shirker's Alley, to avoid saluting, but Daisy gave such an enthusiastic salute as they rounded the corner that the car swung wildly and Daphne was flung against the door. 'For goodness' sake, *salute,*' said Daisy. 'Do you want to be arrested again, or shot?' Daphne meekly stuck her arm in the air. Then, just as quickly, she hid it in her lap.

She imagined Otto seeing her giving the Nazi salute, on the road to ruin in a fast car, and she didn't think she could ever imagine being so wretched.

'We're going to a little place I know. Klaus has arranged everything. There's a doctor there, waiting,' Daisy went on. 'Well, not a doctor exactly, but as good as. It'll all be over by tomorrow, and you'll be right as rain.' Daisy had to shout over the engine.

'Daisy, this is awfully kind of you, it really is, I'm very grateful, thank you so much for coming to the *Kranken-haus* to rescue me, but I'm not sure this is going to work,' said Daphne. 'Would you be terribly sweet and take me back home, to Königin-Luise Strasse? I haven't really got time to think, and I haven't got any of my things. I'll need some things. It's all happening . . . so fast.' She was also feeling – she could now admit this to herself, as the cat was out of the bag and the penny had dropped – slightly sick. She was concentrating on taking deep breaths.

Daisy turned to stare at Daphne as they waited at a light. 'Are you sure?' she said. 'It's all going to be terribly quick, and easy. I don't see what choice you have. You can't have the baby,' she went on.

The lights changed, but at the next one she turned and continued.

'Thing is, Daphne' – at this point, Daisy gave Daphne's face a hard stare – 'it would be so much better for you to opt for, you know . . .'

They were in a line of cars waiting to turn at a crossroads, on Türken Strasse. Daphne looked at the forbiddingly high buildings, the brutal concreted fronts. She'd never seen such ugly, rain-stained, depressing streets. Daisy's Humber was stationary in front of a particularly grim grey edifice, this one with a carved stone eagle above the door. Daphne suddenly recognized it. It was the HQ of the *Stürmer* newspaper. A drizzle began to fall, and she envied Daisy her beret.

Daphne's heart flipped as she realized they were passing Alter Simpl, in the Maxvorstadt. It was a nice bar – not that she had been to many bars. Inside, it was dark, smoky, woody, with black and white framed cartoons on the walls of writers like Hermann Hesse and Thomas Mann, and satirists she hadn't heard of. Otto had taken her twice, and whispered his plans to subvert the regime even though he'd had to join the Party. Everyone had to, he said, if they wanted to work. Which is why it didn't make sense, the whole business of his parents telling him not to see her. He wasn't biddable like that. He was *brave*.

Which meant that if Otto had decided not to see her, it would have been his choice, and no one else's.

The girls didn't speak until they reached Königin-Luise Strasse. Instead of turning into the driveway, Daisy let the car engine idle. There didn't seem to be anyone about.

'Well, the offer stands,' she said. 'I'll just need a couple of days. The medical student I know is very good; all the best girls go to him. Did Bunty only the other day – though you won't say to anyone, will you? It's frightfully hush-hush. She was right as rain in a jiffy. So make your mind up,' she said, as Daphne started again thanking her profusely. 'By the way – I forgot to ask. How many weeks in pig are you?'

Daphne had already counted the weeks backwards many times in her head since the nurse on the ward had told her she was pregnant. She'd counted the days, even the hours.

'At least eight, maybe,' she said. It was either eight or ten. Her stomach lurched horribly. It rather depended. She wasn't sure, and she didn't know whom to ask.

She gazed at her hands, twisting in her lap. This was difficult. How was she going to explain to the *Gräfin* where she'd been last night, and this morning? Not returning before 11 p.m. was a sackable offence.

But she didn't need to.

An angular figure now stood framed in the doorway, waiting, radiating the deepest possible disapproval. For some reason, she was wearing a forbidding black bonnet. Next to the *Gräfin* stood Eric, in his uniform. At their feet were Daphne's trunk and hold-all, her coat and hat. They had packed for her. An awful thought crossed Daphne's mind. It was as if they had been expecting her.

Daphne turned to Daisy and gazed at her sculpted Grecian profile, her blond hair swept off her forehead by the beret, the jaunty scarf around her neck, the rouged cheeks.

'You didn't tell the *Gräfin*, did you?'

Daisy paused just a fraction before answering.

'Certainly not,' said Daisy. 'By the way, there's hair on your jacket.' There was. Daphne was moulting like a dog losing its winter coat. Daisy plucked the locks off Daphne's blue coat, and flicked them, giggling, out of the car, so they were carried off by the breeze. 'I'll wait.

Go and pick up your things, say goodbye to the ghastly *Gräfin* and then we'll nip back to my flat. But make it snappy, won't you? I'm meeting someone for lunch. A high-up, in the Osteria. He's such a perfect poppet, you can't imagine, and I don't want to be late.'

'Daisy,' said Daphne, after she had done what Daisy had said. She sat with her bag on her lap. Everything else was in her trunk: her dirndl from Marquartstein, her Goethe, her Shakespeare in German, all her letters from home, all the relics and souvenirs of her months in Bavaria, the scarf that smelt of Otto. She had to ask.

'Why are you being so kind to me?'

Daisy finished applying lipstick, then dabbed it with her handkerchief. She smiled so her cheeks pouted out, and rubbed some in the apple of her high, pale cheeks.

'Because you remind me of England,' she said. 'Now come on,' she said gently. 'It's time to go.'

A day later, Daisy took the fast road out of Munich, and they were soon in the suburbs, driving past shuttered villas, tennis courts, factories, and then, within half an hour, they were in the midst of lush water meadows. Lakes shimmered blue in the distance and the branches of slender silvery birch trees shivered in the breeze. 'Tutzing 30km'. 'Tutzing 17km'. 'Tutzing 5km', said the signs. And now they were almost in Tutzing, and Daphne began to tremble. She held on very tightly to her bag in her lap, and tried not to think about the next couple of days – the next couple of hours even.

When they got to the main street, with Lake Starnberg to their left, they slowed in the traffic. Then Daisy signalled right, and they turned off the road and wound up a short distance through trees, amid large brick villas set back behind metal gates.

'Here we are, this is where we'll meet Klaus,' Daisy said with confidence, as if they had an appointment with a new tennis coach. The green metal gates were open. There was one car, parked in front of the door, which was flanked by two stone lions. Daisy jumped out as if they were arriving slightly late for a lunch party. She opened the boot and helped Daphne carry her luggage, insisting on carrying the heavier pieces herself, though they both had to haul the trunk.

'Everything's ready for you, I really have to shoot off now,' she said. 'I'll be back on Sunday.' She looked at the car. 'That's not Klaus's car; so maybe he's had to send someone else,' she said. 'You have to pay him. A hundred marks. So,' she said, kissing Daphne briskly on both cheeks, leaving livid prints on her white face, before hopping in the driver's seat. 'You have got the money, haven't you?'

Daphne nodded. She glanced up at the sky, where white clouds moved imperviously towards the mountains.

'In that case, darling, I've done what I can. Best of British, old girl. I'll see you Sunday.'

With a cheery wave, and toss of her blond head, Daisy swept off glamorously in a hail of gravel in the direction of a *Schloß* in Bavaria. Daphne rang the bell, feeling very small, very alone, and very far from home. She suddenly wanted Nesta. She heard the bell peal in the empty-sounding house. Her hand curled around the wad of marks in her coat pocket, and she wondered whether she should give it to Klaus before, or after.

Wouldn't it be ridiculous, she thought, if no one came? She glanced around, wondering what she should do.

She felt unutterably stupid when Otto, wearing a white coat over his uniform, opened the door.

He ripped off the surgical mask covering his face and, with the other hand, tore off his green cap.

'Daphne,' he said. 'Oh no.'

Daphne stared at him. She wanted to cry.

'Don't cry,' he said, reading her expression. 'I've been trying to find you. I'm so sorry – about what happened. My parents – it's hard to explain – it just sounds so awful. I couldn't come. After, I went to Königin-Luise Strasse, but the *Gräfin* said you weren't there,' he said. 'Were you? Did she tell you I came? I tried to find you.'

His eyes took in her tightly belted mac, the hillock of bags, the battered brown trunk with the wooden facings like a Morris Traveller, her name, 'DAPHNE H. LINDEN', painted black on the side. Her eyes took in his Party uniform, underneath the white coat.

Daphne shook her head. No one had told her.

'I waited for you,' she said.

She saw him slip the sharp silver instrument he'd been holding into his pocket. In that second, they both knew why they were there.

As they gazed at each other in horror, they didn't

notice that another car was driving slowly through the green gates. It crunched on the gravel towards them, its windows reflecting the pompous, green-shuttered villa and tall suburban trees.

Daphne saw the car. The Austin saloon was as familiar to her as her own hand. It had a dint in the silver back bumper and a sinuous grey shape, and driving it was Professor Jacob Linden, Reader in Roman Law at Merton College, Oxford, wife of Winifred, and father of Daphne, Demeter and baby John (dcs'd). Daphne hadn't seen her father since she'd left him on the London platform at Oxford station, when she was a clever future undergraduate, dutiful daughter and promising linguist. And now she was Ruined. Shamed.

In fact, she was finished, but not quite in the way he had hoped when he sent her out to Germany.

The car stopped. Jacob Linden untangled himself stiffly from the driver's seat, as if he'd been in the same position for hours, and shoved a large map on to the lap of Teddy Cullen, who was sitting in the passenger seat. Things fell out of the car as he got out, as they always did: one leather glove, a map and a spotted handkerchief. Daphne knew those driving gloves so well and, suddenly, all she wanted to do was go home.

'Daphne, my darling,' said Fa. He looked pale. His hand went up to her face. She almost flinched – he'd never struck her; but then, she'd never done anything wrong before. He rubbed at the marks left by Daisy's lipsticked mouth with his thumb. 'I don't know what you think you're doing here. But I'm taking you back to

Oxford. It'll all be all right. There's a place you can go, which I've arranged, where . . . everything' – her father couldn't say the word 'baby' – 'can be taken care of.'

As Daphne was reeling with this – Cullen had found out from the hospital she was pregnant and had told *Fa* – Linden turned next to Otto. He took in a tall, dark, young man, his surgical cap around his neck on elastic. A bottle of iodine and a sharp metal instrument were visible in a pocket on his green scrubs.

'And, as for you, young man, I don't know you, but I have a pretty good idea of what you do.'

Otto nodded, his eyes huge, his face white.

Teddy got out of the car; loaded Daphne's bags. He avoided looking at her, but opened the passenger door so she could sit next to her father. She sat on the cracked grey leather and stared at the glove compartment, which slightly gaped. She pushed it closed, but it didn't click shut, and fell open again so she had less leg room. She could see why it didn't shut – a letter had been stuffed into it at some stage, but was now sticking out. As her father fussed at the boot, she pulled out the letter and stowed it in her bag. In less than two days, she would be back in Park Town. She glanced back at the steps, for one last glimpse of Otto. He held up a hand, in farewell. She stared back at him until her father turned the Austin left out of the drive.

16

The sun was painting the wide-planked, white-painted floor with stripes of light and shade and, as the wind rose and fell, it intermittently brushed bright-green sycamore leaves gently against the large sash windows. The flat was perfumed with the scent of roasted Arabica beans, with a topnote of Gus's Clinique scruffing lotion. As ever, the Fitzsimon-Folgate domestic mise-en-scène looked like an ad for mortgages or designer–kitchen solutions.

After Wales and Munich, i.e. the few months when they weren't in a good place marriage-wise, things had improved.

Gus had given up going to yoga. Francie had stopped thinking about Nathan – well, she'd stopped thinking about him all the time. She'd sent him a text, saying, 'It's over,' and he'd sent one back, saying, 'What's over xx.' She had stared at this for a while. Only two xx.

For some reason, that hurt a lot.

So she wasn't sure whether Nathan wanted whatever it was they had started to go on, or not, even though she knew that he was also carrying on with Miranda, which was a stretch even for Nathan, or whether he was denying there had been anything between them in the first place.

She debated in her head telling Miranda that she knew that she and Nathan were having an affair. She debated telling Miranda that she'd had an affair with Nathan too. But she decided, in the end, that Miranda was more important to her than Nathan and, anyway, Miranda had bought the flat below her and so was now, as well as being her best office friend, and one innocent party in a lame love triangle, her closest neighbour too.

Yes, she could have had a conversation in which she, Francie, admitted that she'd shagged Nathan, but then poor Miranda would realize that the man she was in love with, who purported to be in love with her, was not what he seemed, and she didn't want to hurt Miranda. Plus, anyway, the whole office knew that Nathan was intent on reuniting with his long-suffering wife in the hope of recreating the family unit with Meredith, Hope and Charity. In fact, the Galsworthys had been photographed at loads of things together recently.

Francie was happy, too, because Gus had switched to Pilates, in a different studio, without Francie even mentioning Shelly Torben, and also, she'd started writing her piece. It was definitely long-form, even though she hadn't got to the bottom of it all yet. She was sure now that Grannie had got pregnant in Germany and that was why she was rushed to hospital – a haemorrhage, perhaps? Uncle Francis had mentioned an abortion in the email, but it was clear there had been a baby, which was her father, Andrew. She had decided that whatever she found out – even if it turned out that Daphne had carried the *Führer*'s own child and given birth in secret in a nursing home in Oxfordshire – she would not, under any circumstances, write the piece for Nathan.

'Mild or grand cru espresso?' Gus said, as he tore at the packaging littered on the chunky maple worktop by the fifties-style cream Smeg fridge that towered coffin-like in the corner.

Gus warmed a heavy-rimmed Italian chestnut-brown espresso cup in the microwave for exactly forty-five seconds then put it under the nozzle. He pressed a button, filled the cup exactly three fifths full of espresso, checked the *crema* and proudly set it before her.

She and Gus had had sex that morning, during which they had kissed each other on the mouth. She felt things might be all right even though, at her suggestion, Gus hadn't used any protection. She was bound to be pregnant now. She might as well start looking for the perfect doula and buying organic hemp onesies.

'I've had an email from Condé Nast *Brides* asking me to tell all about the sex on my wedding night. For £150,' Francie said, staring at her email. She sipped her coffee. It was perfect.

'Sounds like just the gig you've been waiting for,' said Gus, as he ripped at the filmy sleeve that encased his *Guardian* magazine and leaflets rained down on to the floor and table. He gathered them up dutifully, trotted to the recycling bin by the front door and returned.

'Don't be silly. Of course I wouldn't dream of doing

the bridal-sex piece,' Francie said. 'For one thing, I can't even remember our wedding night – can you?'

Actually, she could. They had been in the Bear in Hungerford in a fug of Champagne and cigarette smoke, mingled with the sweet smell of regret. They hadn't, as it happened, had sex. So she would have had to make the piece up anyway. It wouldn't be the first time, or, the way this bloody German thing was going – unless Grannie actually decided to finally spill the beans – the last.

17

Park Town, North Oxford
April–October 1936

Jacob Linden eased the car through the tall pillars stained
by long decades of exposure to damp Thames valley air
that flanked the narrow entrance to 12 Park Town. As
he slowed down, Daphne woke up. They were back.

'Oh look, the blossom's out,' she said, and yawned.
She was hungry, but then she was always hungry, while
her father, like most dons, seemed to have no interest in
food at all, and they had both lived on buns and motor-
ing chocolate since they'd left Tutzing, only two days ago.

At this time of year, North Oxford always looked
lovely. Daphne tried to come up with the right word to
convey how Linton Road, Bardwell Road, Summertown,
North Parade – all the roads, really – looked when it was
branchy between buildings and all the trees exploded
with white froth, as if someone had gone around, overnight, and poured double cream over all the leaves. She
eventually decided that the place still looked like North
Oxford, only younger, softer and greener, as if a Sunday
painter had spent ages rendering each street scene in
smudgy pastels.

'Demeter will still be at school,' Linden said, turning

the key in the ignition of the Austin with an air of finality. 'But Nesta will be home, and Mosey, of course.' He looked tired, his mouth turned down. She gazed at his Roman profile in silence.

He didn't mention Daphne's mother. Daphne knew what was going on, sort of, and he knew she knew. She'd read the letter. And he'd seen it in her grip before she'd had time to put it back in the glove compartment. The letter was from Laurence Lowther. And it was absolutely deadly.

For without any reference at all to his wife, Priscilla, Lowther had suggested it was time for Linden to call it a day, and added that he, Lowther, had recommended Linden – who had spent the last year or so deep in a voluminous study of Roman law as well as Lowther's wife – for a new post being created in Princeton.

Lowther hoped that Linden would be able to start at the beginning of the academic year, in the autumn, but, failing that, January 1937. It was clear from the letter that Lowther's only real regret was that the distinction from the publication of Linden's masterwork, due for imminent publication by Oxford University Press, would now not accrue to Merton, but to Princeton.

Daphne slowly and gingerly levered herself out of the low-slung car while Linden attended to the quantity of luggage. She thought it was unfair on her father; after all, Priscilla was equally to blame. He can't do anything about Josiah Garfield, thought Daphne as her feet touched gravel, because he's at Oriel. The reason Lowther's sacking Fa is because he can.

She took deep breaths to inhale the odour of mulch on the flowerbeds, the spermy whiff of the trees, the green meadows leading down to the dark, peaty deeps of the Cherwell a few hundred yards away. She looked up at her house, hoping to see Dem waving to her from the nursery window, even though she knew she wasn't there.

Wrapping her coat around her, she nobly humped one bag, her overnight bag and her handbag up the short flight of shallow stone steps to the front door. She'd never had a key – she'd never needed one. Nesta always opened it, because Nesta was always there. She found herself longing to see Nesta's round face, her small eyes, and her wispy grey hair, kept off her face with a multitude of grips and slides. She rang the bell, like a visitor to her own house, rather than nipping to the tradesman's entrance at the side, which took you straight into the steamy warmth of the laundry-room and kitchen, and the smell of baking.

The door opened straightaway, and her mother stood there on the black and white tiled marble floor. It was immediately obvious that she had been crying – the end of her nose was red, her eyes were slits and a lace-edged handkerchief dangled from her hand.

Daphne stared at her dumbly.

'Mother,' she said. She longed for her mother to hold her in her arms and tell her it was all right, that she'd missed her, that she loved her. She wanted her to say that Jacob Linden's plan was out of the question; that she, Winifred, would look after the baby, and care for it as tenderly as any grandmother would.

But Winifred just stared at her child as if she was a stranger. She did not move forward, or allow her gaze to drop from Daphne's face.

'I can tell, just by looking at you,' she said. 'You've changed.'

After that awful day, the remaining months passed slowly. Daphne's future was mapped out. She would take the entrance papers again, in October, and get a scholarship; she would have the baby; the baby would be taken care of by Nesta and Mosey; and then she would go up. To Somerville. She would get on with the life her father had planned for her.

Still Winifred was not talking to Daphne, nor to Jacob, whose tenuous grasp of the obligations of matrimony had been stretched past breaking point by the loss of their only son and the disgrace of their older daughter. Daphne had no idea whether her father had applied for the post in Princeton, as Lowther had suggested; or, if he got it, the family would go with him. None of this was discussed.

All Daphne did was read and eat. Nesta had been looking after her. It hadn't been too bad, being back at home. She'd written to Betsy, but Betsy hadn't written back. She'd had a nice letter from Daisy, but Daphne hadn't written back either, because she didn't want Daisy to know she was having the baby, after all the trouble Daisy had gone to for her not to have it.

Once, she'd passed her father's study while Josiah Garfield was in there. It was odd them still being friends, she thought. She heard Garfield say to her father, 'Shot before the Twelfth, eh?'

Later, she'd asked her father what that meant. He'd avoided the question, but she'd worked it out. Shot before the Twelfth meant falling pregnant before being married.

Around September, she was with Nesta in the kitchen, drinking cocoa, and Priscilla Lowther's lady's maid, Agnes, popped in. Agnes usually disdained Mosey and Nesta, as Jacob Linden wasn't head of a college and Winifred was known to be peculiar. But Daphne's condition had made the Park Town house a key destination for the domestic *tricoteuses* of the neighbourhood.

'We're knitting,' said Nesta, her needles clacking and her eyes flashing with pleasure. She hadn't been so happy since Winifred had been pregnant with baby John. And then she used a phrase that made Daphne want to run from the room. 'We're in the family way.'

A tongue was boiling on the range, for Tongue *espagnole* later. Tongue *espagnole* came from a book much used in Nesta's kitchen called *Decorative Cold Meat Dishes*, and was cold tongue, sliced, garnished with black cherries from a tin and served with buttered new potatoes and carrots.

The saddest thing for Daphne was that she was not in the family way at all; as usual, she was just in the way.

In October, Somerville College was reluctant to allow Miss Linden an aegrotat and admit her on the basis of interview only. But the College did allow her to sit the exams at home, as the circumstances that obtained were unusual, if not unprecedented.

So it was agreed. As Daphne was not attending a school, and was by now close to her confinement, the papers were brought round in sealed envelopes to 12 Park Town. She sat the papers upstairs in the nursery. As she was applying to Somerville, the College sent a Junior Fellow.

Miss Carberry, who had a short bob, sniffed, said she was allergic to Antigone and insisted on turning up the gas fire so Daphne felt quite sick, arrived to invigilate.

Miss Carberry sat Daphne down at her desk in the nursery and settled herself with a novel by the fire. First was German unseen, then French prose. She found the papers quite doable, really: the German papers much easier than the French, thanks to her months of grounding at Marquartstein, followed by chatting to the *Gräfin* and listening to Otto and Siegmund row.

As she worked her way through stodgy unseens, she mourned the fact that she would never, at Somerville, get a real chance to show off her conversational German, which was almost faultless. The next day, she had a general paper. It was more difficult. It was clearly designed to elicit that quicksilver quality beloved of schoolmasters through the generations: flair.

So Daphne cranked out long essays on the difference between knowledge and belief and the legality of war. Luckily, she and Demeter had been exposed to such philosophizing from the age of about three.

On the final day of the entrance exams, the penultimate paper was a German unseen taken, according to the small print at the foot of the page, from Harrap's Series of Plain Texts in German. The extract Daphne had to translate was from a book called *Adolf Hitler – Der Führer des deutschen Reiches*, a short account of his life and work by a man called Schulze. And jolly dull it was too.

She laid down her pen and sat quietly at her desk, reading it through until one o'clock. She and Miss Carberry went down to the kitchen, where Nesta had laid out some lunch for them.

After she'd finished, 'Only one more to go,' Daphne had said towards Miss Carberry, who sniffed, then Nesta said, 'And now, young lady, I think a turn in the garden,' leaving their glasses and plates, smeared with Lancashire hotpot, for Mosey to wash and dry and put away. So they'd put on their coats and gone out the side door into the communal garden, where they did a stately turn, Daphne watched by nannies who whispered behind their hands when she passed. Nesta glared at them. She had become very protective of Daphne. She treated her exactly as she always had, since Daphne was a baby.

Then it was time for French translation. Her last exam. It started at 2 p.m.

Halfway through the third passage, Daphne had a feeling as if it was her time of the month, but worse – as if her insides were quickening, churning. She speeded up, her Parker pen racing over the page. It was as if the French was a windowpane – suddenly, she could read it as easily as English, because she had to hurry. Sitting for any length of time had always been uncomfortable lately; now it was impossible. And there was still an hour to go till 4 p.m., the end of the paper.

Without realizing, Daphne had started to breathe heavily. She stopped writing and capped her pen.

'Miss Linden, are you all right?' asked Miss Carberry. 'Can I get you anything? Some water, or a cup of tea?'

She put down her novel and blew her nose into her large, yellowish handkerchief. The sky beyond the window was the colour of a bruise, and it had rained earlier.

Miss Carberry's voice had a note of alarm, conveying to Daphne her anxiety that the baby wouldn't decide to do anything – like start to make a rapid exit in the nursery – that would implicate Miss Carberry in any way.

'I'm fine . . . I think,' said Daphne. And then she froze. Her lower stomach had suddenly clamped itself together. She pushed her chair back from the table and stood up, her hand to her belly.

'Look, I know it's not four o'clock yet, but I've finished. Would it be all right if I went to my room? It's the last paper, and I've finished.'

Even in very early labour, Daphne was her father's daughter. She had read the paper twice before picking up her pen and, after she'd finished, as contractions had got underway, she'd checked it through. Twice. Her stomach unclenched and she could breathe again. This was three weeks before the doctors had told her anything like this would happen. She handed her paper in and thanked Miss Carberry for everything she'd done, then went to her room, lay on her bed with her shoes on and slept.

At Nesta's insistence, Jacob Linden had done a dry run and timed the little trip between Park Town and the Radcliffe Infirmary already. He had made a great show of extracting the Austin from the drive and driving cautiously to the hospital, executing a courtly turn in front of the main entrance and returning to base.

'Seven minutes,' he had said. 'In the rain, too.' He wiped his Ducker's brogues on the mat, took off his mackintosh and hung it in the hall, then disappeared into his study to attend to the much more important matter of his section on the Lex Aquilia. Winifred, meanwhile, would have nothing to do with the mechanics of the inevitable.

'You have to give your mother time,' Nesta said to Daphne, smoothing Daphne's damp forehead when they sat in the kitchen together with cocoa and biscuits. Nesta couldn't understand it. After losing one child to the Lord, Winifred now seemed determined to lose another. It was pitiful.

Daphne had now woken up, and bathed.

She sat in her nightie, dressing-gown and carpet slippers at the enamel-topped kitchen table. She was so big she had to push her chair far out in order to sit down. Nesta had to squeeze past to get to the range, where the bones and skin of two chickens bubbled in a cauldron of scummy water for tomorrow's supper. In the first three months, the smell of boiling chicken would have turned her stomach. Now, it made her hungry.

'I'll have the mite with me; Mosey can help,' Nesta said, lifting the lid off the stockpot. 'You're not to worry. You go off to your lectures and what have you, and then come back as and when. It's not as if I'm not used to it. When you and Dem were tiny, it was me in sole charge. Your mother, poor thing, was much too wrapped up in her own affairs to do much more than pop up to the nursery, at bathtime. She must regret that now, I'd say.'

Nesta's eyes glimmered with emotion, and her face steamed as she replaced the lid. She wiped her brow. She was good with babies. She'd been good with John, wonderful. She couldn't wait for Daphne to produce another scrap to lie all swaddled in the Moses basket by her bed.

Daphne shifted in her chair.

'Nesta,' she said. 'I think it's time.'

She let out a shuddering breath as the cramp eased. She could no longer sit, so she stood and leant her elbows on the table-top, and her breath came faster. She concentrated on a chip in the enamel the shape of a teardrop as she heard Nesta leave the room. She would be getting her father. The bag was upstairs in her bedroom. She wondered whether she should get it, but the thought of climbing the stairs was discouraging.

She'd had an easy pregnancy, after the disturbing bit at the beginning when she'd bled a lot – *pinted* – and now the moment had arrived. In a few hours, Daphne told herself, I won't be pregnant any more. It will be over. Everything will be all right.

'Get in the car, girl,' her father shouted from his study. Daphne heaved herself off the kitchen table. She walked down the tiled passage, slowly. Her father darted into the kitchen while Nesta followed with her things.

Daphne crawled into the back seat of the Austin, still in nightie and dressing-gown, but now wearing outdoor shoes. 'Has this been going on for long?' asked her father, hurling her bag into the passenger seat. It seemed fuller than when she and Nesta had packed it. 'How long? Since when?'

Daphne moaned.

When she opened her eyes, minutes later, they were driving on the Woodstock Road, straight past the sign to the Radcliffe Infirmary.

'Fa, stop! What are you doing? It's right here,' she yelped, leaning forward so she could speak loudly in her father's ear above the sound of the engine, which was like gravel being stirred in a bucket. The labour pains were getting worse. And the car sounded as if it was about to pack in. 'Why aren't we going to the Radcliffe?'

Jacob Linden said, 'We are going to hospital,' as he gripped the wheel, 'but not to this one. There's been a change of plan.'

The Austin left Oxford and nosed its way north, as the sky, heavy with rain, turned a stormy lilac. By the time they reached wherever they were going, it was dark, and Daphne was crouching on all fours in the back seat, and beyond caring. When she realized the car had stopped, she looked up, to see windows shining yellow through the sheeting rain. It didn't look like a hospital.

Just like a big school. The windows were large on the ground floor, and above that they had nursery bars across them. 'Fa,' said Daphne, whimpering like an animal caught in a trap. 'Don't leave me here.' As she spoke, the front door creaked open slowly and a woman in a matron's uniform holding an umbrella stood silhouetted in the entrance.

'Is she able to walk?' the woman asked Linden, who had galloped up the steps to announce their arrival, leaving Daphne beached in the car. They seemed to be expecting her.

'It's her first baby,' said Linden. 'And it's at least a week early. Possibly as much as three. There remains some, er, slight confusion about the due date.' That was easier than referring to conception, which was an indecent event that could never be mentioned. 'I suggest you get her settled, and proceed from there. It's all been arranged.'

Another nurse appeared, and came reluctantly down the steps with the umbrella. She peered into the back of the Austin, where Daphne had now wedged herself between the seats and the floor, wishing she was dead. 'Are you her husband?' she asked Linden, to Daphne's horror.

'No, I'm her father,' said Linden, shortly. 'Here's a copy of the letter I sent to Sister Mary, which explains everything. And, oh yes, here's her bag, with all her things. Wouldn't want to leave that. Now, I'm very sorry, but I know she's in the best possible hands.' He looked at his watch, furtively. 'I really have to go.' He started muttering about having to change and a dinner, and being late, and belted down the steps without looking back, just as he had when he left her at Oxford station so she could spend the weekend with Betsy in Suffolk.

Jacob Linden drove back into Oxford fast, but carefully. If he had a clear run, he could be in Hall by seven. He had to see Lowther. It was his last chance.

Winnie was on the boat to New York, with Demeter, to see about a house in Princeton, but still. There was just time to stop the madness. If he spoke to Lowther, he might see reason. He was a reasonable man. Of course, Linden couldn't explain anything: what was there to say? He couldn't ask for forgiveness, or say he was sorry, about Priscilla. But surely, Linden thought as he slowed down behind a lorry and glanced at his watch, Lowther would understand that the plan was penal in the extreme?

There were many reasons that a Head of College might decide that a don wouldn't cut the mustard any longer: ineptitude, for example. But bedding another don's beautiful wife had never been a sackable offence. After all, Priscilla had moved on to Garfield after she'd finished with him, there was no logic to Lowther's timing at all, and it smacked of cold, calculating revenge. He glowered and stepped on the accelerator.

Linden reached the Peachtree roundabout and turned into the top of the Banbury Road. Lowther must see that the rules didn't apply to wives. He'd try to make him see sense over dinner.

Then an awful thought struck him. It was formal Hall that night.

He had a clear vision of his dinner jacket and dress shirt hanging in the cupboard. He couldn't do the tie on his own. And it was a white-tie dinner. He wondered how he would manage. He would go up to Nesta's room, he decided, and tell her the latest news about Daphne – what was the latest news about Daphne? – and ask her to help.

As he passed Summertown, it had started to rain. The trees along the Banbury Road dripped. There were a few men on the streets, pushing on home with their heads down, hurrying to hot suppers in the semi-detached villas of North Oxford and evenings listening to the wireless and dull accounts of their wife and children's days. The traffic thickened.

As he was passing the turning to Bardwell Road, he saw his pupil, Victoria Berridge, walking quickly. She didn't have an umbrella, and her baby-blond hair shone like a beacon in the dusk.

Without thinking, he slowed the car. He leant over and wound down the window.

'Can I give you a lift?' he said. Her house was about five hundred yards away, towards the Cherwell. It was smaller than the Linden's, but then, the Berridges had only one, precious, only daughter.

'Hello, Professor Linden,' she said perkily. She was leaning into the car, smiling, confident. Her cheeks were wet but fresh and pink and, when she smiled, her young white teeth looked pearly. She gave him a look, a look that said: Go on. I dare you.

Linden made an instant decision. His daughter might, at that very moment, be giving birth to his first grandchild, but it made no difference. 'Hop in, Miss Berridge,' he said. 'And come with me back to Park Town. It won't take long, but I need your help.'

Eighteen hours later, Daphne awoke.

'Where am I?' she said out loud, before remembering. She'd arrived at the place – the hospital? The convent? She still wasn't sure. The pillowcase had a label on it, saying 'St Clare's Hospital for the Middle and Upper Classes'.

She gazed at the ceiling. Her father had left her and just dashed back to Oxford. 'I have to get back for a dinner,' he'd said. 'I don't like leaving you here, but I don't see what use I will be. They'll take great care of you here at St Clare's. Bless you, my dear.' He kissed her on the top of her head and didn't look back as he took the steps two at a time in a relieved rush to be away, as if what lay ahead of him was more important than what he was leaving behind.

The nurse had helped her upstairs – there was a staircase: she remembered gripping the banister, leaning over it, trying not to make an unladylike noise – and into a white-painted room, with the tidy bed headed by two pillows covered by a waterproof sheet. Another hospital.

She had sunk down on to the bed then thrown off her

dressing-gown so she could return to her position on all fours, the only one she'd been able to tolerate in the back of the car. Twenty minutes later, a doctor with a moustache and cold hands had listened to her belly through a trumpet and pronounced the baby's heartbeat strong, 'but rapid'. Then she was left on her own for a couple of hours. At midnight, Sister Mary had appeared again, with the doctor and a cup of hot milk sweetened with honey. By this stage, Daphne was leaning against the corner of her room, pushing against the wall and whimpering. The plain white wall was beaded with moisture, as if the whole building was straining and sweating in sympathy.

'Help!' she'd cried at the doctor who stood in the doorway looking thoughtfully at her. She was dishevelled, sweaty, and tear-streaked. 'Please, help me. It hurts! Don't leave me again. I'm so hot . . .' When they tried to make her move on to the bed she'd shaken them off, so the doctor allowed her to stand where she was, shaking and shuddering, as he applied the cold rim of the trumpet to her straining belly.

Then he went out to the passage. When he came back, half an hour later, he had a pad in his hand. 'I'm going to put you under,' he said. 'Lie down on the bed.' And he'd put the pad over her face. That was the last she remembered.

She lay still. And now, there was no sign of a baby at all. Her white nightgown had been replaced, and she now wore another one, not hers, that opened all the way down the back. Her dressing-gown hung on the back of the door.

Her eyes focused on a crack in the ceiling. She lay there for a long time. Eventually, a different nurse, with pink cheeks, as if she'd just run across a moor, bringing with her the sweet bonfire smell of autumn, accompanied by children in red mittens skipping through fallen leaves, entered the room. 'Miss Linden?' she said. She plucked a yellow leaf off her navy cape. 'And how are we?'

'Where's my baby?' asked Daphne. She decided against raising her voice. She didn't have the energy. And she'd screamed so much last night. 'Is it alive?'

'Ah yes, very much so.' The woman smiled privately, as if she had superior knowledge of Daphne's baby already. 'Don't worry, Nurse will be bringing Baby very shortly,' said the woman. 'He's just having a bath.' Then her face went serious, as if what she was saying would pain Daphne; 'And a little feed.'

He, thought Daphne. I have a little boy, a baby son. She sat up in bed. Then she made as if to hop out. I have to go to him, she thought.

'I haven't introduced myself,' the woman said, closing the door, as if to prevent Daphne's escape. She hung up her cape so it hid the dressing-gown. 'I'm Sister Joan,' she said. 'May I perch here? I've come to talk to you – well, about the future. To help you.'

'What do you mean, my future?' said Daphne to the woman sitting on the bed, who had seen her newborn son, and she hadn't. She looked towards the door.

'As you know, dear,' began Sister Joan, 'it's not going to be easy, at your age, looking after a baby. You have your whole life ahead of you; you're a bright girl, according to your father. You could be a nurse, a secretary, a teacher, and one day, if you play your cards right, despite all this, you might even get married.' She smiled kindly at Daphne.

'I'm going to University, actually,' said Daphne. 'I live in Oxford, so there's my old nanny who's going to take care of the baby. This is all a mistake. You've got the wrong person. I just need to find my baby, and go home.'

As the words came out, they sounded weak and unconvincing. She knew her father had planned this.

There was the sound of wheels outside then a light tap on the door. At the sound, Daphne stared at the door intently. Someone was bringing the baby; then she could see him, and then she would call home and ask her father to come in a couple of days and pick her up, and they'd go back to Park Town, and Nesta would take care of her, and the baby, of course. She was terribly hungry and tired.

A trolley was pushed into the room. Daphne looked at it eagerly – but all it contained was a tray. 'Ah, your breakfast,' said Sister Joan. 'You must be starving, poor thing.'

Sister Joan poured her a mug of tea, placed a plate of buttered toast spread thickly with orange marmalade in front of her and fussed about until the bed tray was just so. The tea steamed and the yellow butter melted on the hot toast. Then she looked at Daphne expectantly, as if she should be happy now.

Daphne pushed the bed-table away. The words of the poem that Jacob Linden had framed and had himself hung in the nursery bathroom returned to her, as they often did after John had died. And when Winifred was spouting tears over Priscilla. And the morning after Siegmund had come to her in the night at Garmisch. When Otto never came to take tea in the English Garden, when she ended up in hospital, when Otto had turned out to be an abortionist and, above all, the words had come to her last night, when she was pushing against the wall, praying for strength, and life.

> Love God our Father
> Keep your face to the light
> Tell the truth at all costs
> Think of others
> Forget yourself
> Stick up for the weak
> Play the game
> Take your beating like a man.

'I don't know who you are,' she said, looking directly at Sister Joan, 'but if I don't see my son within five minutes, I'm going to get out of bed and find him myself.' As she spoke, she had visions of being strapped to the bed and having to stay in this room, possibly for ever.

'Don't be so melodramatic, dear,' said Sister Joan, handing her a cup of tea. 'Drink that, and you'll feel better. It's all been arranged with Mrs Cuthbertson. Janet will be here at two. So I suggest you have your breakfast, young lady.' Her tone had sharpened, as if in readiness for battle, and heaven forbid that Mrs Cuthbertson's plans should be interrupted. She patted Daphne's arm.

'You need to keep your strength up. There's no point seeing the baby – you're not going to be taking him home anyway, he's going with Mrs Cuthbertson.' She plucked her cape off the back of the door. 'It's all been arranged by your father. I'm very sorry if it comes as a shock but, believe me, in time you'll realize it's for the very best – not just for you, but for him.' Then she left the room.

When Daphne woke again, she had no idea what time it was. Her windowless room, with its overhead light, gave nothing away. She lay there, deciding that now she had had a sleep, she could put on her dressing-gown and slippers and find her baby. None of this seemed real. Why hadn't her father come? She knew her mother would have nothing to do with her, or the baby, but it didn't seem possible that Nesta – Nesta, who had loved her as only a nanny could – could abandon her too.

As she was struggling to sit up, holding up her engorged breasts as she tried to straighten the gown under her bottom, a woman who was not Sister Joan slipped into the room. She had a kind face and brown hair, with dark eyes that seemed full of feeling as she looked at Daphne. For some reason, Daphne didn't mind her. She made her feel safe.

'Hello,' she said. 'I'm Janet Cuthbertson, and you're Daphne Linden, aren't you?' Daphne nodded. 'I know you want to see him, and you will see him,' she said. 'I'm not taking him away for ever. Just till you're ready to have him back. After you've done your studies. I've spoken to your father. He says it's important that you go to University. He says any girl can have a baby, but only clever ones can go to University, and you can't do both, unfortunately. Especially since your parents are moving to America, I understand. But remember – Ducklington is not at all far away, and you can visit whenever you like. We're not far,' she insisted. She went to the door and stuck her head round it.

'You can come in now,' she called.

Nesta came in carrying a tightly wrapped bundle.

As she held the newborn, Nesta's face was working with emotion, mainly self-pity. She'd had to keep it secret for weeks. But Linden had told her, and insisted that Daphne be kept in the dark. The house in Park Town was to be shut down, maybe sold, as the family were moving to America; Nesta and Mosey were to look for work elsewhere. For weeks, they'd been scouring the classifieds and personals in *The Lady*.

The problem was, there seemed to be a tiresome glut of professional European women in their thirties and forties looking for work visas who had considerably more experience and polish than Nesta or Mosey. 'Oh lordy, look at this one,' Mosey would say, and read them out.

Happy Home offered to young, educated European refugee, speaking good German and French, to help with girl 6½ and boy 5½, attending day school. Cook general kept.

'And here's another.'

40–43, good packer and traveller, capable and active, good needlewoman, accustomed to large wardrobe, blanket bath.

They both dwelt for a moment on the implications of 'blanket bath'.

Viennese Lady with girl (five years old) seeks post as Housekeeper, Mother's Help.

Her eye raced on.

Companion-teacher, Viennese . . .

Mosey put *The Lady* down and slurped her tea. 'Why don't they all stay in Vienna? No wonder they don't want a maid-of-all-work like me.'

Both Nesta and Mosey sighed heavily. They knew, and Daphne didn't. Linden, Demeter and Winifred were going. Daphne was staying behind to go up to Oxford. And the baby was going elsewhere.

When Nesta had challenged Linden, he had ducked the conversation. 'Let's deal with one drama at a time,' he had ordered.

Nesta held the bundle tight.

News of the safe arrival of her first grandchild was spared Winifred. At the moment of his delivery, she was on a transatlantic liner to New York, sobbing not over her daughter but about the fact that she had left the body of little baby John in the graveyard of the church on the Banbury Road.

Daphne sat up with bright eyes and held out her arms. Nesta handed the new baby down to her.

First Daphne looked at the little red face, about the size of a large Bramley, the eyes tight shut in a line, the tiny nose calmly breathing, flecked with minuscule white dots, and cherry-red lips filled with bright new blood making sucking movements in his sleep. The hair glinted blond and flat on the soft head that smelt toastily of burnt vanilla. Daphne buried her face in the smell and her lips grazed his downy roundness. Then she laid him down on her lap and unwrapped him. First the blanket came off, the Lan Air Cell one with the silky edging she'd seen being handwashed in the laundry-room last week then carefully laid flat to dry; then a tiny tie-front cardigan in yellow, and underneath that, he was wearing a flannel nightie and some white booties with slender silky yellow-ribbon ties.

The booties were tiny, but the feet were even tinier. She took off all his clothes and gazed at him, not even needing to count his fingers or toes. He was perfect, down to his translucent, dinted little ears. 'Don't let him get cold,' Nesta said gruffly, trying not to cry. 'Nice Mrs Cuthbertson knitted him those booties.'

Daphne held the baby close and felt his warmth

against her face, an embrace he allowed without protest. 'He's very good,' she said out loud, with pride. Nesta and Mrs Cuthbertson looked relieved. Daphne was not going to make a fuss. She held him even tighter so her face was pressed against his face. Her bosom felt achey, leaky and sore. 'Nesta, my chest hurts,' she said. At this, Mrs Cuthbertson reached for the baby and Nesta hugged Daphne. 'It will, for a few days,' she said. 'It's to be expected, I'm afraid. It's your milk coming in.'

Daphne watched as Mrs Cuthbertson stuck her little finger in the baby's mouth, and jiggled him up and down. Then the baby started crying. 'Give him to me,' said Daphne, holding out her arms. 'Please.'

She took the crying baby into her lap. He smelt her and started burrowing into her bosom, blindly, like a mole through soil. She began to struggle to remove a breast, but there was no way she could feed him, as she was wearing a gown that, perhaps deliberately, opened only at the back.

As she wrestled with her nightie, the high, lamb-like bleating stopped and her baby son opened his eyes and gazed at her with dark-blue eyes and what seemed like the knowledge of ancients. He knew she had a choice, and that she wasn't going to choose him.

'I'll take him to the nursery and give him a feed there,' said Mrs Cuthbertson. Daphne kissed his face, and his eyes, and nuzzled his head. It was odd; he felt like hers, but he didn't belong to her. She gently removed the baby from Daphne. 'Say goodbye to Mother, little one.'

Daphne lay back, defeated, her breasts now leaking

all over her gown in a spreading stain, still holding the baby's white booties, which had slipped off into her lap.

As she heard the door close she realized: her son didn't even have a name.

18

Faringdon, Oxfordshire
May 2006

'Here we are,' said Francie, as they scrunched up on the gravel. There was an elderly couple sitting on a bench out front, not speaking. The man was bald, his jacket and trousers too big for him, like a suit on a scarecrow, the trousers too short, while the woman was wearing a tweed skirt, blouse and light anorak, all in shades of pinkish beige, accessorized with crimped white hair and a pink scarf.

Francie hoped that they were not unhappily married. She preferred to hope they were two like-minded souls who had found each other at sunset and could therefore serve as poster couple for the proposition that it was never too late for love.

She was a sucker for that sort of thing: she teared up during those interviews in the magazine bit after the news with great-grandparents in their nineties who spoke of never having had a night apart in seventy years, the importance of a 'good cuddle' before 'turning in', and never letting the sun go down on your wrath. Gus turned off the engine, and they contemplated the silent couple.

It cost her a great deal to admit that her marriage to Gus could never match up to those long-serving unions, but – Francie swallowed – it was what it was.

Miranda was now in the flat below White Cube in Little Venice. It was odd, at first: Francie knew that Miranda had 'been intimate with' (yuk) Nathan. But Miranda didn't know that Nathan and Francie had been 'intimate', too. And Francie wasn't going to tell her now that they took in each other's Net-à-Porter deliveries. Now that they shared a bin area as well as Nathan's common parts.

'I do hope we're not too late,' she said, with a brightness she did not feel. She was remembering the knife in her gut she'd felt when she was watering the plants on the patio and had glanced into the street and seen his black Porsche Cayenne in a pay-and-display bay outside. Nathan was visiting Miranda. In fact, every time she saw a black Porsche Cayenne, she still felt a little bit sick to the stomach. But she was OK now. They were fine, in fact. It was so much easier trying to love Gus, she found, than trying not to love Nathan. A real relief actually.

'Yup, this could be decisive,' agreed Gus. Grannie was much 'brighter', the woman had said. Really talking. Gus was keen to find out the dark secret too. It wasn't because Francie was supposed to be writing a piece; in fact, Francie had finally told Nathan (after she'd seen his Porsche Cayenne in Clifton Villas, to be exact, but Gus was not to know that) that she didn't think the piece would work for *Event*, at which point Nathan had pretended amnesia and almost acted as if he'd forgotten commissioning the article in the first place. Then Francie had said, 'Well, that's all right then, as I'm thinking of turning the story of my grandmother's adventures in Bavaria into a book.'

'Fiction, or non-fiction?' Nathan had the grace to ask. That was a good question. Francie wasn't sure. The thing was, there was an awful lot of fact in fiction – novelists spent years researching their subjects, she kept reading – and an awful lot of made-up rubbish in newspapers and articles that purported to be telling the truth. 'Fiction,' said Francie. 'But based on a true story.'

Gus slung his manbag from Bill Amberg over his shoulder as they went up to the front door. 'Let's hope for the sake of your book that she had the total hots for the blond one, the über-Nazi,' he said. 'That would be tremendous, if the monster turned out to be sex on a –'

'*Gus!*' said Francie, grabbing his arm. 'Please. This is serious! We're talking about my possible grandfather.'

'But I thought it was going to be fiction, though, your book?' he said. They hadn't rung the bell yet. 'Still needs a pitch, though.'

'You're the ad man, Gus,' Francie reminded him.

'Debs Shagging Nazis,' he said, waving his forefinger to emphasize each of the three words, as if reading it on a billboard in Hollywood. 'It's got everything. And make sure you get cover approval. They've got to put a swastika on the cover. And the Olympic rings. Or maybe both . . .'

Francie had to admit that Debs Shagging Nazis summed it up, but she still didn't know for sure which one it was Daphne had shagged.

But today would change all that.

They rang and waited together, a united front, a married couple, for someone to answer the buzzer and let them in. Then Gus spoke again; this time, he was serious.

'Now. About today. You know what I think,' he said. 'But I understand why you want to hear it from her rather than me.' He placed his hands on her shoulders and gazed into her face with a meaningful expression. He'd grown his hair longer. It didn't look so stubbly, so Danish, any more. Francie liked it. Their faces were very close.

Gus thought that Andrew, Francie's father, was the spitting image of Siegmund Huber, but then again, if you looked at photos of Andrew as a young man, there was also something about Otto around the mouth . . .

As for Francie, she didn't know what to think. She didn't want it to be Siegmund, for obvious reasons. Given any choice, she would much prefer her grandfather to be Otto, but these things were not a matter of choice.

Milly Goddard was sitting behind the desk in the nurse's station. She replaced the receiver when she saw them, then rather deliberately swigged from a mug and wound the plastic sleeve of HobNobs on the desk into a tight tourniquet, in her slightly aggressive way. 'You can go on up. You know where she is. We're short-staffed today, I have to stay here.'

Francie gave her an air-hostess smile: bright but impersonal. Why was Milly Goddard always like this with her? The whole thing was a mystery. But no matter now: she was pleased that Grannie had undergone this *coup de mieux*. It might make all the difference. She pressed on down the passage, with Gus following.

It was a small bird-like Grannie, her hair tied up in a jaunty blue paisley scarf, who was there to greet them. She was lying three quarters in repose and looked like a dolly that had been carefully tucked into a 'big bed' by a child.

'Hello, darling,' she said. A cup of tea in a pale-green tea cup sat on a saucer, alongside some untouched biscuits beside it. Gus trickled in behind her, and stood there, looking handsome and fit.

'And Gus,' she beamed. 'What a lovely surprise.' Like many old ladies, when the old gentlemen are thinning out, she always brightened at the sight of a man of any description.

Francie kissed her forehead at the place where the scarf and the soft white skin met. Lovely. Grannie smelt like Grannie. Then she sat by the edge of the bed, and took her hand, and stroked it.

'Grannie, it's so wonderful to see you!' she cried, hoping she wasn't sitting too close, crushing her. She seemed so tiny.

'And you too, darling,' said Daphne. 'Apparently, there's something you want to talk to me about.'

'But you asked for *me*,' said Francie, surprised.

She didn't look at Gus. She nibbled a biscuit. She was always hungry now. 'You wanted me to come, and then you had your . . .' She paused, not knowing if Grannie had officially had a stroke or not. 'And Milly Goddard gave me the memory box.'

She looked enquiringly at her grandmother. Daphne's eyes were sticky and bright, and she smiled at her granddaughter fondly.

'Darling, I do – I think – vaguely remember wanting your Uncle *Francis* to come, because I was concerned about how much this place was costing me, and whether I should liquidate some of those investments he'd made, after we sold Hendridge. You were away, weren't you? But that was ages ago . . . wasn't it?' She looked at Francie appealingly. 'Do you know, this room costs £475 a day! I could be in the Connaught. We all could!'

Francie assumed Grannie was dissembling. She had called for Francie, and Francie knew why. It was because the business in Germany had implications not for Uncle Francis or Aunties Sally/ Jill, but for her – and her alone – because it was to do with her father. And now she was burying her head back in the sand. Like Jeremy. He refused to talk about what happened when half his colleagues were burnt to a crisp in a tank in front of his eyes. Francie had tried asking what he did in the war: 'Weren't you terribly brave?', and he'd said, 'We did what we had to do. What's the point of talking about it?' Francie had never asked again.

Gus was sitting in the one piece of furniture from Hendridge that could fit in the room – a wingback chair clad in pea-green wool. A soft Welsh blanket in pinks and creams and paler greens curled cosily over one arm. The object reminded Francie painfully of the lost loveliness of Hendridge: a Georgian red-brick symmetrical manor house with eight bedrooms, an estate that rolled, and had done for many hundred of years, over so many acres.

Gus raised his eyebrows at Francie, as if to say: You've got nothing to lose at this point. Go for it, because this isn't just about you any more . . . it's about us.

Francie found Gus's sudden interest in her Teutonic heritage touching. It had occurred to her that some men, lesser men than Gus, would never have married her if they'd known she was half *German*, but he was taking it on the chin. She took a deep breath. 'Grannie,' said Francie. 'I hope you don't mind me asking. But I've thought about this a lot. And I think I have a right – no, scratch that, I hate it when people bang on about their rights – I think you'll understand my own personal reasons for needing to know. So I hope you'll forgive me for intruding. But the reason I'm – I mean we're – here is, I have rather a direct question for you. I thought you were expecting this. I found the birth certificate. I found Daddy's birth certificate.'

'Oh darling,' said Daphne. She had gone rather pink. She looked a lot more alive than when they had arrived. She looked as if she had years left, in fact. She sat up straight.

'Why did you go to hospital in Munich? And who was Daddy's father? I know it wasn't Grandpa Jeremy. There's a blank where his name should be. So who was it?'

Francie tried not to think about the depressing likelihood that Milly Goddard had somehow muddled everything up and sent her on a wild-goose chase into the past when, in fact, Grannie only wanted to discuss financials with Uncle Francis, and to make the most of it.

So she deliberately narrowed the question; their trip to Ducklington, only last week, had confirmed everything. It hadn't taken long, in the end, to find out that a Miss Daphne Linden had given birth in St Clare's Hospital for the Middle and Upper Classes, and to discover that a Mrs Cuthbertson, of Ducklington, the one who'd registered the birth, had taken in an unnamed baby boy in October 1936. Mrs Cuthbertson's actual daughter, Fiona, still lived at Hospital Cottage (she'd reversed the name from Cottage Hospital). She had shown Francie and Gus a picture of a little boy standing underneath a bare-boughed apple tree to the right of a cottage with a path going down the middle. There was a little wooden cart and a terrier at his feet. He was very blond, as if wearing a cap of light. Francie had stared at the picture of her father.

'Every year, Christmas and birthday, my mother would take him outside and take a picture, and send it to the mother, and keep one for herself,' Fiona Cuthbertson had told them. 'She did this for all her children. Every year, a picture. Well, more for the mothers, of course.'

'It's when he was five,' said Francie. 'Look, it says November 1941.'

'Yes,' said Fiona. 'It must be the last one. Your grandmother had him back. She was married then, during the war, and she could have him back. He was a lovely little chap, wasn't he? Wasn't he lovely and fair? Did he stay very fair?' she asked, then her hand flew to her mouth. 'I forgot! Of course, I heard what happened,' she said, looking at Francie. 'We all saw it in the newspapers. Mum was so upset. She wrote, of course, to your gran. I *am* sorry.'

She had allowed Francie to hold the photograph, as if the act of holding it would help her to understand that her grandmother had given up a baby for years, and that another woman had loved him, and had loved him enough to let him go, and that the boy in the photograph grew into a man, who married her mother and died before Francie had a chance to know him.

'Do you want to keep it?' she said.

'May I?' said Francie. She took the photograph. It was proof.

Francie knew, but she needed to hear it from her grandmother. She took out the photograph and handed it to Grannie.

'Oh darling,' Grannie said again, when she saw what it was. 'The Cottage Hospital. I remember it so well.' She sank back into her pillows. 'Of course, I understand why you feel you have to ask.' She stared at Francie, and then at Gus, almost with defiance. This young couple had turned up, and were asking her to give up a secret, a matter that had been far too significant to mention, and she wasn't sure that it wasn't still too soon to do so, even after a span of seventy years.

'I know. And you – you have an interest in this matter too.' It was a statement, not a question, aimed at Gus.

'Yes, Daphne,' answered Gus. 'I do. Francie's father's parentage matters very much, to us both, and to any children we might have.' The truth was, Francie was ten weeks pregnant, but they had decided not to tell anyone, for the moment. That suited Francie, for reasons that she would also keep private.

'Well. I'm afraid I am going to disappoint you both,' said Daphne. Francie and Gus sat, stunned.

'You may find it hard to believe this, my dears,' she said, 'but I actually don't know.'

'What!' exploded Francie, but inside she felt a joy she could never, ever, tell Gus. For she had no idea, either, whether the baby she was carrying was his, or Nathan's, and nor did she have any intention of her, or anyone else, finding out.

'Hold on,' said Grannie Daphne. 'It's not as bad as it sounds. It's, well, slightly complicated to explain.'

'It sounds jolly complicated to *me*,' said Francie. Despite her own identical condition, she felt rather shocked. She wondered whether she could face, at this stage, a detailed account of Grannie Daphne's early romantic career. The passions of young love seemed awfully far away, and yet awfully close to home at the same time.

'Oh, how rude of me. Here I am, with my tea and biscuits, and I haven't offered you anything. Would you both like some tea?'

So then they had a tea-break. Afterwards, and when a girl had been in to fetch the things, Francie gave Gus the nod.

It was her last shot. He reached into his satchel and took out the softly worn folding leather picture frame in green morocco embossed with gold, which could hold three pictures and yet fold down to the size of a largish wallet. He passed it over to Daphne Fitzsimon, as the words went through Francie's mind: *I really might never know who my father was.* It was so unfair. Most quest novels or memoirs ended with a result. The daughter of the famous film director would find out that she was in fact the daughter of the famous writer, or actor, or rock star.

Whereas all she would be left with would be a strong suspicion – unless Grannie decided to share now.

'I remember this,' she said. 'I sent it to Dem.'

Daphne studied the leather folder that Dem's son Jared had sent to Francie, after Dem had died. The folder contained three pictures: one of Betsy and Daphne, one of Daphne with Siegmund, and one of them with Otto and a dog. All were taken on the terrace of the Huber chalet in the Alps.

'There he is,' said Daphne. 'Just as I remember him. And there's Rudi, such a sweet dog.' She put the leather folder down and looked at Gus. 'You know, after the war,' she said, 'I heard from a friend who disappeared from my school, in Bavaria, where I stayed before I went to be finished in Munich. Marquartstein; that was its name. Remember it so well. When I saw Sophie again, I felt very happy. I thought that, like so many others' – she paused for a beat – 'she would have not survived. We had tea in London – Andrew must have been about eight – he was at prep school, though, of course. Sunningdale. Such a nice school. Where was I? What were we talking about? Did you ask me about Bletchley?'

'You were telling us about a girl called Sophie, Grannie,' said Francie, wondering how to get Grannie back to the identity of the father of her first child. 'When you were at the boarding school. The *Schloß* place.' Then she paused. 'Were you at Bletchley?'

'My dear girl, finally an interesting question,' Grannie said with a merry look. 'If I was, I certainly wouldn't tell you. Some of us still stick to our word, and don't talk about things all the time.'

'Oh,' said Francie. 'Anyway, you were talking about a girl called Sophie.'

'And Prof. Hoff,' resumed Grannie. 'It's all clear as a bell, that time.' It was odd, thought Francie. People her age could barely remember what they had for lunch or the names of their children, yet had crystalline recall of the things they had done and said many decades before.

'People criticized the headmaster, Prof. Hoff, for being a Nazi, but he was a marvellous man, he said if he hadn't joined – the Party – he would have been out on his ear, and he considered it was better for him to be a headmaster than be in a camp somewhere, so he told a lie. I admire him terribly for that.' She tilted her head on one side. 'It wasn't as simple as people think. No one really knew.' She gazed into space, then out of the window. A bird suddenly sang in the hedge.

'How well I remember another boy at the school – and one thing he said really quite startled me. When questioned, he said, "You must remember what went before." His father was a minor canon in the Lutheran Church, upright, religious, and in Bamberg, which was where his family were, his mother would send him and his sisters out to market every day to scrounge the streets for vegetables that had been thrown away, and they were a respectable *middle-class* family. If you don't understand what came before, the hardship, the humiliation, you can't understand, I don't think, what came after. When someone came with a plan, of course, we were all terribly relieved. And that is something that is always forgotten. And of course the German yearning for *Ordnung* and rules.'

'And Sophie?' pressed Francie. She thought it was significant that Grannie had said 'we'. As if she had been one of them. It was as if she'd teleported back to Bavaria in the thirties. Then she remembered that Grannie had joined, as all her teenaged classmates had, the *Bund Deutscher Mädchen* – the girlie version of the Hitler Youth – and had thought it was simply a rather jolly form of Girl Guides.

'Ah yes . . . Sophie,' Grannie resumed. 'I tried to keep up with people after the war but all the boys in my class were killed on the Russian Front. It was so sad. We were the wrong age. I sat with Sophie, having tea in Peter Jones, and I had my photograph album I'd brought with me in my bag – I still have it somewhere – to ask her what had happened to everyone. To my friends. To the boys I'd been skiing with, or done lessons with, or acted with, or sat with having coffee and cakes in the village. And every time I pointed to a boy – they were only seventeen or so – it was heartbreaking. Sophie said, as I pointed at the photos over the tea cups, "Oh, haven't you heard?", and "Oh, haven't you heard?" Every single one of them died. Every single one.' Daphne's eyes burned into her granddaughter's, and then she cast her gaze down and held the silence for a minute.

Gus and Francie knew in that second that Grannie was honouring the German dead, many millions of whom were innocent victims of the regime too. Like Otto: who had been part of a student protest movement in Munich in the late thirties, and had been sent to the Eastern Front, and died.

'Like Siegmund Huber,' said Francie. She had put his name out there. She watched Grannie for her reaction. 'Siegmund died, too.'

Grannie regarded her stoically. 'I expected he had,' she said. 'Otherwise . . . well, he might have made contact.' This was the closest Grannie came to an admission.

'He died on 28 October 1944, eleven kilometres east of Munio, in Posen, North Finland,' Francie told her in a flat voice.

'Did he?' said Daphne. 'And how did he die, may I ask?'

'Well,' said Francie, who had taken out a couple of photocopied sheets of A4 from her bag. 'Officially, Kamerad SS-Obersturmführer Huber died a hero leading his company into battle, according to a letter I've seen. It begins, *'Liebe Frau Huber!'* and ends, *'Heil Hitler!'*

'But the word on the street was,' Francie pressed on, determined to finish, 'he was popped off. Shot. He was so fanatical, so determined to carry out orders, that he was leading his men to certain death, so determined not to surrender, that his own men took him out. Killed him.'

'Ah,' said Grannie. 'I can't say I'm that surprised. Unlike my other great friend in Munich, Otto' – she paused after she mentioned his name – 'Siegmund always excelled at being a German. You could always say that for him.'

She seemed sad, and shrunken, then she resumed in a brighter voice, as if thinking of happier times. 'Jeremy, of course, wouldn't go back after the war. He never said why, but I knew. He said, "German friends – they can come and see us."'

Francie knew that Jeremy Fitzsimon had had a 'good war', but she also knew what that meant: he had seen unspeakable carnage, witnessed friends being blown up, dying in ditches, and personally saved the lives of several of his regiment, and carried on doing his duty. Francie, Francis and the twins, Sally and Jill, had only known the extent of his heroics, in fact, when they read the *Telegraph* obituary. The details haunted Francie to this day, especially the bit about Grumps having extricated two wounded men from the tank which had been knocked out and having tried to inject one of them in the arm with a painkiller – only to find that it had no effect because the limb was not properly attached to the body; and the man died. The MC Fitzsimon had been awarded was, the *Telegraph* obituarist reckoned, 'as good as any that was won in the war'.

'I think what darling Jeremy felt was, some things, you don't pursue,' said Grannie, looking at them both in turn.

'The truth is,' she said, 'it's so long ago now.' And sighed.

'Please, Grannie,' said Francie softly. 'I won't love you any less. I won't love Grandpa any less. You know that. You are all I've ever had, really. Nothing can change that.'

'Oh darling, I do know that,' Grannie said. 'But it costs me a great deal to admit . . .' This was how Grannie always preambled topics that did her some slight discredit, such as her Aga meringues not being chewy, or her failing to complete the *Telegraph* crossword.

'It pains me to admit more than I can say, that when I got pregnant, in February 1936 – your father was born a little early, on 30 October – there was not one . . .' She paused, sighed heavily, and her hands plucked at the dark-red jacquard counterpane. It didn't look like something that could have come from Hendridge. '. . . but two possible fathers.' She pointed to the photo wallet, the picture of the four of them with the dog.

'And those were the two.' There was a silence.

'It's just how it was. I don't want to go into any details; I have long ago forgiven Siegmund, the man who, I can see now, forced himself on me while I was his guest, and I was too silly, I suppose, too ignorant, to resist. I'm sure nowadays everyone would call it rape and get into a frightful stew. But I've never really seen it like that. I wasn't' – she hesitated – 'what you might call the most willing party. Siegmund certainly never waited for any *answering gleam*. I was asleep in my room – well, it was Betsy's room, but we'd swapped. Betsy said hers smelt of cabbage. But I never stopped him. I let it happen. I was young. I had no idea . . . and the awful thing is, you know, it's hard to admit this even now. But I don't think . . . he even knew it was me. He thought it was Betsy, I think.'

'Jeez, Grannie,' said Francie. 'That's tough.'

Grannie smiled brightly. 'Oh darling, it's too late now, to blame others, but you may find this hard to believe. I'm not remotely angry. I wasn't really angry at the time. I blamed only myself. It was just bad luck, really. So much worse things happened to so many of my friends. Betsy lost both her brothers. It was far, far, worse for her. I had no proper idea, Francie, where babies came from. I thought they came out of your navel until I was at least seventeen, and then I had no idea about contraception whatsoever. We were not told, and what my mother told me was, to say the least, entirely misleading.'

By this stage Francie had come close to the single bed – she recognized Grannie's special pillow – and was holding her grandmother's hand, and stroking it. She understood. Better than she could ever say to anyone.

'And as for the other young man, Otto. Well, darlings, we were in love.' She looked bright and younger for a moment at the memory. 'Maybe he wasn't, but very soon it was too late. I was pregnant. And those days, of course, having a child outside wedlock was a terrible disgrace. And abortion – we called it miscarriage of course – was illegal.'

'Illegal?' Francie blurted.

'Of course, darling. But then Fa was in disgrace anyway, he didn't invariably behave well. He had a thing – another thing, I should say – with one of his students. She was called Berridge, as I recall. Then he went to Princeton, joined the family, but just before the war, Ma decamped to New York. She became a writer. A good one, as you know. Her novel, *Stillborn*, was very well received. So it was rather unfair, I suppose, on me, for a few years, but I went to Somerville, I got my degree, and then I got married, I worked, and had Andrew back as soon as I could. So it did turn out all right in the end, up to a point anyway. Didn't it?'

Gus and Francie sat and digested this.

'Grannie, thank you so much for telling me. I think you're very brave. Very brave indeed,' said Francie, hugging her. 'What happened in the end, between you and Otto?' she added. 'If it's not too cheeky my asking.'

'Oh darling, you can ask away, anything you like, and if I want to tell you, I will, and if I don't, I won't,' Grannie said. 'Well.'

Then Grannie explained about Otto. She told her visitors about life in Munich, about bicycling in the cobbled streets, the balls, the beer halls, about lessons at the *Gräfin*'s skiing in Garmisch, opera in the evenings. When Francie asked why Grannie had ended up in hospital, she looked puzzled for a second and then said, 'Oh, it was something to do with the early pregnancy, it's thought I might have lost a twin,' and Francie thought, my father might have had a *twin*, does that mean twins run in the family, and glanced towards Gus, then Grannie said sadly, 'I thought he was the love of my life, and then he never came.'

'Who never came where?' asked Francie, thinking, I do hope she means Otto.

'Otto. To the English Garden,' said Grannie Daphne. 'The day I found out that Betsy was being sacked, we were going to meet there. It was rather awful, really. I thought he'd stopped loving me. I was terribly sad. And that was the end of that. Well, almost. There was one other time, when we sort of met by accident. I was in terrible trouble, and had to leave the *Gräfin*'s, and I saw him, but he didn't have time to tell me much, because Fa showed up, in the Austin, and drove me back to Oxford.'

'Why didn't he come? Why did he stand you up?' asked Francie hotly. 'How dare he?'

'It really wasn't his fault,' said Grannie. She turned her face to look out of the window, as if she didn't want to talk any more. By now, the room had darkened, and they were sitting in the gloaming. Outside the windows, the trees were silhouetted against an indigo sky, and rooks were cawing. It was nice being in the country, even if they were only in a nursing home in suburban Oxfordshire, Francie thought. The air was always cooler, full of the smells of earth and mulch and grass and leaves.

Maybe she and Gus should get out of London, and make a go of it, somewhere like Wales. She'd liked Wales.

Nothing seemed to matter so much, and the people seemed happier there. Or they could go to France. Since she'd got pregnant, she'd been attracted to the deep countryside in a way she'd never been before. But when she mentioned moving to France, and buying a vineyard, Gus said, 'That never ends well,' and made a point of showing Francie magazine pieces with standfirsts saying things like 'Terri and Robert Hallpike dreamed of a better life in France but ten years later her burnt body was found encased in concrete and he was charged with murder.'

Francie repeated her question, as it looked as if Grannie had gone to sleep. Her face was still turned towards the window. 'Why wasn't it Otto's fault?' asked Francie.

'Darling, there was no way of reaching me,' said Grannie. 'He tried. He came, but they never told me. And the telephone at the *Gräfin*'s had been cut off, as she was poor as a church mouse. There were no mobiles, or anything, or laptops or whatever you call them. His parents wouldn't let him see me anyway; they said that if he saw me, it would ruin his chances of a career in medicine. He was very brilliant. They knew Otto had no interest in the Party, he made that very clear right from the start. No, they blackmailed him. He had to join the Party. He had to stop seeing me. They said if he didn't it would not only ruin him, but it would blight his cousin Siegmund's career too.'

'But why?' asked Francie.

'Darling child, the Hubers had been told I was Jewish, that was part of it. I heard, much later, that Otto had been forbidden to see me, on the grounds –' She shook her head slightly.

'It never occurred to me that it mattered, and no one ever mentioned it at home. But the Hubers found out and, to them, it mattered an awful lot. To consort with a Jewess – my nickname in Munich, among the German families, was *Die Jüdin* – was to disown the whole of Germany. It was very painful, that time. Very, very painful. But that sort of thing went on. And it wasn't long after that I met your grandfather,' she said, with a smile to Francie, 'and it all fell into place.'

'Well, I must say you're being very forgiving.' Gus couldn't help himself. 'Sounds like Siegmund was the sort of Nazi that even the Nazis couldn't stand.'

Francie switched on a standard lamp so she could see her grandmother, who lay back on the white pillows. She looked at her grandmother protectively, and said, 'I can't believe Siegmund Huber shopped you on top of everything else he did, and screwed up your relationship with Otto.'

Grannie sat up. 'Oh Francie,' she said, matter-of-factly. 'Language! Everyone's getting too worked up! I'm sure Siegmund did many terrible things – well, I know for a fact he did. And he paid a terrible price too, from what you tell me. But I don't think he ever betrayed me.'

'Who did then?' said Francie.

'Why, it must have been Betsy, of course,' said Daphne. 'Not that it matters now. We fell out in Munich. She was paying me back. She spread it around I was Jewish, even though she knew perfectly well that I was only, if anything, half Jewish. What she was paying me back for, I can't even recall. Something to do with a young man, I expect. With Betsy, it usually was. Now, do you think it might be time for a cocktail? Anyone feel like a drink?'

Both Francie and Gus shook their heads.

'Now, of course, I am not completely gaga, despite appearances. I read the paper. I am well aware that with DNA testing and whatnot that it would be perfectly possible for you two to discover somehow – God knows how – who Andrew's father was, and then you, dear Francie, will know for the first time for certain whether Andrew was Otto's or Siegmund's.' She paused. 'And so, of course, would I.'

They all pondered this, until Grannie broke the silence.

'But I don't want to. I have never wanted to. So, all I would like, darlings, is to leave you with the following.'

She snapped a gingernut in half with her elegant, bony fingers and picked up one half and nibbled it, like a squirrel with a nut. Tiny bites. 'When I met Jeremy I had a child by another man. But it was the war. And he took in Andrew as his own. He was his father. He never asked me who Andrew's father was, not once. I told him it had been an accident, and I was very sorry, and that was that. To Jeremy, Andrew was his son, and that was all there was to it. Jeremy loved Andrew deeply. And if it was good enough for Jeremy, for Grumps, I hope it will be good enough for you.'

Francie nodded. She was pleased Gus was hearing this, in case things got sticky later on, when the baby looked nothing like him.

'You see –' Grannie hesitated, as if weighing up what she was going to conclude. 'An awful lot was expected of our generation, and an awful lot was given. It was how it was. Now, I read the papers, and sacrifice these days means rinsing out a jam jar before recycling it, or buying an electric car, installing solar panels, or not going skiing. It's hard for you to understand.' She looked very tired now.

There had been no need, in the end, for Grannie to draw the distinction more explicitly between the Hero and the Me Generation – a simple mention of Jeremy Fitzsimon MC was enough to remind Francie that her quest, in the end, had been all about her.

'We had a wonderful life together. So many marriages – I've seen it so often – turn into a kind of *Totentanz*, a dance of death. Ours started with a slight hiccup' – Gus and Francie glanced at each other at this heroic understatement – 'but then it really did go from strength to strength. I miss him,' she said. 'I miss him every day.'

'I know, Grannie, I know,' said Francie. She didn't know what else to say.

'And now, my dears, if you'll excuse me – it's time for an old lady to indulge herself in one of her few remaining pleasures.' She reached out to the small Roberts radio next to the side plate, held together with red rubber bands she'd saved from her morning-post bundle – she was an inveterate writer and receiver of letters – so the batteries didn't fall out.

She fiddled with the bands and made sure they were all straight. 'I loathe it when people say "passed", she

burst out, for no apparent reason, 'instead of "died".'
She held the transistor. Francie wondered whether, perhaps, someone in the nursing home had just died, and
they'd all been told. 'Passed what? A gall stone?' Daphne
went on. 'It's silly beyond words. I remember how
annoyed Ma was when our cook, Mosey, said that John,
my brother who died, was "sleeping in Jesus". I don't think
Ma ever recovered from the phrase! As for everyone
being "gathered" for the Great Beyond . . .' She trailed
off. 'It's like saying "price points", instead of "price", or
"station stop", rather than "station". Maddening! Why
can't people just say someone's died any more? That's
what they've done. They're just dead.'

She switched on the radio. It was tuned to Radio Four,
and it was just after seven. As the tune tum-ti-tum-ti-
tum-ti-tummed, Francie and Gus both kissed Daphne
on her dry, lined face, its surface like crumpled linen, as
they said goodbye.

Francie's eyes filled with tears, as they always did,
because she thought it might be the last time. But as they
were halfway into the passage, Grannie turned down the
radio as the *Archers'* theme tune was fading out and
before David and Ruth were about to have words on the
vexed subject of their daughter Pip in the milking par-
lour. She called out after her favourite granddaughter.

'Oh darling, just one thing,' she called. 'You remember what I always said about running around the castle
barefoot in the snow?'

Francie paused at the door, imagining her grandmother aged eighteen, bolting barefoot round the *Schloß*

in a clinging one-piece made of grey cotton. Grannie always complained about having to do it and how frightfully indecent it was cantering braless among the boys in shorts as a master in lederhosen shouted, *Schneller! Schneller!* at her.

She turned around and smiled. 'How could I forget?' she said. She loved Grannie's stories – how on New Year's Eve the whole school took their skis to church by sleigh, lit by braziers, sleigh bells jingling, for the skis to be blessed for the following year, and how she ate doughy white buns with a slab of chocolate in the middle at tea, and how they made patties of lard and slept on straw pallets in the hut on the mountains.

If you tuned out the Third Reich, it was all very Heidi, her grandmother's little Bavarian rhapsody.

'Goodbye, Grannie.' She didn't say 'Take care.' She didn't say 'Love you,' let alone 'I love you.' Now, she and Gus always said 'love you' before they hung up, even though they knew there was a world of difference between the sign-off 'love you' and the words 'I love you.'

But one never said either with Grannie. It was generational.

Daphne didn't answer. She raised a hand in farewell. Francie understood. They'd already said goodbye once, and that was sufficient. It was time for *The Archers*; she'd listened to every edition, sometimes twice, since 1951, and she wouldn't want to miss a word now.

'So what did Grannie always say about running around the Bavarian *Schloß* in the snow?' Gus asked, as Francie paused outside the door to collect herself. Her heart felt full. She knew she would not see Grannie many more times, and that Grannie might not live to see her first great-grandchild.

She wondered whether, in life, you are loved even more for the questions you don't ask than the ones you do.

Francie stood outside her grandmother's room. She and Gus were alone in the passage, decorated in pale-yellow stripes down the wall and a mushroom carpet on the landing. The sound of the Channel Four news came from the room opposite Grannie's, and an old man in a paisley dressing-gown and yellow cravat was creaking towards them down the passage. For once, she didn't feel like bolting away, back to London.

'She said she used to hate running round the castle barefoot in the snow, in the dark, before breakfast,' she replied. 'But afterwards, for some reason, you were always warm, for the whole of the rest of the day.'

Announcement in the Deaths column of *The Times*,
31 January 2007

FITZSIMON, Daphne (née Linden), on 29 January,
in her 90th year. Funeral service outdoors at Mob
Quad, Merton College, on 2 February at 12.30 p.m.
No mourning, no flowers please.

Acknowledgements

This book is dedicated to my dearest mother-in-law, Margaret, and to my late maternal grandmother, Bice, but could not have been written (or would have been much worse written, I should probably say) without the help of many. I would particularly like to thank for unstinting attention Joachim von Halasz, an expert on Hitler's Munich, and Brendan McGurk, my tour guide in Bavaria. For historical help – and this is a work of complete fiction – I turned to, among others, David Pryce-Jones and Anne de Courcy, who couldn't have been kinder. I would also like to thank Julian Turton for help with Marquartstein, the staff of the Vier Jahreszeiten, Munich, and the Intercontinental Hotel, Berchtesgaden, for their hospitality, ditto Martin and Miranda Thomas for allowing me to use Martin's manshed in Wiltshire when I was in the agonizing final throes of composition, and Bella Mates for transcribing interviews.

I would also like to thank Juliet Annan for being my publisher. I am lucky to have one who possesses impeccable judgement and a faultless ear, as well as the bravery to be occasionally brutal. I would like to thank Sarah Day for zealous copy-editing, Ellie Smith, Caroline Craig and Sophie Missing for all the things they do, and of course Peter Straus, my agent.

But my main debt is owed to the following: Betty

Lawson, the late Margaret Budd, the late Michael 'Micky' Burn MC, Elizabeth Lowry-Corry, Elsbeth Juda, Rose Mary Macindoe, Daphne Brock and, above all, Prilly Crowther, who granted me long and in some cases repeated interviews about their time in Germany in the thirties, which was a lot more fun, and even hairier, than I've made it sound here.

RACHEL JOHNSON

SHIRE HELL

Mimi and Ralph have left social climbing, pushy parenting and their marital problems behind them in London, and moved west to the bucolic green depths of the country. Or so they thought. Yes, there's mud and masses of fresh air, plenty of handsome hayseeds and there's Rose, Mimi's new best friend and Dorset's answer to Martha Stewart. But what should be Shire Heaven is, it turns out, just as tricky to navigate as Notting Hell.

There's low-level conflict between the racehorses in vintage/Diesel/Ralph Lauren and the brood mares in Barbour/Boden, there's guerrilla warfare between the landowners and eco-warriers and naked hostility between Old Money, New Money and No Money. Yes, in honeybourne, if you don't have:

• A landscaped garden within 1000 acres (minimum) of prime land
• A helipad for your trophy guests
• An organic farm shop selling 16 sorts of home-made sausages
• Four pony-mad polo-playing children
• A literary festival in your mini-stately
• A bottom that looks smackable in jodhpurs

Then, well . . . you're Mimi basically. And that's just the start of her problems. Mimi also has a secret. But can she keep it?

'An irreverent romp through the wilds of the English countryside . . . hilarious. Johnson's humour is wickedly delicious' *She*

RACHEL JOHNSON

NOTTING HELL

'Our neighbours divide into the haves . . . and the have yachts.'

Meet Mimi and Clare, two married women making the most of their Notting Hill postcode. New best friends, and close neighbours, that doesn't stop them being rivals, in fact it compels it. Both are aspiring Notting Hill Mummies (Clare needs the baby, Mimi needs the six figure income) and, keeping up with all the area's fads, fashions and fabulousness is a full-time job. But the arrival of sexy billionaire Si in their exclusive communal garden strains loyalty to friends, family, spouse and feng-shui guru alike . . . and only one of them can win. But who will that be? Clare or Mimi? Are they friends, or just . . . neighbours?

'Shiveringly brilliant' Jilly Cooper

'Witty, sharp, outrageous and cringingly real. I was riveted!' Sophie Kinsella

'A wickedly funny comedy of modern manners' *OK!*

RACHEL JOHNSON

A DIARY OF THE LADY

'The whole place seemed completely bonkers: dusty, tatty, disorganized and impossibly old-fashioned, set in an age of doilies and flag-waving patriotism and jam still for tea, some sunny day.'

Appointed editor of The Lady – the oldest women's weekly in the world – Rachel Johnson faced the challenge of a lifetime. For a start, how do you become an editor when you've never, well, edited? How do you turn around a venerable title, full of ads for walk-in baths, during the worst recession EVER? And forget doubling the circulation in a year – what on earth do you wear to work when you've spent the last fifteen years at home in sweatpants?

'A total romp . . . wonderfully readable' *Guardian*

'Hilarious' *Daily Mail*

'Action-packed, entertaining, marvellously indiscreet' *Sunday Times*

He just wanted a decent book to read ...

Not too much to ask, is it? It was in 1935 when Allen Lane, Managing Director of Bodley Head Publishers, stood on a platform at Exeter railway station looking for something good to read on his journey back to London. His choice was limited to popular magazines and poor-quality paperbacks – the same choice faced every day by the vast majority of readers, few of whom could afford hardbacks. Lane's disappointment and subsequent anger at the range of books generally available led him to found a company – and change the world.

'We believed in the existence in this country of a vast reading public for intelligent books at a low price, and staked everything on it'
Sir Allen Lane, 1902–1970, founder of Penguin Books

The quality paperback had arrived – and not just in bookshops. Lane was adamant that his Penguins should appear in chain stores and tobacconists, and should cost no more than a packet of cigarettes.

Reading habits (and cigarette prices) have changed since 1935, but Penguin still believes in publishing the best books for everybody to enjoy. We still believe that good design costs no more than bad design, and we still believe that quality books published passionately and responsibly make the world a better place.

So wherever you see the little bird – whether it's on a piece of prize-winning literary fiction or a celebrity autobiography, political tour de force or historical masterpiece, a serial-killer thriller, reference book, world classic or a piece of pure escapism – you can bet that it represents the very best that the genre has to offer.

Whatever you like to read – trust Penguin.